Unsolved

Heather Critchlow grew up in rural Aberdeenshire and trained as a business journalist after studying history and social science at the University of Cambridge. Her short stories have appeared in crime fiction anthologies *Afraid of the Light*, *Afraid of the Christmas Lights* and *Afraid of the Shadows*. She lives in St Albans.

UNSOLVED

HEATHER CRITCHLOW

First published in the United Kingdom in 2023 by

Canelo
Unit 9, 5th Floor
Cargo Works, 1-2 Hatfields
London SE1 9PG
United Kingdom

A CIP catalogue record for this book is available from the British Library.

Print ISBN 978 1 80436 258 7
Ebook ISBN 978 1 80436 257 0

Look for more great books at www.canelo.co

Printed and bound in Great Britain by Clays Ltd, Elcograf S.p.A.

I

For Will, Rachel and Adam

PROLOGUE

LAYLA, 1986

Layla presses her face against the horse's flank, soothed by the warmth of her body, the softness of the chestnut hair. Eager to be out, Ruby skitters; her hooves clatter on the chuckies and she traps Layla against the fence. As she pushes the animal's side to move her away, Layla feels the thoroughbred's coiled energy, a sense of danger and unpredictability. Quick to temper when crossed, the mare has bitten other riders in the past. Layla understands the impulse. Some days she wants to tear chunks off everyone around her, to gnaw her way out of her life.

She tightens the girth and springs into the saddle, a fluid, effortless movement. Stephen has told her more than once that she looks at home on the back of a horse, though these days his admiration is tinged with something else, resentment at the way she treats him, or maybe envy – that there is one place she feels happy and it isn't with him.

She doesn't need to press her legs into Ruby's sides, just takes the reins and thinks *forward* and they are away, trotting out of the yard. She relishes the feeling of power beneath her. One touch and they could fly and be free.

Then Jim rounds the end of the block, carrying a full hay net over each shoulder, wisps trailing in the breeze.

She had hoped to make it up the track before he came back.

'Layla, wait,' he calls, his face dark with anger that she has left him the byres to muck out, the ricks to fill. It isn't just that, she is sure. His words still echo in her mind. *Cock tease.* It makes her stomach clench, but she swivels in the saddle, waves, pretends not to hear or to care. She doesn't have time for him today. She doesn't have time for any of them.

'Bitch.' Jim spits the word but, thanks to Ruby's rising stride, by the time it reaches her it has lost its power, falls to the ground, flaccid.

At the top of the track she pauses to look back at the view, holding the side-stepping mare in place. Twenty-one years of growing up beneath these hills and the landscape is never static. Beyond the stables, she sees clouds racing across the patchwork Aberdeenshire countryside, notes the purple smudge of a distant rain shower. Now that she is free, her anticipation releases – delight spins beneath her navel at the thought of what lies ahead.

She scans the yard below, makes sure no one is watching, then she turns the horse up towards the wood, gathers her for a burst of speed and the jump – up and over the ditch, wall and wire. Layla's breath catches at what feels like a vertical spring. The breath-holding danger, and then she is out of sight, her heart galloping.

They weave through the tight-knit trees, following the path that is not a path, the one only they use. The forest is close and primeval – alive with brilliant moss, neon-green and soft where it covers rocks in thick layers. Above her head, lichen is strewn among branches, as if some forgotten river rose here and left it stranded. The trees drip with moisture and the air feels alive, as if everything is pushing her forward, conspiring, leading her astray. Layla shivers at the notion.

But then Ruby snorts, shakes her head to loosen the pull of the reins, and the feeling vanishes. The horse's hooves slip a little on the sodden ground and Layla has to concentrate – must take care not to catch her leg on one of the tree trunks that crowd the narrow gaps they shimmy between.

As they leave it all behind, she starts to breathe more evenly, to allow the tight defensiveness she wears to loosen a little. The horse walks more easily; they flow together, away from the things and the people that try to hold them down.

She glances at her watch. Still an hour before she has to be there and the thought of it makes the hairs rise on her arms. She has time to take Ruby to the edge of the trees, to the wide fields where she can let the horse loose and her hooves will churn the soft ground. When the gallop is fast enough that fear flashes through Layla and the wind makes tears pour down her cheeks, then she can forget the world for a moment, forget her place in it and the cage closing in on her. There is only movement, nothing more.

–

It is dark when Ruby thunders into the stable yard: riderless, panicked. The horse's red coat is dark with sweat; her eyes roll white and she foams at the mouth, her whole body shaking. The stable hands come running.

Jim catches her bridle but she wrenches her head away from him and rears, squealing in pain. It is only then they see the deep gash on Ruby's back leg, the blood pouring from her hock. It takes four of them to coax her into a stable but they cannot get near her. At midnight the decision is made. A vet shoots the horse.

The decision to stop looking for Layla takes longer.

CHAPTER ONE

WEST MIDLANDS

CAL

Cal pauses as he turns the car into the farm track that leads to their house. From this vantage point, with the sun setting behind the trees in the distance, it looks peaceful, idyllic. The lights are off in Allie's studio. Unusual. She is always out there, splattering paint on huge canvases, her brow furrowed and mind lost to her art, preparing for the latest exhibition or fulfilling the occasional corporate commission. She doesn't enjoy those as much, he knows, but recently those jobs have been keeping them afloat.

Reluctantly, he puts the car in gear and drives slowly between the fields to the house, with the American-style covered porch they fell in love with the moment they saw it, Allie heavily pregnant with their daughter. Then, it represented the promise of everything.

When he gets out of the car, Rocket emerges from the house, the Labrador's whole body wagging. At least someone is pleased to see him. Inside, there is a stillness that makes Cal's heart judder – he used to have this sense of doom if he couldn't immediately see or hear them when he came home. Over the past sixteen years those fears have become wisps of memory. But they're coming back and he doesn't know how to stop them.

'Allie? Christina?' he calls, following the dog towards the kitchen and relaxing when he sees his wife at the table, though her expression is not a happy one.

'Where have you been? Didn't you get my messages?'

'I'm sorry.' He is always apologising these days. 'I was in the library. Preparing for… tomorrow. I had my phone on silent.'

Something like fear sweeps across her face.

'You're seeing him again.' Her voice is incredulous.

'I have to.' He sets down his bag, takes a breath to steady himself. 'I can't just walk away. Please try and understand, Al.'

It's the journalistic opportunity of a lifetime, and yet more than that. A chance to understand. He has to keep going.

'For God's sake, Cal, I thought you were listening.' Allie's cheeks are pink, and her eyes fill with tears. It strikes Cal that he can't feel her distress, only see it from a distance. 'Ever since those letters came you've been different. It's scaring me.'

It's not just the letters. It's the research, the rabbit hole, freefalling into impenetrable darkness. Allie used to be his champion, but she can't get behind him this time. In his mind the crime scene stills, the silent screams and the broken bodies. They're always there, on the periphery, demanding answers.

'Is this because I missed your gallery opening? I told you I was sorry.'

Allie's eyes darken with hurt. 'It's so much more than that, Cal. You're changing; you're different. Please don't go and see him tomorrow. Not again.'

'I have to go. You know I do. It's all arranged.' He turns away, alarmed at the sudden bolt of anger inside him. He

6

is mildness, not temper. This is coming from somewhere new. Or someone else. Allie's words have rattled him. 'It's just a few more times. Then I'll be done and we can move on.'

'What if it's too late by then?'

'What?' He spins around, searching her face. 'You don't mean that.'

Allie's voice breaks, she drops her head into her hands. 'I don't know what I mean. You're not yourself, Cal. You haven't even asked me why I was calling.'

He takes a breath, grips the back of a chair to steady himself.

'I'm sorry. What's happened?'

'It was Chrissie. She disappeared from school.'

'What?' Cal's heart starts a race in his chest. In his world, vanishing has terrible consequences.

'It's okay. She came home eventually. Walked half the way. She's upstairs, but she won't come out of her room. I just… needed you.'

His wife sounds exhausted – their daughter has never been a challenging child. Neither of them knows how to deal with these recent developments. At sixteen, Chrissie is clammed shut and any attempt to prise her troubles from her only increases her vice-like grip on her secrets.

'Has she said anything?'

'No.' Allie shakes her head and a tear runs down her cheek. She turns her face from him and swipes at it as if she no longer trusts him with the deepest parts of herself. Cal thinks about reaching out for her, pulling her to him. It seems such a simple, human way to react, and yet the chasm between them is jagged and impassable.

'Shall I try and talk to her?'

He doesn't want to do anything without Allie's permission, feels he has invalidated his right to decide by not being here earlier.

Allie sighs, a twisting of frustration and sadness that he tries not to see.

'You can try.' She bites her lip. 'Anything to avoid talking about *him*, I guess.'

As he walks to the stairs, he hears the back door slam behind her.

–

Cal stands at the foot of the stairs for a moment. Blackness crowds his vision, images flicker on and off in his head. It frightens him; these snapshots of pain have come from nowhere. Have come from *him*.

When he is calm, he ascends and knocks softly at his daughter's bedroom door. Normally there would be music drifting out, the sound of chatting or a YouTube video, but today there is nothing. Maybe he can draw her out and they can all spend the evening together, do something normal, banish this creeping darkness. He has always been able to get through to Chrissie, their connection is a golden thread, unbreakable.

'Go away, Mum.'

'It's not Mum, it's me.'

No reply.

'Can I come in?' he asks, turning down the handle slowly, and waiting. 'I'm coming in unless you tell me not to.'

He quickly steps into her room and his breath catches in his throat. She's sitting on her bed, her hands wrapped around her knees, defiant pale face turned to him. The living, breathing reincarnation of another teenager.

Her image is Margot's, startlingly so. The power of genetics astounds him when he gazes at the inherited waves of reddish hair that frame her face. It takes him back to when he was nine years old. Nine years old and about to lose a sister.

Cal looks sadly at the chair by the bed. Chrissie used to keep it clear for him, demand that he cuddle whichever soft toy was in favour, settle a blanket over his knees. Now it is covered with discarded clothes and papers.

'I'm busy, Dad.'

'Things to do, people to see?'

She scowls, no hint of softening.

It's inevitable, he tells himself as he perches on her bed and she turns her face away like her mother did moments earlier, that a daughter will draw away from her father. It doesn't mean anything.

He forces himself to take a breath, struggling not to say the wrong thing.

'You had Mum worried today.'

It is the wrong thing.

Chrissie snorts. 'But not you. Because you didn't even pick up your phone.'

Cal's heart rate stutters, he feels a closing down inside himself. It's all too hard. He hasn't felt this way for years, not since Margot vanished. He feels the urge to shout, to shake her, to get through to her. It frightens him. He does not want to be his father.

'I'm sorry,' he says instead, baring himself to her in the way he couldn't to his wife, admitting it. 'It's this series I'm working on. It's getting inside my head.'

Some of the victims were Chrissie's age. Snatched on the way to school, terrorised, discarded. Images seared in his brain. Close-ups of narrow wrists, bound with rope that burned and cut the skin. He swallows.

Chrissie stares out of the window at the purple leaves on the copper beech shading the side of the house. Even through the fog of his own crisis he can see she is not okay.

'What's going on? This isn't like you, walking out of school.'

Her head jerks round.

'How do you know what's like me? You don't know me. Not any more.' She fixes him with sea-green eyes that brim with tears she is trying to hold back. He feels afraid of her, like he's failing her without knowing how.

'I want to help.'

'Then leave me alone.' She makes the words sharp then turns, facing away from him, eyes on the tree that has sheltered her since childhood.

He doesn't know what to do. Sits, for a moment, withering under uncertainty. Then he rises, slowly, goes to the door, wishing she would turn and tell him to stay, hating himself for floundering.

From the doorway he glances back, torn, wanting someone to tell him what to do. In that moment he wishes for Margot: ten years older than him, sparky, wise – always on his side. He has tried to run from the pain of her loss but it is impossible, it only grows, finds new ways to work at him. Now, looking at Chrissie, he wishes so desperately that she were here. She would understand.

But then, if she hadn't gone, maybe none of this would be happening at all.

CHAPTER TWO

The building is daunting to approach. After several hours in the car Cal is stiff; he shifts the bag that holds his recording equipment further up his shoulder. He gazes up at Broadmoor's Victorian façade, taking in its arched windows and the imposing gate that stands between him and the man he is here to meet. The famous clock tower shines in the weak sunlight.

Dread runs through him. Every time he comes he is sure Dubois will cancel, change his mind, even at the final moment. Today he wishes he would. Last night's upset folds shadows over him, but it's more than that. He is afraid.

Getting in takes even longer than previously. When he shows his photo ID, the guard studies it intently, no hint that he's seen Cal before. He has his fingerprints checked; his bags scanned. The staff are always alert, on edge.

'Leave your things in here.' The man gestures to an open locker.

Securing permission to take in even the most pared-back recording equipment required months of letters and the approval of the Secretary of State. He unloads the essentials – an ambient microphone only – and slides his bag into the locker. Even solicitors are not permitted to take in more than pen and paper.

Alone in the blank interview room, he waits. He needs to settle his nerves, to pull on a mask quickly, or Dubois will see. The man is a snake, watchful, deadly. Cal is aware that he is being recorded by the cameras that litter the institution, mechanical eyes that probe every movement. He smooths his trousers with his palms, breathes deeply.

As much as he knows he should, he can't just walk away. His ratings have been on a downward slide for a while now. He may have been one of the first British true crime podcasters, shifting rapidly from dry radio documentaries to the new medium, but a tidal wave of competition followed. Cal's producer, Sarah, barely conceals her impatience and he knows she is aggrieved to be landed with him, would take any excuse to offload the dead weight she inherited from her predecessor. He is on a knife edge.

But then the letters arrived. Dubois – Woodland Killer, the Face of Evil – had never once granted an interview. Cal was given exclusive access; hints were dropped that there was more to reveal about the other victims, the missing who vanished without a trace. Police estimated there could be twenty more, thirty. Maybe Cal could be the one to find them.

Even Sarah seemed excited. This series would be the one to elevate the podcast. But Dubois is a slippery subject and every time Cal tries to tighten his grip, the man slithers away. Instead of baring his soul, he has inveigled his way into Cal's head; his dreams teem with terrifying details, heart-breaking pain. Feelings that bring back memories.

Before Cal can fully collect himself, Dubois steps into the room, handcuffed to a minder. The man's diminutive stature and ferret-like features are infamous – his picture published so many times in the papers that every time it startles Cal to see the echoes of that image in folds of fat. His skin is even paler today and he wears nondescript jogging bottoms, a loose T-shirt. A far cry from the strong, fit man who lured young women with his striking looks and easy charm.

Dubois spends much of his time alone – other patients don't take kindly to him and there have been attempts on his life. Cal's eyes can't help but slide to the jagged scar on the man's neck, evidence of the time that the rigorous procedures to protect him failed and a fellow inmate made it through the cordon with a shard of shower tile.

Dubois sees him looking, tilts his head back proudly to expose the vivid line, concrete hardness in his eyes. He is always shackled while Cal speaks to him. It's either that or have several other people in the room. The hospital team will be right outside, behind glass, watching the body language, ready to intervene. They never speak to Cal. He wonders if they disapprove of this endeavour – of giving the wicked a voice.

'Good morning.'

The killer nods at Cal. Doesn't smile. Waits for everyone to arrange themselves. The chains clank as they are locked, tugged. Sweat breaks out on Cal's forehead. *Get a grip.*

'How did you sleep?' He keeps his tone polite, hides the sudden plunge of foreboding, the feeling that today is a mistake. He isn't up to it.

Dubois smiles and Cal sees his pointed canines. The bite marks Dubois left on the bodies of nine young women were not post-mortem. He steels himself not to shudder, reminds himself this man will never be released.

'I don't really sleep these days, Mr Lovett. I don't need to. Doesn't look like you had a good eight hours either, though.' The voice – rusted, grating – curls around him.

Cal slides the chocolate bars he has been instructed to bring across the table, changing the subject from his own sleeplessness.

'I brought your Twixes.'

There is a flash of fury behind the man's eyes. The rage burns the air around them, scorching the atmosphere.

'I asked for fucking Mars Bars.'

He didn't. But there's no point in trying to convince him.

'I'm sorry,' he says.

'You're just like them.' Dubois' eyes glitter. 'Can't get anything right. Fucking useless. Shame I can't make you understand. If you walked on broken bottles you'd think more carefully.'

His tone is petulant rather than threatening now, but his fists clench and the chains shift. Cal swallows nausea. His mind springs to Janine Rollins, one of Dubois' victims. Her feet were completely shredded. The pathologist pulled 200 splinters of glass from her soles. That wasn't the worst thing that happened to her.

Dubois fixes him with a look of hatred that seems to pierce Cal's core. The moment hovers between them. He wants to look away but he cannot break the gaze, cannot hear anything other than the rushing of blood in his head.

Then the man shrugs, drags the package nearer. Cal's chest releases as Dubois peels the wrapper from a Twix and bites into it, closing his eyes in bliss. He chews with his mouth open and Cal can see the caramel sticking to his teeth. The shift from rage to relaxation takes place in a fraction of a second.

When he has eaten, the man – the monster – opens his eyes, leans forward conspiratorially, makes a show of looking around. Cal sees the flash of charm and the dangerous charisma that still lurks inside him, though in the bloated body with its dirty fingernails and pungent smell, it seems grotesque.

'What do you want to know today?'

'You hinted in your letters that there is more to be told about your... story?'

They both know this is why Cal is here, why he comes again and again. There are people out there who have no answers, who need to know.

Dubois mimics his hesitation, feigns surprise. 'You want to know about my... crimes?'

He tilts his head back and laughs. The sound jangles Cal's nerves.

Cal knows that Dubois enjoys playing with him. There is little else that passes for amusement in his life. That is the bargain he made, the deal with the devil. But he's starting to wonder if he will ever get paid.

He ploughs ahead with his questions, ignoring the barbs. Dubois answers them mechanically but Cal can see his attention is slipping. He is bored, unchallenged. His fingers stretch as far as the chains allow to scratch at dry areas on his arms, dead skin drifting from them. Cal tries to look interested in the stock replies, searching for a chink in the standard narrative. Normally he is good at this, enjoys the thrill of the chase, but there is something about this man that slices through him.

'Tell me more about your mother,' he says. This subject is off limits but he is desperate. Dubois gives yet another shrug but there is something in the set of his shoulders that convinces Cal it is the route to more. 'She died when you were young. Maybe you don't remember her?'

'I was twelve. But she wasn't exactly worth remembering.'

'That's a shame.'

Dubois moves uncomfortably in his seat; his fingers return to his arms. It fascinates Cal to see the discomfort and the distaste on his face. All the more reason to push at the bruise.

'My father is the interesting one,' Dubois says, picking now at a fingernail, his voice dangerously quiet, warning Cal away.

'Really? What did he think of your mother?'

He regrets the challenge almost immediately.

Dubois jerks his head up, his face contorted, his body pulling at the restraints. 'He thought she was a fucking whore.'

The violence of the hissed words is stark. Cal knows what this man has done, what he is capable of doing, but even so, the instant hatred, the veins popping in his head, shocks him. He gathers himself, concealing the rattling feeling inside.

Dubois spits out his venom. 'She was fucking half the village.'

'Is that true, though?'

Patricia Dubois. The model for her son's loathing and lust. In truth, she was having an affair with one local farmer, seeking solace from the reputedly ferocious temper of her husband.

'I remember one night.' Dubois' pupils dilate, and Cal represses a shudder at the snake-like expression that slides onto his face. 'My father got us out of bed to watch. He used his belt. Made sure she was sorry. She screamed. I can still hear her, you know.' He taps the side of his head with a chained hand.

'Then he told her she could go but not with anything he'd paid for. He took it all off her. Every last stitch. Kicked her out into the snow and made her run. Naked.'

Cal's heart beats faster at the vacant delight in Dubois' eyes. He tries to imagine a father waking his young children to terrorise their mother in front of them. It doesn't take a psychologist to understand the origins of the man's sadism: he learned it on his father's knee. Dubois made his victims run too. But he never let them get away.

'How did she die?' His voice comes out a whisper.

Dubois holds his gaze. 'A farm accident. Such a shame. But you do have to be careful around tractors, I've heard.' He barks out a laugh. 'Her face when she realised.'

'When she realised what?'

His mind fills with pictures of the tractor shed, runs away with thoughts. Dubois wasn't there. No one was. That's the story.

But retelling his mother's death seems to have refreshed the man, woken him from his stupor. He lowers his voice to a flat whisper that Cal has to strain to hear. 'She wasn't the first, you know.' Dubois holds his gaze as if craving the reaction.

'Your mother?' For a moment Cal can't grasp what he is talking about.

'Noooo,' he says as if it were obvious. 'Mandy.' He wets his lips and all Cal's journalistic instincts stand to attention. This is it. The payoff for these hours of oily revelations and the images that will never leave his mind. Dubois flicks his eyes to the glass, behind which a nurse stands, motionless... '*They* think she was.' He stretches and lets another superior snort free. 'All of you do.'

'You went to college together. She was unkind to you.' Cal stumbles, aghast at the way his thoughts are slipping from him.

He knows this is a distortion. It was Dubois who showed an unhealthy interest in poor Amanda Lyons. She turned him down and he waited months to retaliate, nursed the rejection, fed it. But Cal has to be willing to play along.

'She wasn't the first to treat me that way.' His eyes shine. 'I made them all sorry. In the end.'

Amanda Lyons was found tied to a tree, tortured. There was river water in her lungs but no river nearby. He'd moved her from place to place. He kept her alive. Cal forces his mind away from the known victims. They have their justice, such as it is.

'So, who was the first?'

Dubois shrugs, leans back again, apparently having lost interest. He stretches a hand for more chocolate, takes his time unwrapping and savouring.

Cal wants to scream. He pictures himself wrapping his hands around the man's neck, squeezing out the truth. The vividness of the image shocks him. There is something about Dubois that makes the air cold, changes you. It's like a contagion.

A few moments later and Dubois is glassy eyed with the sugar rush, following another manic tangent. 'One woman: her husband was playing away,' he leans forward and cackles wheezily, 'and they pinned it on him. He died in jail last year. Appeal denied.' He folds in two, laughing, as if this is a joke.

It is hard to navigate the ping-pong nature of the man's thoughts. There are no rules, there is little to cling to.

'Tell me about her, then.'

Dubois shakes his head, irritated. 'Maybe another time.' He smirks, returns his gaze to the window and starts humming, an old tune Cal recognises but can't place immediately. Eventually it comes to him. *Daisy, Daisy, give me your answer, do.* The sweet sound is incongruous in the small interview room. He can smell the man's sweat, mingled with the sickly odour of the chocolate, the closeness of the air in a building where so many windows are sealed.

From the room, you can see twelve-foot walls, flanked by security fences, topped with razor wire. Beyond is a forest, the nearest trees felled to increase visibility. All of Dubois' victims were found in woodland. All of his known victims. Cal wonders what he thinks when he looks out and sees the dead stumps.

'The Woodland Killer. That's what they called me.'

It is as if he can read Cal's mind. The notion sends an icy chill through his blood. He swallows, nods. It's irrational, it's just this place getting to him. All the same, he is relieved when Dubois turns back to the window and he can collect himself for a moment.

'They don't know the half of it,' the machine voice grinds out the words. Before Cal has time to digest them, to understand, Dubois swivels to face him again.

'Don't you ever feel like you might just... snap?'

Cal shakes his head. Can Dubois see his thoughts? The sick feeling that nestled inside him after Margot went stirs. He has never truly rid himself of it, but mostly it slumbers.

'I think you're lying.' Cal's eyes are drawn to the man's mouth, his tongue probing at cracked skin. 'To yourself.'

'Maybe.' He forces the word out. For rapport. For the story.

'All men feel it. The sight of *them*.' Dubois returns his gaze to the window. Cal wishes he could breathe fresh air. 'Tell me again why you want to interview me?'

He has been through this over and over. It's nothing more than ego stroking.

'I think my listeners will be interested in what you have to say,' he parrots. 'In why you did the things you did. They want to understand you.'

'They want,' Dubois leans forward again and Cal catches a whiff of stale sweat, 'to see the monster under the bed.'

'You weren't born a monster,' Cal says, though he struggles to believe the words now he is sitting in front of unrepentant evil. 'Things happened to you. That made you this way.' Margot flutters inside him like panic.

Dubois rocks back, his scorn bouncing off the close walls.

'I know what you really want. You're just like the rest.' He shakes his head in disapproval, as if curiosity is the greatest crime. 'Do you have a dog?'

Confusion empties Cal; leaves him numb. 'Yes, one,' he says, his voice faint.

Dubois sniffs. 'I had dogs. Lots of them.'

'I know.'

He had seventeen dogs when he was arrested. Kennelled at his home, they were well cared for, but they attacked the people who came to rescue them, flying against the wire of their cages, thrashing, snarling, drooling. Only three of them survived. The others had to be destroyed.

'It's hard to find enough for that many dogs to eat,' Dubois says, staring at Cal. 'Enough meat, I mean. You have to do a lot of hunting.'

Cal thinks this time he will be sick. He feels completely dislocated; the interview has slipped from his control.

There is a rap on the glass and he startles, making the killer laugh.

'Tick tock. Time's up. Lock me up, throw away the key. It won't make a difference. In the end, we're all dumped in our own scrapyards, aren't we?'

Cal's brow creases in confusion at the words that sound like riddles. He is desperate to leave the room, and yet anchored in place by the horror, by the need to know. 'Can you give me a name, before you go?'

The key is turning in the door, the nurses start to file in. Dubois shakes his head sadly, pondering. 'A name? But which name would I give, *Christopher*?'

Cal freezes. Christopher isn't his name any more. It hasn't been for years.

His mind tumbles over itself. How does Dubois know his old identity? How? It's crowded in the room now: the six designated staff circle their patient. Cal flounders in the heat and revelation.

But then Dubois turns, looks back at him and everything around them seems to fall away.

'I suppose I could give you one name,' he says, his tongue darting over his cracked lips. 'Just for now.' There is a strange false kindness in his eyes. 'How about Margot? Would that do you?'

Cal's mouth falls open, his blood drains. He gasps a breath of stale air, but he cannot speak. Is this the truth? Is this what he has been waiting for? He wants to rewind and run, to have never set foot in this place. It has all been a terrible mistake.

Fast, so fast he can barely see it, a hand between the shoulder blades turns Dubois. They whisk him away as if on rails, adhering to an immovable timetable of routine, stopping for nothing.

'Wait,' he calls, but they are gone.

Cal staggers. He reaches for the table as the blackness intrudes on his vision and sinks into the chair, winded and destroyed, hearing only the door clanging shut at the end of the corridor. Locking his answers on the other side.

CHAPTER THREE

Cal retreats the way he came in, gathers his belongings from the locker in a daze, and emerges into a cold wind. His mind is a scrambled tapestry. How does Dubois know about Margot? He can't know. This isn't happening. It is years since he escaped being Chris Longacre and the shadow of what that meant.

He drives fast through ordinary residential streets, the monolith of Broadmoor behind him. These quiet roads have protocols, living in the gaze of the hospital. If a patient absconds, the sirens will sound and the schools will close, the hatches come down. It has been decades since an escaped inpatient killed a local child, but the town remembers, has to live with the failure. It knows the worst inhabitants are not people you ever want near your family. Even in memory.

Cal needs time to think, to assess, to untangle the threads of his conversation with Dubois. But on the two-hour drive he cannot get a grip. Fear roots inside him, raw and blinding. He can feel stress building between his shoulder blades, is conscious of the weight and the tension, knows he is barrelling towards something awful but he cannot face it, not yet.

There is no one at the house. He dumps his bag and takes the dog for a long walk along the river. The water is surface-still. It should be calming, but the feeling doesn't reach him. Rocket bounces ahead, his tail wagging, joyfully snapping at insects that rise around him, burying his nose in the reeds.

His sister's shadow joins them. Echoes of the life he deliberately left behind. Margot is the reason Chris became Cal. But how did Dubois know? He cannot stomach the thought that tries to rise inside him, doubles his pace, trying to escape it. *We're all dumped in our own scrapyards.* The words nudge at him, insistent.

There has to be a rational explanation. Another rational explanation. It's not as if he has tried to conceal his old life, he tells himself. It's just that no one has thought to look before now. Of course a man with an obsessive personality and endless time to wonder would seek to satisfy his curiosity about the journalist interviewing him. That's all this is.

And yet. The knowledge that Dubois has hidden scores of terrible crimes chases Cal along the riverbank, sullies the clear cold sky and the flash of kingfisher blue in the distance. What if there's another reason he knows too much?

Not that. Anything but that.

Cal stumbles, then sinks to the ground in a crouch, a moan escaping his lips. A second later, Rocket's wet nose snuffles his neck. He grasps the dog's collar, uses it to anchor himself, to stop the tide of distress pulling him away. He ruffles the velvet ears and forces himself to breathe.

He will gather his resources about the killer, he decides, letting the dog go and scanning the empty horizon. The piles of articles, news reports and copies of police files, the tattered biographies, he will go through them all again.

Then he will be ready, armed for another conversation. Not like today, when the man danced circles around him.

Margot's face spins into view, not blurry like she usually is, but tangible, distinct. He grits his teeth so hard they hurt. Then he whistles for the dog, turns for home.

—

The atmosphere in the house is glacial. He means to talk to Allie, but every time he tries to form the words his resolve withers. She won't ask how it went. She is angry, but he has also always kept the details of his investigations away from her and Chrissie. How can he change that now? He can't share the images imprinted in his mind: the blood-spattered silver birches; the torn skin; the manic enjoyment in Dubois' swollen features as he remembered.

Chrissie doesn't come down for dinner and Allie retreats to her studio, leaving Cal stranded on an island between them. He eats alone at the table, laptop open and dog at his feet, plagued by memories of the day, anxiety billowing inside him. He holds it in, afraid to speak, refusing to make it real.

In the morning, he watches the dog follow Chrissie along the track to the school bus. He feels a sudden impulse to call her back. From here she is a flash of daughter-sister-daughter again. His hands shake as he grips the windowsill.

Allie is filling the dishwasher when he leaves. She doesn't notice the film of perspiration on his skin, or if she does she doesn't comment.

She turns to him. 'We need you.'

'I just have a meeting with Sarah. Then I'll be back to do some research. I'll be contactable,' he says, knowing that isn't what she means but unable to comfort her.

25

She turns back to the sink, her shoulders slumped. 'Good luck.'

For a moment he can see the opening, the extended hand. He opens his mouth to tell her what Dubois said. *The killer knows my name, knows Margot's. Help, Allie, help me.* But the words stick in his throat and he thinks he will choke. He closes down. Just like always.

–

In Birmingham, it feels reassuringly busy. Pausing at Victoria Square, he takes comfort from the people around him, the sense of safety they offer. But as he gazes, the thoughts darken. What secrets do they hide, these people, whispering around them, falling between their outlines?

The now-dry statue of the reclining woman looks strange in her bed of foliage. He can't get used to the decision to turn off the fountain, beach the goddess. Leaving the square, he glances at his watch: he is late. The metallic body of the Bullring towers over him like an alien life form and he quickens his step, conscious that Sarah will not like being kept waiting. Sure enough, he sees her at a window table in the cafe, glancing at her watch and tapping her foot.

Cal's last producer was sitting out his years until retirement. Either he understood that interference could ruin the carefully calibrated tone, the fragile relationships with his subjects' families, or he didn't give a shit. Whichever reason, it suited Cal perfectly. Sarah is different. She wants to co-ordinate, market, push.

To be fair, she probably doesn't like him very much either. She's on the up and he's dragging her down. She wants star ratings, publicity, forward motion. He knows the ratings slide has placed him in the production company's crosshairs.

Her latest idea is a live audience event. He has tried to explain to her that no one is going to pay ten quid to sit in a hall and listen to a middle-aged stubbly bloke in a mountaineering T-shirt talking about missing people. This is not strictly true – he knows he has some very dedicated fans, but he doesn't have any desire to meet them and shatter their illusions.

He's going to have to tell her, he realises as he weaves through the chairs to her table, struggling to squeeze past a harassed mother with a buggy and screaming child. He can't keep it a secret. He feels jittery even before the caffeine, as if the killer's malicious gaze has branded him somehow. As if she will know as soon as she looks at him.

'Sorry,' he says, putting his rucksack on the chair and shrugging off his coat. 'Can I get you another?'

Sarah frowns, taps a manicured fingernail on the table, where a tiny cup sits empty. 'Espresso.'

He marvels at how she has managed to get here from London so early, looking immaculate in a white shirt, black trousers and heeled boots. She wears jewellery that looks like modern art and always behaves as if she's just downed seven coffees. He has a feeling Chrissie and Allie would love Sarah.

He has to queue for a while and he can see her staring at her phone, increasingly frustrated at the delay. As he places the coffees on the table, he tries to arrange the words in his head, but she launches straight in before he can speak.

'How did yesterday go?'

'Good.'

'Really? Because I've listened to the other recordings, Cal. There's no substance. Just hints.'

'It's early days. I'm getting him to trust me.'

He shivers at his own words. What parts of yourself do you have to sacrifice to earn a killer's trust?

'We need something juicy, to get the ratings. People like a specific case. A victim. Find me a pretty face and a distraught family or we've got nothing to go on.'

Cal sets down his coffee cup too hard, slopping hot liquid over his hand, onto the table.

'Shit.'

She doesn't say a word, passes a napkin, but he can feel the contempt. He inhales and tries to calm the red heat of anger he feels. She doesn't know what she's saying.

'It's Dubois. Marc Dubois. The first interviews ever. This is a massive coup. With or without a new victim.' He shouldn't have to explain how compelling the fear that weaves itself around this killer is. People will listen.

'Did he give you any names yesterday? Anything concrete?'

This is Cal's chance to come clean. He tells himself to speak. To explain. But he hears his sister's voice, and he remembers the way the sun hit her hair through the kitchen window and her hand setting his cereal bowl in front of him, and if he says her name right now he will start crying and never stop.

Sarah is oblivious to his distress. 'We only have two advertisers lined up so far. It's not enough. I need clips I can use to hook more. We need to start psyching up your fans.'

The producer's words tumble over him – costs, times-cales, audience, episode length. Time, time, time.

Guilt and fear and secrecy pound inside Cal, tying him in knots and paralysing him. Then another thought intrudes: what if he tells her and she pulls him off the story? It is the kind of thing she would do.

He cannot risk it.

'I have another session with him next week. I'll get him to talk.'

After that. He'll tell her after that.

Sarah sighs, then knocks back her espresso in one swift movement. Standing, she looks down at him from her vertiginous heels, disdain in her eyes.

'You had better.'

CHAPTER FOUR

Cal doesn't go home straight away. He has parked near the library at Paradise Circus and is drawn instead to its post-modern latticed design, rising before him like the tiers of a cake. Inside he goes to the true crime section, searches for Dubois' salacious history. Half a dozen attempts at dissection, nestled alongside tomes on the Yorkshire Ripper and Myra Hindley.

Everyone in the country knows his name, his face. Cal doubts his victims would be recognised by anyone. Their lives are a footnote to his notoriety. When one of those missing names, those fractured lives, could be your own sister's, it is less easy to understand why the perpetrators get all the attention. Deep down, he knows it is fear, the monster under the bed, the need to tell ourselves that if we are vigilant, well prepared, it cannot happen to us. It can, though. He knows it can.

The library is distractingly quiet. He skim-reads the books, going back over the details, searching in vain for the period of time he is interested in. He wants to know he is wrong, that it cannot be. But there is nothing that covers that year.

He works feverishly until lunchtime, barely looking up as he scans and scribbles, rushing past the pages that bear the gory details. In the last book there is a section of photographs in the middle. He doesn't want to look, he knows he shouldn't, but his hands turn the pages automatically.

It's the policeman he notices first, young and ash-grey in the background, smoking a cigarette. It could seem disrespectful, but Cal can forgive him, he knows the twenty-year-old found the woman lying under a blanket at his feet. Her shoes are next to her, high heels set carefully in the mud, and a bleached arm protrudes from the makeshift cover, fingers curled, broken nails encrusted with dirt.

His mind connects the image to Margot, to what might have happened to her, and his vision swims. He grips the corners of the desk, lays his forehead on the wood, taking in slow, long breaths. When he finally stretches from his cramped position, he gathers his sheets of paper, which are peppered with dates and question marks, and returns the books to the shelves with a shaking hand.

Exhausted, Cal grabs a sandwich to eat in the car and escapes the library's echoing atrium. Instead of Margot, he makes his thoughts turn to Chrissie and whatever has suppressed her usual quiet happiness. He should have tried harder the other night, he thinks, biting into the sandwich as he walks to the car park, too hungry to wait. He's going to talk to her properly later. They'll get to the bottom of whatever is going on.

His phone vibrates in his pocket and he juggles sandwich and water bottle in a panic, knowing he must not miss any calls from his wife today. But when he looks at the screen it isn't her number. How odd that, today of all days, Andy should call.

Though the voice is older, tired and worn, Cal's mind springs back to the tall, fair-haired man who took him to the pub that terrible summer when no one else could see him through their tears. He remembers Andy crying into his pint: his sister's boyfriend as lost without her as he was. They've stayed in touch since then. Not often, a call or two a year these days.

'How are you, Andy?'

He thinks he hears a wheeze in the man's throat that wasn't there when they last spoke. Andy has never managed to give up smoking. There are lots of things he has never managed to do – find someone else to love, get married, have children.

'Thought I'd check in with you.' Andy coughs. 'I dreamed of her last night.'

Cal could tell Andy about Dubois. He's one of the few people who would feel the horror as keenly. But the man is frail. Can he do that to him?

'It's coming up, you know?' Sadness and resignation travel down the line to Cal and find a mirror image.

'It is.'

Andy never forgets her birthday. She would have been fifty-four this year. The anniversary seems significant, the mystery of her disappearance a failure that hangs over them all. Cal's mind flashes to the woman beneath the blanket, the useless arm, the broken nails.

He swallows. 'Will I see you at the park? At her bench?'

'I'll be there.'

Cal always goes twice. Once with his mother and later with Andy. Never together. The bench is their touch-stone.

That's the thing about a missing person. She is unanchored in the world. There is nowhere to go to mourn her. There is no closure. The best possible fantasy is that she upped and left, is living her life somewhere without you. But now Cal has to live with the worst possibility. He can't tell Andy what he's thinking, not yet. It would torment him.

He reaches the car and fumbles for his keys.

'Well. Best get on,' Andy says, as he always does, though what he has to get on with isn't clear. Their calls are never more than a few minutes long. 'You give my regards to those girls of yours.'

Andy hasn't met them. He has never asked, and Cal would refuse if he did. He never lets Allie come with him to the bench – though she's asked year after year, so badly wants to be there for support. He keeps it separate. Chris and Cal. Then and now. Chris isn't really alive any more. He slipped away when Margot vanished. Cal wouldn't know what to do with him if he came back.

–

By the time he drives home, Cal feels bone tired; hopeless and dark. He takes the steps up to their once-adored porch slowly. The air feels heavy.

'Allie?'

The house is quiet. Too early for Chrissie to be back. He dumps his bags on the floor of the kitchen and takes two beers from the fridge. A peace offering. The back door swings shut behind him and he follows the over-grown path to the studio in the old barn at the edge of their property. The trees have thrust their branches into his way, the grasses are long and wet. He can see the route that Allie weaves daily so he follows her footsteps, the beer bottles clinking between his fingers.

He is going to talk to her about Dubois. He needs to reach across the divide that has grown between them. He is thinking how best to approach the conversation, is so intent on formulating the right expression that he doesn't immediately realise what he is seeing through the back door of the barn. There is a square window at eye level, only a small frame in comparison to the wall of glass that overlooks the fields on the other side.

The first thing to catch his eye is the canvas she is working on – it must be fifteen foot high and half as wide. In it he glimpses the talent she displayed in her twenties, great slashes and splashes of colour that left her when Chrissie was born. It takes his breath away, recognition bursting over him like sunlight. But then he falters, slides his hand from the door. Because Allie is standing only a few metres away, her lips pressed to another man's, his hands tangled in her hair.

Cal lurches to the side, only just catching the beer that slips from his grip, mercifully stopping the bottle smashing at his feet. He stares in shock until a hot feeling of shame and terror pours over his mind. He staggers back a step and his legs take the cue to retreat, stumbling along the pathway, the foolish offerings cold in his hands.

As Cal trips into the house and dumps the beers on the table, terrified he will be noticed and pursued, his phone starts to ring. If he was in his right mind, he wouldn't answer. But he doesn't have time to make that assessment. His brain screams out at him as his fingers slide automatically to the screen. Sarah. Why is Sarah calling him? He has only just seen her, he thinks stupidly, as he holds the phone to his ear.

He doesn't have to speak.

'Have you heard?' She sounds breathless, he can hear her heels clacking on a pavement somewhere.

'Heard what?' That his life is in freefall?

'Dubois.'

Has the man given another interview? Cancelled their arrangement? Admitted to other crimes? His thoughts speed around pointlessly, his fingers cold, his mind only half on her words.

'They found him in his cell this morning. The news just broke.'

'What?'

'He's dead, Cal. They found him hanging from the door handle.'

CHAPTER FIVE

Cal paces the kitchen. His hands jerk to his face, he tugs at his hair. The dog whines at his frenetic movements. The image of his wife entwined with another man competes with a vision of Dubois kneeling on the floor of his room, all of his secrets taken with him forever. Twin strikes of grief. He has lost his opportunity to find out what happened to his sister. The podcast, the hope, the plan – all gone. Shattered.

'Fuck,' he moans, and the sound is animal, wild.

The dog whimpers at his feet. Cal stares at the room and it looks different, like he doesn't belong to it. He wants to talk to Allie. He loves her. He hates her. His mind flashes to Dubois, to his scorn for women. He has to get away or he will do something awful. He grabs his keys, feels them bite his palm as he runs to the car.

He drives. All good intentions dissolve. The life he built so carefully is collapsing. Deep inside, maybe he always thought it would. For the first time in years he wants his mother, his childhood. He wants to be back then, before everything changed.

He holds the wheel steady for an hour, going in no particular direction, choosing roads for no reason, pressing on the pain and the blame until it blinds him, eclipses everything good.

Eventually it is too much, he is too tired to go on. He parks in a woodland car park and rests his head on the wheel. Grief pinballs inside him: for Allie, for Chrissie, for Margot, but he cannot cry.

It is stifling in the car, so he cracks open the window and the cool air makes him shake. It's the shock, he realises, distantly. He takes deep breaths. Catastrophic thoughts chase their tails around his head.

Outside, the sun sinks behind the woodlands. People come back to their cars with dogs and children, only to be replaced by others, all casting a wary glance at the lone man who remains in his car.

This is just the kind of woodland Dubois favoured. The sort of place he took his victims, where they were later found tied to trees, eyes glazed, screams still on their lips. They did not die quickly. How many times was Dubois a man in a car, glanced at and forgotten? He closes his eyes for a moment, steadies his breathing. He can't let himself fall down that rabbit hole. He will never come out.

It is dusky dark when he arrives home for the second time, excuses on his lips. He will not reveal what he saw earlier. He needs time to take it in. To decide what to do. But the knowledge of Allie's infidelity is poison in his veins.

When he reaches the kitchen and sees her concerned face, he is floored. Did she see him outside her studio? Is it now? Is this when it ends?

'I saw it on the news,' she says, taking his bag from him, setting it down. 'What are you going to do?'

He looks dumbly at her, only then notices Chrissie at the table, her face an equal mask of concern.

'I'm really sorry, Dad. It was such a good scoop.'

Dubois.

He wants to cry at the sight of them. His family. United for a moment. Too late. Cal runs his hand across his head, playing for time and composure. Allie rubs his arm and he feels himself recoil, but she crosses the room to the wine rack, oblivious.

'Sarah keeps phoning,' he says. 'I need to get back to her.'

'We've ordered pizza,' Allie says, handing him a glass. The red sloshes against the sides like blood as he takes it. Her finger curls over his for the briefest second. He pulls his hand away.

'I'm going up to the office – I need to go through the recordings I have, see what I can do with them.'

'No problem, we can bring you some up.' Allie is always good in a crisis. She is able to put herself to the side until it's over. But he can't appreciate it today.

Upstairs, he clears old papers from his desk and piles them on the floor, trying to shift the image of Allie and the other man from his mind. Who is he? Tremors of rage compete with despair. He is afraid of himself. Work is the only place he can escape for a while.

From his bag he takes the books and the notes, gathers anything related to Dubois. He starts to arrange his thoughts, using a piece of paper to create bubbles of possibility, linked to each other by arrows and lines. He is putting it off. Listening. Ordinarily he loves the editing stage, cutting and slicing the words to create something new, tell the story. Not this time.

He starts the recording.

All at once the room is filled with the killer's scratchy tones. He listens to the wheedling charms, the pointless small talk, the time he now knows was wasted. He can hear the way the man ran circles around his conversation, only really said what he wanted to, slippery and conniving.

It's a myth that you need to hang from a high rope to die – Cal knows that. Dubois could asphyxiate himself if he had the motivation. But there's something about the death and its timing that makes Cal uneasy. Dubois was having fun with him, taunting and provoking. Would he drop a tiny clue and then kill himself without waiting for the punchline? It just doesn't make sense.

His heart beats faster. He has reached the part of the last recording where the man seemed to lose sense of reality – the strange singsong floats around him. Only now he can't listen without seeing Margot's face, imagining Dubois gripping her perfect skin, picturing her terror. What if her final moments were with him? There is nothing worse, surely there is nothing worse? And all his life he has believed not knowing is the ultimate pain.

The door to the room opens and for a moment Margot is standing there, her hair framing her face: no marks on her skin, no pain in her eyes. Then the vision disappears and it is Chrissie, a pizza box and the half-empty bottle of wine in her hands. Her brow furrows with confusion as she listens to Dubois.

He slams his hand down, clicks the mouse frantically to pause the interview. She cannot have this inside her head. Silence pours in, cleansing his ears of the tarry feeling. He has spoken to murderers so many times before, but this is different. This one has crawled inside Cal's head and laid his eggs there. Waiting to hatch.

'Pizza's here.'

'Thanks, Chris.'

There it is: the name he relinquished. He gave it to his daughter. It's hers now. He notes her fragility, the sad way she moves. Does she know what's going on with her mother? Is that it? Could he ease the burden if he tells her it's okay, he knows? She places the box next to him and peers at his scribbled thoughts, lingering. He reaches out and pats her hand. It's cold.

'You okay?'

She nods. The veins in her neck are faintly blue against milk skin; a reddish curl falls across her face and she brushes it away.

'You know you can tell me anything, Christina, don't you?' The words spring from nowhere. He says them gently but she startles all the same, like a deer in the woods. 'I mean it,' he says. 'There's nothing so big it could ever come between us. Nothing you could do. You know that, right?' Cal isn't sure what he is trying to say; he feels so emotional, as if the world is about to end. Their world. 'I'm here. If you ever need me. For anything.'

Chrissie puts her palms flat on the paper chaos, studies her fingernails in the lamplight. Then she nods.

'Thanks, Dad.'

And like the deer in the woods she is gone, leaving only the imprint of her absence and the voice of evil behind her.

Cal stares at the door for a moment. Then he clicks the mouse.

I suppose I could give you one name. The voice taunts him. *How about Margot?*

CHAPTER SIX

By the morning, Dubois is everywhere. Every news channel, every talk show leads with his death. His face – the old slimline version – is plastered across both broadsheets and tabloids. Smaller portraits cluster beneath him, his victims' smiles betraying nothing of the horror to come, worth fewer column inches than their killer. It makes Cal itch to see them. He may never know, now, if his sister should be one of them.

The news channels scrape so low they even interview released convict Jason Barr. The man briefly shared a cell with Dubois fifteen years ago. Cal's skin crawls at the sight of the broad, suited shoulders, the presenter's courtesy, the rapt attention afforded him. Barr, a man who did twenty years for clubbing women over the head when they left pubs and nightclubs, is soaking up the attention.

He knows Sarah wants to release their recordings too but he avoids her calls. His mind is collapsing in on itself. He can't even look at Allie. He stays in his attic office all day, waiting for the courage to deal with it all, hating himself more the longer he delays, listening to the recordings over and over again.

At midnight, he folds the laptop closed and stares at the shadows on the wall. A headache pulses at his temples, now nudging behind his left eye. He digs in his bag for painkillers, swallows them with wine, stares into the glass as if answers float in the tannin. The house is quiet. His wife and daughter have gone to bed. He needs to sleep but his mind is wired.

He wishes he could go back to that interview room and wheedle more. If only he'd known. Cal cannot bear the thought that the monster is at rest. He wishes for hell, for torture, for regret. Margot's birthday is so close. Fifty-four years old. She should have been here. His stomach churns but he slugs another mouthful of wine anyway. As he does, his eyes drift to the files on his bookshelf. There are stacks of cases there, families calling out for his attention, loved ones desperate for help.

A particular file catches his attention. The date on the spine. 1986. The same year Margot vanished.

Layla. He says her name aloud and it leaves an imprint on the air in the empty room. The family contacted him last year, convinced he could help solve the case of their missing daughter. He receives hundreds of case suggestions and most aren't suitable or, when he looks into them, they dissolve into something different. Her file is one he's kept. Yes, it is a compelling mystery with a likely suspect, but it's more than that – something about her reminded him of Margot. Fierce independence maybe. Women ahead of their time.

He crosses the room, traces the numbers on the spine, his head fuzzy with wine. The family are sure they know who killed her, but there is no body and they need help proving it.

Cal pulls the file from the shelf, flicks through print-outs, newspaper cuttings and notes in his incomprehensible shorthand. A dot on the map, the edge of the Highlands on the road to Inverness. Only twenty miles from Aberdeen, but so very far away from everything plaguing him. He stares at the contours of the map until they blur and he sways with tiredness.

His phone buzzes on the desk, bringing him back to himself. Sarah. Again. She'll have seen he's been online. He thinks about not answering, but he can't hide in this attic forever.

'Cal? Why haven't you been taking my calls?'

'Sorry,' he says. 'Had a few... family issues to deal with. It couldn't be helped.'

'Unfortunate timing.' He knows she won't ask details – she doesn't care. She sounds more annoyed at not being able to get mad at him than anything. 'So. We should release the recordings.'

'Not yet.'

'What do you mean, not yet? He's dead. It's over. What are you waiting for? They're interviewing anyone who ever had any connection to him. Even some low-life he shared a cell with, for Christ's sake.'

'I saw that. Our recordings will get lost in the noise. Let's wait it out. Go big when it dies down.'

Sarah is quiet. Cal can almost hear her doubt, like little metallic cogs turning in her unfeeling mind.

'I'm not sure,' she says finally.

'He referred to other victims. Give me time to investigate.'

'You don't have any names. It's pointless.'

Cal swallows. An image in his mind: the black-and-white crime scene shot of a woman tied to a tree, her chin on her chest, streams of darkness on her skin. He wishes he'd never seen it, that he could erase it from his mind. His shoulders slump as he makes his confession.

'He gave me one name, right at the end.'

'What? You didn't say. Whose? This is great.'

43

At his arm, the phantom of the woman he misses.

'Margot,' he says.

'Surname?'

Here, he hesitates. 'Not yet. But I'll do some digging. I just need some time.'

Sarah is quiet for a moment and when she speaks he can hear the burden, almost feels sorry for her. She sounds so young.

'But we have a series scheduled to go out. We're so close to being cut, Cal. I can't tell you how close.'

So their fortunes are tied. Cal's gaze falls to the file in his hand. Without realising, he has carried it to the desk. His tired brain hums with the edge of the migraine.

'There's another case. I've been working on it for a while.' He hopes Sarah doesn't hear the exaggeration.

'Go on.'

'Layla Mackie. She vanished when she was out riding in 1986, in Aberdeenshire. The horse came tearing back into the stables, blood pouring from its leg. They've looked everywhere for her but she's never been seen again. Her family are sure they know who killed her. It's an easy win.' He hates himself for saying this, for thinking this.

'How long would it take before you could supply an episode?'

The vulnerability vanishes. This is the Sarah he knows.

'A month?'

'No way.'

'Three weeks, then? Two? At a push.'

'Two weeks.'

He doesn't let himself think this through. The times-cale is just not possible. These things take months to set up, years sometimes. You have to cultivate people, tread softly, not blaze in for quick results. But forcing itself up through him is the knowledge that he can't stay here and, more than anything, he needs to buy himself time. He's going to have to use Layla to do that.

CHAPTER SEVEN

He shoves the pile of boxer shorts into a corner of the battered holdall, weighed by the pressure of Allie's gaze, feeling the urge to leave it all behind, get away as fast as he can.

'I thought we talked about this. You can't just vanish at a moment's notice.'

'There are lots of things we can't just do, and yet we do them anyway.'

'What's that supposed to mean?'

He bites down the temptation to confess what he saw only days ago.

Allie's hands are on her hips, frustration in her brown eyes. Dubois' death sits between them, the darkness has spilled in. He can't bear the tension in her voice, roping him to her when he needs to be free to think. He grabs for some T-shirts but her hand stills his, cool fingers that he shakes away, frightened to feel her touch, remembering what he saw through the doorway.

'Cal? You're not listening to me. Can you just stop for a minute? How many times do I need to say it for you to listen?'

'It's my job, Allie. It's not going to be for long.'

'But something's wrong – you've changed. Ever since you started talking to that man.'

She hisses the words through her teeth, because Chrissie is somewhere in the house and she wants to leave her out of it. This feels different to fights they've had in the past. Like they're standing on the edge.

'What are you talking about?'

'You're carrying him with you, Cal. More than you ever have before. It's getting to be too much. You bring this atmosphere into our house, our lives. I can't keep living with the dead, with the effect it's having on you.'

Her words are sharp darts of truth. He hates her for them.

'I'm sorry I'm not cheerful enough for you, Allie.' His voice rises. 'If my need for answers, my past, is inconvenient, then I'm really very sorry.'

Allie's mouth drops open. She throws her hands up and her eyes blaze with anger.

'That's not what I mean, Cal. Don't make this about her. About Margot. I've always been there for you.' Tears threaten. 'I would have been if you'd let me.'

A whisper of shame crosses his mind but he tucks it away because he doesn't want Allie to be right and reasonable, he just wants to get the hell away from her.

He throws a shirt on top of the bag.

'I can't keep doing this.' Her voice is low enough that he has to concentrate as she enunciates. 'You aren't listening to me. It's scaring me, Cal. This has been months now. We need to talk properly, or...'

'Or what?'

He can feel himself pushing her, backing them both into a corner. A tiny part of himself cries out to stop but he doesn't listen.

'Or… maybe there's no point any more.' Allie's eyes are brimming. She's waiting for him to rescue them. He can feel her despair and it scares him that he doesn't care.

'Maybe that would be for the best.'

The words are out before he can stop them.

'What do you mean?'

'I saw you, Allie. In the studio. With *him*.'

Her face flares with heat, regret and guilt filling her eyes.

'Oh God. I'm so sorry. Cal, it was one moment. I… Why didn't you say something? I could have…'

She reaches for him but he pulls his arm away.

'Who is he?'

He doesn't want to know, but he needs to. His mind keeps cataloguing everyone it could be. One of their friends from the village pub? A gallery contact? Who? It's making him hate all other men. He needs one man to focus his anger on. One other man.

'I can't… It doesn't matter who he is, Cal. It was a foolish moment. It isn't about him. It's about us. I'm sorry, I made a terrible mistake.'

'Tell me.'

He sees the light change in his wife's eyes – a stubborn determination he used to love. But in those days it was never used against him.

'No.'

'I have a right to know.'

Allie sucks in a gasp of air and he knows he's gone too far.

'You have a right to nothing.'

She turns on her heel, a smudge of green bright on her cheek. Her long brown hair flows out as she pivots. It's his last glimpse of her – striding away from him in her baggy artist's overalls. He hears her feet on the stairs, then the door slams and seconds later the car's engine guns, gravel complaining beneath angry tyres.

Then silence.

Cal finishes putting clothes into the holdall. He places it neatly in the hallway, beside the recording equipment that will take up most of the room in the car. He concentrates on every movement, trying not to let reality rush in.

Chrissie walks in through the back door, her curls standing out around her head, catching the sunlight. He is relieved she has missed their argument. The dog trots after her, nudges her side with his golden muzzle.

'Where did Mum go?'

Cal sighs. 'She's mad at me for going away,' he says, not able to answer her question.

'But you have to.'

He meets her eyes. They are Allie's eyes, but he can't tell what they're thinking any more then he can fathom his wife. He has a sudden flash of terrible foreboding and loss. Before they know it, she'll be gone. If he wants to stay, it's for her, so he doesn't miss any more moments.

He nods. 'This is important, something I have to do. I'm sorry.'

She helps him load the car. Rocket sits on the porch, his gaze reproachful. He scratches the top of his head.

'Take care of them, boy.'

Over the years, Cal has won awards and developed a following, an online army of sleuths committed to helping him trace witnesses, find documents, parse clues for meaning. He has hidden the cost from these people.

Chrissie stands back, her arms wrapped tightly around her skinny torso, her legs like bean shoots running between her denim mini skirt and a pair of clumpy boots, laces trailing. In her checked shirt and with black-framed glasses, she looks bookish, fragile. His heart tears a little at the sight.

He pulls her into a last hug and she wraps her arms around him, squeezes tight.

'Be good for your mum. Tell her I'll call later.'

She doesn't see him off – just bounds back up the steps and into the house, Rocket at her heels. Her whole life has been marked by this – her father rolling in and out like the tide.

–

At the end of the driveway, the postman is shoving their letters into the mailbox. Cal drives slowly so the van has gone by the time he reaches the turning. Now that he has left home, the implications of Allie's infidelity and their disintegration are hitting him. The back of his throat hurts and his cheeks are red – he feels stoppered by tears. It has been this way since Margot vanished, as if something inside him is blocked. He has locked the pain inside and no one has found the key to it, not even the people he loves. It frightens him sometimes, as if a part of his personality is missing, grief suspended in the absence of answers.

He leaves the engine running while he gets out to check the mail, sifting through the jumble of circulars and bank statements, extracting a couple of items addressed to him. He throws his letters into the seat behind him and pauses to look back one last time, his hand on the top of the open car door.

He is running, giving up on his marriage when he should stay and fight. But for the first time in years, he is more afraid for himself than his family. He can feel himself sinking, the old dark thoughts returning. If he doesn't save himself, he is going to drag them under.

CHAPTER EIGHT

ABERDEENSHIRE

The first place he goes is the last place Layla Mackie was seen. Start at the end. He steps from the car and slams the door so it echoes into wild countryside, awed at the vastness of the landscape.

The track is bordered by slumped drystone walls and barbed wire. Yellow gorse prickles beside them, and small-holdings and farms cling to the hillside as if they could be washed off it at any moment. The sky is huge, the sense of space intimidating.

Cal walks the road that leads to the stables. As he passes under the shadow of a wood that is up a steep bank and behind a wall, he can see horses grazing in some of the fields, their coats thick with mud. The owners retired to Spain a few years ago and it is the daughter who runs the place now.

He won't go there today. First, he needs a sense of what he is dealing with: the possibilities and likelihoods. He needs to know the questions to ask. He also needs to fast-forward through the initial stages of the process. Usually, he would be better prepared. He's agreed with Sarah that this will be different – less polished, more fly on the wall. He'll take the listeners along with him from the start. That's the only way he can get it done.

As he stands gazing across the distance, following a line of pylons with his eyes, Cal returns in his mind to the blank cell-like space where they spoke, he and Dubois. He can almost smell the antiseptic tang of the floor cleaner. Regret for the missed opportunity fills him. The country is delighted Dubois has gone, glorying in his unpleasant end. Cal knows it's irrational of him, but he still finds it impossible to believe that Dubois was a man on the verge of suicide. The air of mischief, anticipation at revealing to Cal how clever he was in deceiving the experts; the request for chocolate. These aren't the actions of a man not intending to stick around. Even without those final taunts.

Could someone else have played a part in asphyxiating the killer with his torn bedsheet? The institution claims a mistake with shifts meant usual checks weren't made in the night, but isn't that a bit too convenient? Or maybe Cal is deluding himself. People can sink into depression in a moment, can act before they have time to think straight. It happens every day.

Dubois was an outpost on a road for Cal: fame and fortune, or at least a steady income and some recognition. But those final words have turned him into something else, something he is afraid will haunt him forever.

He returns to the road and takes out his recording equipment. Poetic narratives have become his trademark. Where others have a newsy, reportage style, he chooses to flesh out the world, tries to draw his listeners into the places and communities he sees. It surprised listeners at first, probably lost him some hard-bitten crime followers, but he is unapologetic about it – for him the people left behind are everything.

CHAPTER NINE

EPISODE ONE: THE HORSE CAME BACK
ALONE

The single-track road that leads to Hightap stables is a lonely place, even in daylight. The walls that border it are generations old – slumped but not tumbledown, each stone placed by hand. They are jacketed in a greeny-blue lichen that looks like it belongs under the ocean. But the shingle beaches of Aberdeen's coast are twenty miles away, battered by the salty might of the North Sea.

Thirty-five years ago, a chestnut thoroughbred named Ruby charged riderless into the stable yard, her body shaking and blood pouring from a gash to her leg. Her reins were tangled; one stirrup was missing. Stable hands reported a foam of sweat on the mare's back, her eyes rolling in terror. The clotting blood showed that it had been some time since her injury. It was almost dark.

Searchers walked the road for hours looking for the rider, initially convinced there had been an accident – perhaps a collision with a vehicle, or the horse spooking and throwing her. They pictured the woman lying injured, unable to get to help. As the temperature fell, volunteers returned for blankets, flasks of warm tea, so that when they found her, they would be prepared. But they found no sign of an accident – no tyre tracks, damaged walls or verges. Gradually they extended the search area – she had been gone for hours, could have ridden far into the hills, so they roamed *the moorland. As it grew dark, they kept calling her name but no one answered.*

The name they were calling was Layla Mackie.

No one has ever answered that call. Throughout the night, volunteers increased from local farms and the hotel where twenty-one-year-old Layla waitressed. In the following days, barns and outbuildings were searched. Nothing has been seen of her since that day. It is as if she vanished into thin air.

In the weeks after her disappearance, suggestions were made that Layla wanted a different life. Her friends from school had moved on, to university, jobs, marriage, but her world had barely changed. It is possible that this influenced the effort put into tracing her. But more than three decades later, Layla's bank account – into which she had saved £917 – has not been touched. There have been no credible sightings.

Layla's family believe the answer lies in the community. They believe they know who is responsible. That man still lives there, in the shadow of a lonely mountain. All her parents, Tam and Jean, want now is to find out what happened to their daughter.

This is Finding Justice, *and I am your host, Cal Lovett.*

CHAPTER TEN

LAYLA, 1986

Layla loves this time in the morning. When she isn't on breakfast shift at the hotel or too hungover to get out of bed, she drags on her boots and coat and walks through the fields to the stables as early as possible, not stopping to eat first.

Doug, the stable owner, lets her ride in return for the work she puts in. Sometimes she teaches, but patience with hysterical children isn't her forte, so when she can she volunteers for the mucking out, grooming, filling the hay ricks and checking the water troughs. She isn't afraid of hard work; the driving rain or snow doesn't put her off. She knows that's one of the reasons Doug likes her. On sunny days there is no shortage of help. When the mud is ankle deep and the wind is tearing into the hill, Layla will still be there.

Today the dawn is a line on the horizon, grey clouds moving fast across the lightening sky. There is a bite in the air but it's not as sharp as the cold winter mornings when the darkness lingers and it feels like she's the only one left on the planet.

'Morning.' Doug is already leading two horses into the bottom field. He will have been out for the last thirty minutes feeding them. 'Ruby and Joey need doing.'

Layla nods, slips into Ruby's stall gratefully. The mare shakes her head up and down, anxious to be out. Her breath steams in the cold air. She shoves her nose into the head collar Layla has taken from the hook outside, spooks at the wind as she steps into the yard.

'Easy girl.' Layla strokes her soft neck, buries her nose in the horse's sweet-smelling flank for a moment. 'Steady.'

Ruby's hooves clack on the concrete as she follows Layla to the end of the block where Joey, an old faithful of the stables, patiently sticks his head over the door for his head collar and lead rope to be fitted. He walks calmly out when she pulls back the bolts; he would take himself to the field if they let him.

Joey nudges Layla with his nose. She rubs his muzzle affectionately and digs in her pocket for a treat for him while Ruby side steps and angles for her share. Flanked by the pair, one lead rope in each hand, she takes the track to the field, feeling a sense of calm and rightness she only gets in fleeting moments like this one, away from people and life and the sense of purposelessness that has plagued her since school.

An hour later, all the horses are fed and turned out, their stables mucked out and fresh sawdust added to their beds, water buckets refilled. Numb with cold, she follows Doug into the farmhouse kitchen where his wife, Sal, is frying bacon and his daughters are getting ready to walk up the track to catch the school bus.

He holds the door for her and she slides in past him, feeling his breath on her face. It makes something in her stomach flip.

She leaves her muddy boots in the porch, nodding at the girls as she slides across the tiled floor in her socks and sinks into a chair, rubbing at her hands to warm them.

One of the collies noses her and she strokes its head then shoves it away so it returns to the range.

'All right, Layla?' Sal is never particularly warm to her. 'Bacon?'

'Thanks,' she says, the feeling creeping back into her fingers and the cosy kitchen dissolving her unease. 'If there's some going.'

She pours herself a tea from the ever-present pot on the table and takes a piece of toast from the rack, ravenous. During the day the stable hands and riders use the kitchen off the tack room to make themselves hot drinks and microwave food. Access to the main house is a privilege reserved for the most devoted and Layla knows others resent her for it. Sometimes she wonders if Sal resents her too. She is never as easy with Layla as she is with the other helpers.

Sal sets a plate of bacon on the table and Doug sits opposite Layla, passing her a bag of floury rolls so they can make fat sandwiches, dripping with grease and warmth. His feet touch hers under the table, so she bends her legs, draws her toes under her chair. As she squirts ketchup onto her bap, Layla feels Bridget's eyes on her, glances up and meets her gaze. Bridget's curiosity slides away quickly, her cheeks flame.

The girl must be thirteen. Layla knows she is jealous of her freedom to stay here for the day with the horses, has heard her begging her parents for the day off before the shows. Bridget has no idea that Layla burns with jealousy at the difference in their lives.

Doug and Sal are strict with both girls, have high expectations of what they can and will achieve. It's only now she has been spat out at the end of her education with nothing to hope for that Layla sees this is the true gift. Not the freedom and the disinterest that characterised her own parents' attitude to school. It's not that they don't care, she thinks, more that they have never believed that she had it in her to rise to the top.

So she didn't. She messed around, flirted, smoked and drank her way through her teenage years, enjoying her popularity, not noticing that most of the others had plans and were studying in the background, however much they claimed to be slacking off. In the last couple of years those friends have fallen by the wayside, largely deserting Aberdeen for Glasgow and Edinburgh, meeting new people and forging new lives. When she sees them in their university holidays, she feels more alone and adrift than when they are away.

'Girls, time to leave.' Sal points to the clock and Bridget and her younger sister Paula grumble as they slide their feet into boots, pick up bulging schoolbags and pull waterproof jackets on over their blazers. The sun is a phantom in the sky, shrouded by cloud – it doesn't look like rain. But this is Aberdeenshire, and in half an hour it could be completely different. The changing moods of the weather are the only constant.

'How long are you here today?' Doug speaks through a mouthful of bacon sandwich and Sal slaps his arm in admonishment.

Layla finishes her last mouthful before answering.

'Not on shift until evening.' She wraps her fingers round the mug of tea, feeling the heat rushing back into her cheeks now she is out of the cold and has eaten. 'I can stay as long as you need.'

'I was thinking you could exercise Ruby this morning, then maybe take Dapple for a slow hack – see how that stiff leg is doing.'

Sal looks sharply at him.

'And who's going to teach the lessons, like?'

'Will you not be around?'

Sal gestures at the post-breakfast carnage in the kitchen.

'Aye, but I have plenty to be getting on with and I wouldn't mind a ride.'

Layla knows from experience that Sal will not thank her for trying to clear up the kitchen. There's an invisible line that she's acutely aware of – she is not family. But she feels the tension in the room, knows it is caused by their differences in opinion on her.

'I could do one of the lessons,' she offers. 'You could take Dapple...' She doesn't want to offer the golden task but she feels she has to. 'Or Ruby.'

'No. I want Layla to ride Ruby,' Doug tells Sal. 'You can take Daps.' He slaps his hand on the table and pushes back his chair, conversation over. Sal picks up a pile of dishes, carries them to the side and drops them in the sink. The splash they make is the only sound that breaks the uncomfortable silence.

Layla follows Doug to the door with her head down, careful not to look at Sal, feeling the venom in the air as well as the usual thrill of pride.

CHAPTER ELEVEN

LAYLA, 1986

Breathless with the rush from stables to shower and out again, Layla wraps the apron strings twice round her waist, glowering at the head chef. He is red in the face, sweating as the orders pile up in front of him, little white slips fluttering in the breeze from the fan, plates sweltering under the heat lamps. The rostered chef is sick and the kitchen porter AWOL. Again.

'This isn't my job,' she protests.

'It isn't my fucking job either, but you were here last and if that useless shit hasn't turned up then someone has to do it. We can't have the fucking dishes piling up, can we? Stop your whinging and get on with it.'

He dings the bell. 'Service!' and one of the other waiting staff scuttles forward.

'You need to sack the useless fucker,' she hisses, pulling out pots that have been piled into the vast sinks and picking up lumps of concealed food to allow the plug to unblock. 'This shouldn't be my problem.' She raises her voice. 'I did my nails, for fuck's sake.'

'Can you hear that?' The chef bellows, holding a sweaty paw to his ear. 'Can you? That's the sound of precisely no one giving a shit.'

She grits her teeth, loads as many plates as she can into the tray and slides it into the industrial dishwasher, pulling the lever to lower the top down. She presses a button and immediately the sound of water pounding the dishes fills the nook of the kitchen, shutting out the effing and blinding as Chef vents his anger on the commis chefs. One gets a clip round the ear. He looks like he might cry.

'Anyway,' Chef yells during a lull in service, as she gulps water from a pint glass and sets it on a high shelf. 'It's your bastard boyfriend who should be here as cover, not me.'

'He's not my boyfriend.'

'I live in the next cottage, I ken what goes on, you wee slapper.'

He's joking with her, trying to make amends, but Layla feels irritation creep across her skin, doesn't want to be yoked to Stephen. It's casual, that's all. Not exclusive. She wonders what else he hears through the walls. The bruise on her back still hurts when she lies on it.

Two hours later, she is bedraggled; flushed from the relentless steam and grime, irritated by the sympathetic looks from the other waiting staff, none of whom have offered to swap with her. Released for ten minutes, she stands outside the back door to the kitchen, breathing in the smell of the pines and furiously sucking on a long overdue cigarette.

'All right, lovely Layla.'

She smiles, huffs her fringe out of her face when she sees Glen rounding the corner in the darkness. The barman is rolling an empty keg. She notices the muscles through his white shirt, pouts, wishing she wasn't so sweaty, so red in the face.

'They've had me washing the pots,' she whines, enjoying the way he fumbles the crates when she speaks to him.

'That's not on,' he says, his voice soft, and she holds his gaze a beat too long, enjoying the effect it has. He steps closer.

'Laaayla, coffee!'

Irene's voice punctures the moment and she rolls her eyes, stubs the cigarette out on the wall and throws the butt at his feet. She touches his arm as she passes.

—

'Wait up.'

Layla pretends not to hear Stephen. She increases her pace on the gravel, crunching quickly to her car, a small packet of leftovers warm in her hands. Chef isn't always an unreasonable bastard. Sometimes he gives her spare food for her mum and dad. Her mum is always excited to unwrap the parcels. She plates them up like they're in a restaurant. It makes Layla feel ungrateful and sad, maybe because she sees this food every day, eats it regularly, scrapes it into the slop buckets. It doesn't seem special to her at all.

'Layla, wait!'

Stephen has to run to catch her. He grabs her arm tight and whirls her around. She almost falls but he pulls her against his chest.

'What the fuck, Layla? Why are you ignoring me?'

'Ow. Get off. I didn't see you.'

She rubs her arm. He leans down to kiss her, hard. She wriggles, barely concealing the sense of revulsion she feels, annoyance at him rising inside her. Sometimes she gets like this. Doesn't want to be touched, doesn't want to talk to anyone.

'Are you coming to the pub tomorrow?' His gaze is constant. His arms fix her in place, allow no wiggle room. 'I haven't seen you in ages.'

'You saw me the other night. A lot of me.'

'Aye, I don't mean that.' His hands on her make her hot and uncomfortable so she pulls away. 'Don't be like that.'

'It's been a long day. I've got to get this home.' She holds the foil parcel aloft by way of explanation, though it is too late to eat and it will be going in the fridge.

'Fine.' He backs away, shaking his head like he doesn't understand her at all. She doesn't understand herself either.

'Stephen, don't be like that… I'll come down after I've had my supper tomorrow. For a bit.'

He pauses, looking hopeful. 'Are you sure?'

'I've said I will.'

'I'll see you, then.'

She slams the car door harder than it needs. Knows he watches her as she drives away. Her arm still hurts. But she'll go tomorrow because something is better than nothing.

Her parents have left the hall light on. It's always like this at the end of a shift – it's late, she should go to sleep, but she's exhausted-awake; her feet throb with pain and heat. She won't be sleepy for at least an hour. She unbuttons her sleeve and inspects her bicep – a bruise is already flowering, tender to the touch.

Layla slots two slices of bread into the toaster and massages her feet while she waits for it to ping, lifting each in turn and rubbing the arches, the balls, flexing her toes.

'You should wear flat shoes.'

She jumps. Her mother has come down in her pink velvet dressing gown and is standing on the threshold looking in at her, the buttons done up to her neck.

'Mum! Don't creep up on folk. How long have you been standing there?'

Surreptitiously, she rolls her sleeve down to cover the marks.

'Not long. You should get to bed if you're riding in the morning.'

'Aye.' Layla grabs the toast and slathers butter on. 'I will do.'

Jean watches her, saying nothing, and Layla half wants her there and half wants to turn and shout: *what*? She lays her knife on the side and takes a bite of toast. Her mother huffs and bustles in beside her, lifting the knife and taking it to the sink, putting the lid on the butter, walking it to the fridge.

'Leave it, Mum, I'll do it.' But Jean ignores her, takes a cloth and wipes away the grease, follows it along to parts of the surface that are perfectly clean. 'Mum, I said leave it. I might have some more. I'll do it after.'

The walls close in a little more.

'You never do though, do you?' Her mother stares at Layla, looking for more faults. 'You'll eat us out of house and home. Make sure there's some of the loaf for your dad in the morning, will you?'

'For fuck's sake,' Layla huffs under her breath, taking her plate through to the lounge and flicking the TV on to one of the few late options – a talk show filled with sick pranks that hospitalise the participants.

She waits for her mother to start on at her about her language, but when she turns to look through to the kitchen, the cloth hangs neatly over the tap and Jean has gone to bed. The darkness pulses at the window, its emptiness filling her.

CHAPTER TWELVE

LAYLA, 1986

'He's a wee shite.'

Layla catches the threads of conversation from the back door of the hotel, where she is eking out her cigarette break as long as she can. Her name is mud as she was late again for the breakfast shift and Chef bawled her out; she can't afford to push it at the moment. Being treated like a child has made her feel huffy, trapped. She's tempted to lash out at everyone, so she's taken herself off for a breather. Hearing some gossip might still her restlessness, quench the boredom.

'Who's a wee shite?' she calls, stepping out onto the gravel to where the bar staff have clustered, taking their break before the lunchtime requests begin.

'Yon idiot. He thinks he's God's gift.' Irene huffs on her own fag and folds her arms.

Glen gestures to where a spotty boy is staring at a box of empty bottles, a sulky look on his face. 'Full of it, that one.'

'Who is he?'

'The nephew of one of the boss's friends, so we have to put up with his bollocks,' Irene tells her. 'Otherwise, he'd be long gone.'

'Ssshhh,' another of the barmen says. 'He'll hear you.'

The boy kicks the box and the glass crashes against the side.

'Watch it,' Glen shouts over. 'If they smash, you'll be picking the bits out of the gravel.'

The youth looks up and pushes his floppy hair out of his eyes.

'*I* won't be.'

'See?' Irene turns her back and raises her eyebrows at Layla. 'It's his first week. Gobby wee shite.'

The boy walks over to them.

'Who's she?'

He points at Layla and she almost laughs as he makes a play of checking her out. He must be three or four years younger than her.

'Have you done any of those boxes yet?' Glen steps in front of Layla and fixes the boy with a glare.

He holds his hand up, steps back with a cocky swagger. 'All right Grandad, keep your hair on, I'm doing it.'

'He's been doing it for the last hour. It should have taken him five minutes, tops.' Glen grimaces.

'Someone needs to take him down a peg or two,' Layla says as they watch him saunter back to the cellar.

Glen stubs out his cigarette. 'Aye, and it might just be me if he carries on with his nonsense.' He sighs. 'More than my job's worth, though. Better get back to it. Funny day for a wedding, Thursday, but I don't imagine it'll change the amount they drink.'

Irene echoes his sigh, picks at the corner of her lip. 'It's going to be a long afternoon.'

'I wouldn't put up with that,' Layla tells them, watching as the boy talks back to the usually unflappable Glen.

'Any ideas are welcome.'

'I'll give it some thought.' She laughs and returns to the kitchen.

–

It's a hell of a shift. No one is in a good mood and the minutes drag as the wedding runs late and the food threatens to be dry and inedible.

Chef is in an unbearable state, turning the air blue with his ranting, so when the duty manager attempts to calm him, Layla takes advantage of the moment to sneak into the ballroom and breathe some fresh air. As she flips back the door into the corridor, one of the younger waitresses, a schoolgirl who normally helps out at weekends but came in early evening to help with the wedding, brushes past her, cheeks red, tears in her eyes.

'What's with you?' The girl turns her head away, doesn't slow her pace. 'Hazel?'

'Nothing. Need the toilet.'

Layla frowns. As she swivels, she glimpses the boy ahead of her, tucked into a dark corner of the corridor. The brazen look sends chills through her.

'What did you do?'

He says nothing, just shrugs then drops his gaze to her chest and moves his hand to his crotch, so briefly she thinks she might have imagined it. She hears her name called.

'Better go,' he says.

–

She can't get the boy out of her head. As the afternoon progresses and she stands pressed against a wall with a tray of drinks, listening to yet another variation on a best man's speech she's heard a thousand times, she lets the memory wind her up. She can see him washing glasses behind the bar. When he comes out to collect more, he catches her eye and smirks. Hazel is quiet, keeping her head low.

By the time the meals are cleared and the band is tuning up, Layla has reached a satisfying boiling loathing. The weather is dry enough for them to have kicked the guests out onto the lawn while they clear and the tables are moved back off the dancefloor. She needs the reprieve – the bride's father has wandering hands and more than half the guests are already half-cut. Glen slips past with a tray of empties and she catches his eye.

'Is he still winding you up?' She gestures to the bar.

Glen rolls his eyes. 'He's worse. Doesn't shut his trap. Ever.'

'I think he upset Hazel.'

'What did he do?'

'She won't say. Don't let him near her, though.'

'I won't. You come up with a way of sorting him out?'

He's joking but Layla flushes with an idea.

'I might just have…'

Glen draws closer and she leans in as she tells him her plan. She can smell his aftershave, his arm grazes hers and she feels a flutter of excitement as the lights dip and the first guests reappear.

'Layla!' The head waitress sticks her head out of the kitchen. 'You can take a break while they start.'

'Tell the others,' she murmurs to Glen. 'In the car park after work.'

–

The word goes round and the smirks and smiles carry them through an arduous shift. It's one in the morning by the time the music wraps up and the guests stagger off to their rooms or the main bar to continue drinking. Layla surprises a couple behind a potted palm, giggles at the flash of thigh and their red faces as they scuttle off.

The crowd in the car park isn't big – just the waiting staff, the bar staff and a couple of chefs. Hazel went home early with a headache. The boy has no idea what's about to happen and Layla relishes the shock on his face as Glen and another barman grab his arms while the others cluster around him, laughing.

'What's going on?' His voice has already lost a fraction of its cockiness, the sound of his confusion makes her giggle.

'Off, off, off,' she chants, and the others follow her lead.

The chefs step forward to help as he realises what's happening and tries to make a run for it. He's outnumbered but it doesn't stop him kicking and lashing out.

'Fuck off. Get the fuck off!'

There's a whirl of movement and someone manages to get his trousers to his ankles. This is where it ends, a harmless warning, or it should do, but a cloud of adrenaline and excitement seems to have settled over them all. Layla can almost taste the shift in the air.

Maybe it's him. The boy is yelling obscenities, writhing, making it all so much more dramatic than she imagined. A different person is holding each limb so he can't escape and they don't let go. She doesn't tell them to. His underpants have Donald Duck on them. Layla thinks of Hazel, of her shamed tears, hoots in glee at the retribution. She catches Irene's eye and shakes her head at the look of worry on her face.

'It's just a bit of fun. Don't look so serious, Irene.'

'Aye, but...'

Layla ignores her. She cups her hands to her mouth and shouts, 'And his kecks!' not really expecting them to do it, but she is in control now, holding the puppet strings. No one questions. All they hear is the direction. One of the other waiters dashes forward and tugs them sharply down and then they drop the boy and dart back.

Maybe it's the dark, or the residue of the excitement, but it's only when their laughter dies away that they realise he is crying, curled in a ball. He drags up his underpants, his face distorted and his body shaking.

There is a moment of silence, the sense that it all went too far swirls around them.

'Shit,' someone says, as the boy sniffles at their feet, his face hidden behind his curtain of hair. 'You okay, like?'

'It was only a joke,' Layla says, stepping forward, arms crossed. 'Can't you take a laugh?'

He turns, looks up at her.

'You're a fucking bitch,' he screams, and she steps back at the hatred on his face.

CHAPTER THIRTEEN

CAL

The cottage isn't tumbledown. That's too picturesque a description. The harled walls have weathered a grubby beige, the wooden window frames look rotten. Weeds stand a foot tall and automotive equipment is scattered across the drive. Parked on the edge of the road, Cal takes in the bleak horizon: fields rolling endlessly, exposed to the weather. In the snow, the road would be cut off, the steep track treacherous.

He has miked himself in the car. As he moves towards the front door, he narrates the scene before him, notes the pitiful windchime, threads twisted and knotted, unable to sound any longer.

The door is answered by a short man whose face is carved with the anger of decades, his hair a grizzled white, whiskers poking from his chin. He hasn't shaved and his checked shirt is not fresh.

'Mr Mackie, I'm Cal Lovett. We spoke on the phone.'
'Aye.'

The man turns and makes his way back through the house without another word. He moves quickly. Cal hefts his bag of equipment over the threshold, closes the door behind himself.

The house smells of soup, animal and damp. A ginger cat loops its tail around the door frame to the kitchen, then flees when it sees Cal. The narrow corridor leads to a conservatory that leans against the back of the house. Added later, it is more pleasant. There are two cane chairs, a matching two-seater sofa, and a small electric heater. He takes in the views of the countryside, the breadth of the sky before him. This is a place where you could sit and watch the weather pass, see everything. It is also exposed: there is nowhere to hide from the raw openness before you.

Mrs Mackie – Jean – is the one who contacted him. She rises from her chair and stretches out a hand. Small and thin, she looks older than her seventy-five years. He feels like a giant beside her. Her fingers are knobbly and arthritic – the skin tight and red across pronounced knuckles. He is careful not to grip too hard.

'Mr Lovett. Thank you for coming.'

'Thank you for seeing me. And it's Cal, Mrs Mackie. Call me Cal.'

'Jean.'

'That's quite a view you have there.' He smiles.

Mr Mackie – Tam – shifts from foot to foot, the less comfortable of the two. He scowls and Cal recognises the recalcitrance, understands that he has been persuaded. An old dog is curled on a piece of fleece beside the chair, its eyes on its master. It is some sort of collie–lab cross and when he bends to pet its greying head, its tail thumps twice.

'Who's this?' He speaks directly to the dog, not the man, knowing instinctively that this animal is the best route to him. You can see it from the way the dog's blanket

74

is placed, just the right position for Tam to reach down from his chair and touch its head.

'Bessie.'

He ruffles the dog's ears; her eyes half close with pleasure at the fuss. He misses Rocket, hopes Chrissie is walking him as much as she promised.

'Tea?' Tam's tone remains short but Cal senses an infinitesimal thaw.

'Yes, please, milk and one. Can I help?'

He straightens and the dog settles back, head on her front paws, moving only her eyebrows as she watches them.

'No, you're fine.'

The man stomps from the room and Cal can tell by the way Jean stares, the one step she takes forward then back, that he doesn't usually do the honours, that he has gone because he wants to escape conversation.

'He's nervous,' Jean tells him, perching on the edge of her chair and gesturing for him to take the two-seater.

'I understand. It's not easy to talk about it.'

She nods and he takes in the pile of photograph albums to her side. Neatly stacked, prepared for his arrival. He unzips his bags and draws out the microphone packs he will need.

Tam takes a long time with the tea. Finally, he returns with a tray on which three cups have been placed in a triangle formation, along with a plate of pink wafer biscuits. Cal accepts the cup of tea and takes a pink wafer, smiling his thanks. The wafer is like sweet cardboard, but he knows they will feel more comfortable if he eats one.

'What do you need from us for this, then?' Tam slurps his tea, eyes the recording equipment.

'Today let's just talk about Layla, if that's okay? It would really help me to know a bit about her, who she was and what happened that day, from your point of view, the people who knew her best.'

Jean sniffs and her hand is already on the top album.

'Knew her best,' Tam repeats the words as if they are foreign.

He focuses on Jean, who wants him to see her photographs, wants him to make sense of the pieces she has left of her child, to wave a magic wand and take away the pain.

'Horses.' She sighs. 'It was always about horses.'

—

He stays so long that they can't keep putting on a front for him. As he sits, listening to their stories, Dubois and his monstrous crimes recede ever so slightly.

'Such a bonny baby.' Jean smiles, lost in the pictures. He sees a cheeky face that turns into an elfin child with a pointed chin and deep brown eyes beneath her fringe. As she grows, her smile changes, he thinks. It's not always present in the pictures – as she gets older she glowers or simmers more frequently at the camera – but when it is there, he sees something guarded. Or is that simply fancy? Knowing what he now knows.

'They called,' Jean says. 'To say she'd fallen off the horse and they couldn't find her. Tam went out.' She nods to him. 'Didn't you? Didn't you, Tam?'

He sees that she wants to share the burden of telling it.

'Aye.' He sucks his bottom lip under. 'I went out with them to look for her, like.'

'It got dark.' Jean's lip trembles. 'They walked all the roads she could have taken, searched the dykes.'

He doesn't need to imagine the creeping fear, the gradual knowledge that this would be more than bumps and bruises, more than a good tale to tell. Not a good tale at all.

'Everyone's moved on,' Jean says, sadly. 'She's forgotten but we…' She stares out at the fields, her thoughts trailing away for a few moments before she looks back and he sees the hunger. 'We just need to know what happened.'

In the other chair, Tam clears his throat.

'What do you think happened to Layla?' Cal asks.

A thundercloud passes over Jean's face. Her husband remains pale and silent.

'That chef. He did it.'

Cal leans in towards them. 'Stephen? Layla's boyfriend?'

Jean huffs at the word *boyfriend*. 'It wasn't serious.' She fixes watery eyes on him. 'He's still there. Living in that cottage like nothing happened. He knows. I know it was him.'

'What makes you so sure?'

Jean closes her eyes in pain. 'The bruises. She tried to hide them but I saw. God help me, I never said a word.'

CHAPTER FOURTEEN

After three hours in the cottage, Cal emerges into a twilight glow, cold and clear, sucks fresh air into his lungs, places his equipment carefully in the back of the car. He is exhausted. His mind whirls with ideas, images of Layla, of his sister, his home. He is overcome with a desire to speak to Allie, despite everything, but when he dials his wife's number she doesn't answer. He wonders who she is with, what she's doing, or if it is as simple as her promise that it is over between them. Is that why she won't tell him the man's name?

He has found himself a small bed and breakfast close by. Ideally it would come with a gossiping farmer's wife who knows everyone and everything to have happened here in the past fifty years, but the owner, Marilena, has been here less than five.

Cloistered in his room, Cal spends an hour jotting down notes from his afternoon interview. He has names to follow up on – the lad Layla was supposed to ride out with that day is still local, there are people from the hotel, from the stables. He pauses the recording and stares at the page. Their reaction to his questions about her school friends surprised him. He sets it going again.

'She stopped seeing them.' The tightness of Jean's voice reminds him of her hands gripped so tightly together.

'Really? Why was that?'

Silence. He remembers Jean looking at Tam, who'd shifted in his seat.

'They went their own ways.' Tam's words sound dismissive. 'Off to university or whatever. She had her horse riding.'

'Was there no suggestion Layla might go to university?'

It was Jean who answered.

'There wasn't the money. And she didn't need it. She was just fine here.'

Cal ends the recording and sets down his pen. There were grants back then. The money feels like an excuse for low expectations. Maybe that's unfair. He thinks of the bleak cottage on the hill, wonders if it was as desperately lonely back then or if that comes from the grief that now hangs in the air. Is it possible Layla faked her disappearance so she could escape? The thought nags at him. He knows the urge to run, that it can make you take rash decisions. If Layla is alive that's a good resolution, but he dreads another story blowing up in his face. There are only so many times you can start again.

He pours a drink and dials Chrissie's number, keen to hear her voice, to connect with home in some way, to be there for her in a way he cannot, or at least does not, manage in person.

Her voice is tight.

'All right, love?'

'Yeah.'

'What's up?'

He wonders if the way he left, the argument with Allie, still reverberates in their home.

She sighs.

'Nothing. School... Nothing.'

'Tell me.'

'No, it doesn't matter. What about you? Are you there? Have you been to the *scene of the crime?*'

She hams up the last four words to make him laugh and he knows she is changing the subject, but he is relieved that she still wants to talk to him so he lets her.

'Not yet. We don't know if there is one, to be honest. I met Layla's parents today, though.'

'And?'

'They just want answers.'

'Will you get them?'

Her voice is wistful.

'I'll try, love.'

There's a moment of silence and then the words seem to burst from her.

'Mum says you're always chasing Auntie Margot's ghost and that we'll never be enough. That you haven't dealt with it.'

He feels a spark of anger, sadness, that Allie confides in their child. Chrissie knows only the barest details about the aunt she never had. His parents clammed up the year after Margot went missing and never unlocked themselves again, so his side of the family is a disappointment, composed of broken people, ghosts and the absence of cousins. He likes that when his daughter talks about his sister, she acts as if she knew her, like it matters, but it worries him that Allie's anger spills out when he isn't there.

'Mum shouldn't say that to you. It isn't true.'

'Isn't it?'

'No. Margot's been gone a long time.'

'But you don't have answers.'

He is silent for a moment, listening to his daughter's breath down the line. From the window he can see the full cold moon bathing the countryside in silver.

'Sometimes there aren't answers,' he tells her.

That isn't the truth and he wonders if she knows he is lying. There are always answers. Finding them is another thing entirely. He can't escape the belief he has missed the only chance he had. That his answers hung from a hospital door.

'Is Mum there?' he asks.

There is a pause, then his daughter's voice tightens again, this time with regret. 'She can't come to the phone.'

'But she's there?'

'Where else would she be?'

'Nowhere, love.' He curses himself for involving her. 'I should go. Maybe speak to you tomorrow?'

He waits for her to tell him she's busy – out with friends.

'I'll be here.'

—

Unable to sleep, he goes back out to the car for his bag of paperwork. It's breathtakingly cold; stepping into the pure darkness is like plunging into a pool of ice water. A thin fog drifts around the building. Cal jogs to the vehicle, pressing the button to unlock it, the car's lights flashing and illuminating the path in the mist.

He leans into the back seat to grab the rucksack and notices the letters lying there. Was it only yesterday that he stood at the end of the drive beside the mailbox? He grabs them and rushes back to the warmth of the bed and breakfast. If he doesn't throw them away here, he'll only have to do it later.

In his room, Cal sets the little plastic kettle to boil and tips the paperwork onto the desk by the window. While the water bubbles noisily, making the tiny kettle bounce and judder, he tears open the letters, discarding the inevitable offers of WiFi and insurance. The last letter is different – a neat handwritten direction on the front. He half-recognises it but his mind is elsewhere as he slides his fingernail under the seal.

When he sees who it is from, Cal throws the paper onto the bed in shock – as if it's capable of burning him. The sight of the elegant penmanship makes his skin crawl. It's a letter from beyond the grave. He has unwittingly driven all this way with a piece of the Woodland Killer in the car behind him.

The kettle clicks off and he wipes his forehead. Suddenly the peaceful dark beyond the window seems to encroach on the room. He closes the curtains to shut it out, pours himself a cup of tea, all the while conscious of the discarded letter on the bed. He is sure whatever is in there will make sleep impossible, but how can he leave it until morning? He takes a deep breath, sits down and lifts the page.

Dear Mr Lovett,

Christopher. Do you mind if I call you that? It was a pleasure to see you again today. I find I rarely have the opportunity for such stimulating conversation and I hope to speak with you again soon.

I hope I didn't alarm you. My little surprise, earlier. You must forgive the indulgence. It gets a little dull in here and the look on your face was a picture. I expect not many people remember her these days, do they? A person's loss is reduced to scrap. Perhaps we can talk about her sometime. I may be able to help you. I would like to help you.

However, I must confess that I am disappointed that you failed to grasp the truth of my mother's betrayal of my father – a man simply trying to provide for his family and who did not deserve to be treated so boldly. I hope you're not going to be tedious, Christopher. I hope you can keep an open mind.

Do feel free to write to me, Christopher. Once we have smoothed this petty wrinkle in our under-standing, I feel sure we can continue our conver-sation and that I can provide the illumination you are lacking. This can only be good for us both.

Yours,
Marc Dubois

Cal stares at the words, reads them over and over until the letters blur and his eyes hurt. There it is again. *Scrap.* It itches at the edge of his mind. He thumps his fist into the bed, wishes he could scream with frustration but the sound is stuck inside him, bouncing around until his stomach feels heavy with dread. Gradually, the weight of the words sinks through him. He paces the room, scouring the letter for more, searching between the lines for certainty, a concrete clue.

It is all so tantalisingly out of reach, and yet he knows. He knows deep down that he sat across the table from his sister's killer. He bought him chocolate bars, agreed with his delusions, watched the lines of his face and the look in his eyes. The letter only adds to Cal's instinct that Dubois didn't orchestrate his own death. He was having far too much fun for that.

The words circle his mind, the killer's essence lingers in the room. Feeling sick, he crosses to the window, thrusts it open so he can breathe, taking deep gulping breaths. The cold makes him shake but he stands at the window for a long time, numb with grief, the letter resting between his fingers.

CHAPTER FIFTEEN

Cal wakes early, anxiety a pall around him, thick, viscous. He forces himself out of bed, tries to quell the jitters by breathing deeply. His mind is busy, tumbling over itself with thoughts of Dubois and the lost shadow of Margot. In the early hours he made his resolution. He will contact the police force at home and tell them his theory.

Bleary-eyed, he sweeps back the curtains and what he sees makes his breath catch. Mist coats the land like a thick white blanket, from which trees protrude like ghosts. Above the ground fog, the sky is clear and the sun illuminates the view, burning away the fronds where it touches them. It is indecently beautiful. He pictures Layla, riding her horse through the mist, galloping up the heather-covered hillside.

Showered and dressed, he drives to a bakery. Curious about local pastries called butteries, he buys a bag of them and a large coffee, tearing pieces from one as he sits in the car and logs into the Facebook account for his podcast. Die-hard listeners are already speculating about the subject of his next series.

He's losing his touch. What's he even working on? Cal forces himself to the next comment, finds he doesn't need to leap to his own defence.

It'll be great, whatever it is. He recognises the handle: 'Star-kissed Dreamer' – an anonymous listener who follows everything he does. He wishes he had her confidence.

He knows he is putting off the call. Eventually he forces himself to take the first step. He remembers the name of the detective who last reviewed the case, but after long minutes on hold and being passed around, it is a different voice that he hears. His hands are shaking.

'Christopher Longacre? I'm Detective Foulds. I'm sorry for keeping you waiting.'

'That's okay. And it's Cal now. Cal Lovett. I changed my name.'

There's a pause. A sympathy beat.

'I see. Detective Carson retired last year and so your sister's case falls under my department. I understand you might have some information about Margot?'

She is making it easy for him. He can do this.

'Yes.' He breathes. 'I'm a reporter now, I have a true crime podcast.' He waits, but she gives no hint of recognition. 'I interviewed Marc Dubois. Before he died.'

He feels the intake of breath, the change in the air that always accompanies that name.

'No one knows who I was, who I used to be. Not even anyone I work with. But he... he knew things about me. He knew my real name.'

'And you think...?'

The voice is careful.

'I think he killed my sister.'

There is a moment of silence. He tries to imagine her face on the other end of the line, her thoughts.

'I know it sounds crazy, but he wrote me a letter before he died. I opened it last night. That's why I'm calling.'

'And what did he say? In the letter. Did he give you a location?'

Cal falters.

'Nothing specific. Just hints. But he keeps mentioning scrapyards.'

'Mr Lovett.'

'Cal.'

'Cal. Look, I don't know what we might be able to do with this information. But why don't you email me a copy of the letter and any other information you have and we'll take a look into it.'

Her voice is professional. It gives nothing away. It isn't enough – the understated reaction to a seismic revelation. He wants fireworks, horror, validation. But it will have to do for now.

'I have recordings as well,' he tells her. 'I just don't think he was a man on the verge of suicide. I think maybe there must have been foul play...'

Foulds becomes brisk. 'We are not investigating the death of Marc Dubois, Mr Lovett. I'm sure you know that. Any concerns you have about that need to be directed to the force in charge of that investigation.'

'I know, I'm sorry.' For a moment Cal worries he has blown all his credibility, turned her against him with lunatic accusations.

'But as regards your sister, I'm happy to take a look at the letter and listen to the recordings you have. That's all I can do.'

'Thank you,' he stammers. 'I appreciate it. I'll send them through.'

When she hangs up, he stares at the letter. The word 'scrap' dances in front of him, clicks into the memory of the recording. *Scrapyards*, he remembers. *Scrapyards of our lives.*

The cottages sit in a row of three. The furthest one is as neat as a pin, garden blooming with flowers and regimental vegetable rows – he sees courgettes, carrots, lettuce. The other two are less maintained. One has a scrubby patch of ground strewn with children's toys, faded plastic diggers filling with rainwater. Stephen's house is the middle one – a soggy deck chair sits next to a sand-filled bucket that appears to be two inches deep in fag ends.

Cal is conscious that he hasn't been invited onto the estate. Microphone ready, he knocks on the door in the centre, waits. When no one answers he presses his face to the glass in the door, cups his hand over his eyes to see.

'He's not there.'

The voice makes him jump. A woman in a blue dressing gown stands on the doorstep of the cottage with the abandoned garden toys, her hair wild, her eyes puffy. She gestures at the trees with an unlit cigarette.

'Stephen. He's up at the hotel. On the breakfast shift.'

'Oh. Thanks.'

Though she doesn't ask for one, he feels he owes the woman an explanation.

'I'm Cal. I'm making a podcast about someone Stephen used to know.'

'Layla.' The woman supplies the name without hesitation.

He pauses. Surprised.

'Nothing stays a secret around here.'

Some things do, he thinks.

'Did you know her?'

The woman concentrates on clicking the lighter, holding it up to the cigarette. The air is cold and her feet look blue on the stone step. Once she has taken a long drag, she shakes her head.

'We only moved up a couple of years back. From Yorkshire.'

'Do you work at the hotel?'

She nods. 'I did bar work, like. Before I had the nipper. Phil's the meat chef. He's the reason we're here.'

'But you've heard about Layla.'

'People talk.' She looks at him in disbelief. 'Nowt else to do, is there?'

'What do they say happened?'

She shrugs, inclines her head in the direction of the empty cottage. 'A lot of folk think it was him.'

'And you?'

'He's a miserable bugger, right enough, but...' Cal waits. She only shrugs again. 'What do any of us know?' A cry starts from inside the cottage and she rolls her eyes, stubs the cigarette out on the wall then throws it over the fence into the sand bucket. 'I'd best get on. Stephen will be back about ten for a break, I'd guess.'

Cal steps back, waits for her to go in and snaps a quick picture of the row of cottages in the woods. Then he makes for the path through the trees.

His call with Detective Foulds feels a lifetime away from this haunting place. He follows the path until it creeps out from behind a bank of rhododendrons that have run wild, and crunches onto a gravel driveway. In front of him the hotel presents its elegant face: grey pillars flank a large door and the tall glass windows to either side gleam. Cal skirts the building, finding the kitchen easily enough. Tucked at the back of the building, away from the lawns and the views. Boxes of vegetables stand waiting to be taken in, alongside crates of milk and juice.

'Guest entrance is that way.' A thin woman dressed in a white blouse and neat tartan skirt emerges from the open door. Her dark hair has a purple tinge but her face dates her, lined with past troubles. She must be in her sixties, Cal guesses.

He channels his most winning smile and humble pose.

'I'm not a guest – I was looking for Stephen.'

'Oh right. I'll tell him. He's making bread at the moment.'

She peers curiously at Cal. He notices she's holding a pack of cigarettes and a lighter.

'I can come back, it's no problem. Don't let me stop you.' He gestures to her hands.

She nods and flips the lid on the pack open.

'Who shall I say was asking for him?'

'Cal.' He shifts a little, watches her inhale the first long drag, sees the lines on her face relax. 'Have you worked here long?'

'Aye. Too long.'

He decides it's worth the ask.

'As long as thirty-five years?'

She snorts. 'Maybe. I've stopped counting.'

'I'm actually making a podcast about someone who used to work here. Maybe you knew her? Layla Mackie?'

At the name, the woman's hand freezes halfway to her mouth. Something crosses her face and he can't tell if it's suspicion or grief.

'I worked with Layla.'

'Would you be okay to tell me a bit about her? Sorry, I didn't ask your name.'

'Irene.' She looks back at the kitchen. 'I suppose I could. But not here. I can meet you at the end of my shift.'

He strolls the grounds while he waits for Stephen and Irene. The lawns and the tended areas are lush and pristine but fierce nature tumbles from their edges – the hotel and its immediate surroundings a fingerprint of elegance impressed on the wilder landscape.

He thinks of his own garden, still suffering from last summer's parching. Everything here seems brighter, a more significant shade of real. Did Layla ever walk across this manicured green with its croquet hoops and tidy edges? Probably not. The staff entrance and car park are hidden from view, reality kept at bay.

Cal waits a little way between the hotel and the cottage, hoping to intercept Stephen. His mind keeps drifting to the letter, to the repetition of the language, the sense that it means something. Flashes of cold bodies left in empty woods, broken, defiled.

He has just decided that the chef isn't coming when a man in whites strides into sight. The man is tall, extremely muscular – if it weren't for the ingrained frown maybe he would still be good looking. Inexplicably, Cal thinks of Dubois: folded with fat in his hospital unit.

'Stephen?'

The man startles, halts and the etches of his frown deepen.

'What?'

'My name's Cal. I spoke to Irene a bit earlier – maybe she said? I'm making a podcast about Layla.'

A hunted look enters Stephen's eyes. Cal thinks he sees pain before anger masks it.

'I've got nothing to say.'

He sets off walking again and Cal scurries to keep up. Layla would have been powerless against such size and strength.

'I don't have an agenda. I just want to talk to you.'

Stephen stops. The blood has risen into his cheeks.

'You're just going to say what everyone else does. That I was the boyfriend, it must have been me.'

'People say that to you?'

'Not to my face, but I know they're thinking it. It's the way they look at me. The silences when I walk into a room. It's been like that for a long time.'

Cal is surprised to see the distress surfacing. He senses Stephen wants to walk away but he's also bristling with the unfairness.

'You never thought of moving away?'

'Maybe I should have.' Stephen looks directly at him, his eyes a hollow challenge. 'But I don't have any reason to run.'

'Look.' Cal takes his most reasonable tone. 'I don't have a theory I'm trying to prove.' Stephen snorts. 'I just want to find out what happened to Layla. This could be your chance to put your side of the story across. All those people who turn away from you, who look at you differently. They'll be listening.'

There is a long pause, into which cold wind blows and Cal shivers in his warm jacket – noting that the chef doesn't react even though he is only in his whites.

'No.'

'Can I leave my card? Just in case?'

The man shrugs but takes the card Cal offers. It's all he can do for now. Hope that time and a chance of redemption will erode his resistance.

He meets Irene in the car park and they decide to do the interview in her car. Cal likes people like Irene. She's straightforward, happy to be recorded. You can see her edges.

'I'm glad someone is looking into it,' she tells him. 'Still think about Layla sometimes and wonder what happened to the lassie.'

'Tell me what she was like.'

Irene looks out of the window at the looming hotel.

'You know, I rated the kid. She was sparky, smart. But some people found her… difficult. She could be cruel.'

Cal waits, knowing silence will be the key to keeping her talking. Irene looks uncomfortable, as so many are – the aversion to talking ill of the missing means he gets a sanitised version, a softened sense of their nature, overlaid with kindness induced by loss.

'There was this one incident. With this boy who worked on the bar. I mean, don't get me wrong, he had it coming to him and all, and it wasn't just her but, I don't know. It went too far.'

Cal makes a sympathetic noise. Tilts his head. 'What happened?'

'Everyone got carried away. He'd been giving lip all day and he was so up himself it was unbelievable. Thought he was God's gift. He was driving everyone mad. Layla said we should debag him, teach him a lesson.'

Cal frowns, not understanding.

'Let everyone see his pants and then see how cocky he felt after that. It was just supposed to be a laugh.' She rubs her head. 'I haven't thought about this in years.'

'Take your time.'

As she tells him, she stares out at the gravel as if she can see backwards through time. 'It was supposed to be in fun, sort of. We didn't realise how upset he was until it was too late. The lad was greetin' – proper tears, his face red as a beet. We were all shocked at how out of hand it had got. No one was laughing by the end, like.'

'What about Layla? What did she think?'

'That's the thing. I saw her face as she walked away and she looked… she looked… happy. Like she'd won.' She shakes her head. 'He didnae come back after that night. Everyone was feart because he was the nephew of one of the boss's friends or something. Thought there might be blowback but there was nothing.' Irene shudders. 'People got carried away. No one stepped in and said "enough". I thought about it a lot after that. How easy it is for things to get out of hand.'

CHAPTER SIXTEEN

EPISODE TWO: WHO WAS LAYLA MACKIE?

It is tempting to canonise the dead or missing. To paint ordinary men and women as saints or martyrs in their absence. It's easier then, isn't it? To believe in angels and demons instead of flawed human beings like you and me, people who made a misstep, or strayed into the wrong place at the wrong time, the wrong relationship. It feels safer if they are different to us.

In the course of this investigation so far, the people who knew her have had a mixture of things to say about Layla. And no, not all of them are flattering or kind. The underlying anger beneath some of their recollections has made me pause a couple of times, stunned that she made such an impression they still feel it so many years down the line. But then, they haven't had the chance to air those grievances with her as they would usually do. Perhaps it is understandable they have festered.

I'm grateful to those people for speaking honestly to me, because the only way we're going to make progress, to discover what happened to Layla thirty-five years ago, is by building an accurate picture of her.

Before we examine that day and night in greater detail, let's look back at Layla's childhood in the remote croft on the side of a hill, speak to some of Layla's school friends as well as her parents Jean and Tam.

'She was wild, you know? Didn't ever listen in class — she used to drive the teachers mad. Chewing gum, wearing make-up. She was funny. If it was a dull day you could count on her to liven things up.' That's Elidh Cameron speaking, one of the girls in Layla's form class at secondary. 'I didn't hang around with her or anything. She was off with older kids. The boys. They all loved Layla.'

Another friend who prefers to remain anonymous: 'I don't like to gossip. There was one school trip where I think she ended up in the boys' dorm. You heard things. I don't know if they were all true. She was a bit of a bitch, to be honest. I was bullied by her in S3. Obviously, it's not like she deserved what happened to her or anything. But... you know.'

However, not everyone will talk.

Layla's parents, Jean and Tam, are convinced Layla's then-boyfriend Stephen holds the key to understanding what happened to Layla. So far, Stephen has refused to speak to us. Stephen, if you are listening, maybe it's time.

CHAPTER SEVENTEEN

LAYLA, 1986

'I feel a bit bad.' Irene catches her as she reaches her car. 'He's really upset.'

She nods in the direction of the bar door, where the arrogant boy had limped moments earlier like a deflated beach ball, his hair in his eyes.

'You shouldn't,' Layla says. 'He needed to learn.' The satisfaction of his humiliation curls cat-like inside her. She is sick of the way boys treat her, like they are so much better. Hurting him felt good, overdue.

Irene shrugs, but the worry etched on her forehead stays in place.

Too wired to drive home, Layla leaves her car and takes the path through the woods towards the cottages, relishing the cold air on her arms, the shock of the chill after the close fog of the kitchen: steam, heat and the stench of food. Animals scuffle in the undergrowth and the leaves rustle around her. A delicious sense of vulnerability traces its way down her spine.

The lights blaze from the middle cottage so she raps on the door and goes in without waiting for an answer. Stephen is slumped on the sofa, still in his chef's whites hours after the end of his shift, clogs discarded on the floor, a beer in his hand. A wave of… something… passes across his face when he sees her. Mistrust, maybe.

She flops down next to him. 'Got any more of those?'

He nods towards the fridge. Doesn't move.

Layla huffs across the room, grabs a beer. The sight of his boxers drying on a rack in the corner turns her stomach. Why is she here?

'You missed the fun,' she tells him.

'Oh, aye?'

'Yon new boy with the floppy hair – works in the bar?' Stephen nods, blankly, his face puffy with tiredness. 'Got what was coming to him.'

She cackles, feeling again the soaring sense of angry power. It isn't that lad particularly. Just a million like him. Never doing a hard day's work, arrogant as their fathers. She knows the type. Met one, met them all. She can still hear the beat of music from the wedding disco ringing in her ears.

'What did you do?'

'Wasn't just me!' She turns wide eyes on him. 'Everyone got involved.' She slugs her beer. 'Took his trousers off him.'

'You didn't?'

'And his kecks…' She laughs again and swigs fast so the bubbles of beer foam in her throat.

Stephen rubs at the red-gold stubble on his face. 'Ach, I don't think that's funny.'

She snorts. 'He deserved it.'

'He's just a kid.'

'He's a dickhead.'

She flounces back on the sofa, irritation filling the hollow, hungry parts inside her. After a moment, Stephen's hand creeps up the inside of her thigh; she brushes his thick fingers away, pushes her legs together, smooths her skirt.

He makes an exasperated noise. 'Fuck's sake, don't sulk.'

'I'm not.'

'Why are you here, Layla? I'm the one that should be pissed off. You didn't show up at the pub the other night after you said you would, what's going on with you?'

'Sorry, I forgot.'

The silence he allows to fall around them makes it clear he doesn't believe her. He stands and puts his bottle of beer down hard on the overflowing coffee table. It makes a hollow thud as it hits the wood.

'I'm off to bed. Are you staying, like?'

Layla shrugs, turns away from him. She wants to feel special but Stephen never seems to understand that.

'Do you even want me to? Maybe I should just go.' She spits the words at him, pushing when she wants to pull. Something sparks in his eyes at her anger, like she is better when she fights him. More interesting. He stops, returns to her, sliding his hands around her waist even as she pushes him away. He fixes his grip and holds on as she backs away; his breathing heavy, the weight of him against her.

'Fuck off, Stephen.'

'You don't mean that.'

He holds her gaze and grips her wrists, forces her back so she is leaning on the laminate worktop. She bucks her hips against him. He laughs.

'Fuck's sake, Layla. You're a prick tease.'

'Go on then,' she says, gritting her teeth and turning her head as he tries to kiss her, glad when it makes him angrier.

He isn't gentle and she doesn't care. As he drags her skirt, tights, underwear down and lifts her onto him so carelessly her back scrapes against the cupboards, she doesn't close her eyes. Instead, she stares, slack-eyed at the mess around them – the washing, the dirty dishes and the beer bottles. The void of night beyond the window gapes and threatens to suck her into its darkness but she doesn't care, even imagines she sees a flicker of movement. Let them look. They grapple and sweat and as he comes, she grips him tight inside her and digs her nails into his back. She thinks of the boy on the gravel with his pants around his ankles. She's glad.

CHAPTER EIGHTEEN

LAYLA, 1986

Layla balances the heavy tray on one arm, hooking her fingers over the edge onto the starched napkin that lines it. She uses her spare hand to flick open the swing door and lurches through, the silver cruet set rattling and the ice tinkling frantically in the glass.

She hates people who have room service – lazy arse-holes who can't be bothered to use their legs and make it down to the dining room. They always want the works as well: heavy full breakfasts, racks of toast with jams, fruit, precarious coffee pots. Sometimes there's a tip, and that almost makes it worth it. Sometimes it's generous. Other times it makes her want to spit in their faces.

She makes her way along the hall and knocks, lifting one knee to help balance the tray and then holding it up for long minutes, feeling the burn in her arms, composing her face for what will lie beyond. They don't send the sweet and innocent waiting staff up if they can avoid it, not after one fifteen-year-old weekend waitress got the fright of her life – full frontal from an old man. Dirty prick, she'd have dealt with him. They know that, so she gets more than her fair share of laden trays.

She sighs, furious at being made to wait. Part of her is tempted to dump the tray on the floor and hammer on the door but she pictures the complaint and can't be arsed. Eventually, it swings back and she steps forward with a breezy tone designed to needle any hangover.

'Morning!'

She is disarmed by the neatness of the room, the smartly dressed occupant. The curtains are open. He is handsome.

'Thank you.' He holds the door open to allow her to pass through and then strides back to pick up the phone handset. The room does not have the fuzzy morning smell of alcohol and sleep. He gestures at the table for her to put down the tray and she does, then turns to go.

'Wait,' he whispers, covering the handset with a palm, his eyes crinkling at the corners.

She hovers while he concludes the call, business that sounds like a foreign language, some deal, lawyers, paperwork, most likely oil related. She rocks on her heels, her feet sore, and takes in the details of the bedroom, an unfamiliar place in a building she knows like the back of her hand. The view of the grounds offers a new perspective. She wishes she was riding one of the horses across the lawn, churning the precious green stripes.

He puts down the phone but doesn't immediately speak. Layla knows he is looking at her, huffs her fringe away from her face. She is not used to being disarmed by men. She is irritated and yet also curious.

'Thank you,' he says. 'It must be a pain to have to bring this all the way up here.' He holds out a neatly folded ten-pound note and his fingers touch hers as she takes it. 'I just can't get away from the telephone.'

Though he gestures at the paperwork behind him, his eyes remain fixed on hers.

She smiles.

'It's not a problem.'

—

Jim is thudding about in the last stable. Layla has finished mucking out, sustained by bacon rolls and a warm coffee in the farmhouse kitchen when she arrived. She saunters towards the final door, watches him sweeping the sawdust back into a neat bed where Jasper has spread it around the stall like he always does. A barrow of sodden clumps sits beside him.

'I'll take that for you.' She steps in and reaches for the handles.

It's close in the rich-smelling space. His face colours pink and he lets the hair flop over his eyes.

'Thanks.'

She smiles, enjoying the way it makes him even more flustered, then hefts the handles of the barrow and wheels it round the back of the block to the six-foot-high pile that is decomposing there. She pushes the heavy load up a plank onto the top of the pile and dumps it at the furthest point, compacting it with her feet. A few flurries of sawdust whisk away as she stamps. She stares at the distant clouds, wondering if the lessons will be called off later, if the weather will be too bad for the delicate little snowflakes whose parents drive up here in their shiny cars. She feels an odd falling sensation, like panic. Shakes herself and returns with the barrow, propping it against the wall.

Jim holds up a head collar and lead rope. 'Doug says we can take Duchess and Ziggy out for an hour.' He looks so excited, unguarded.

Layla watches him stride ahead towards the field, resisting the disjointed feeling that plagues her before she jogs to catch up. When she reaches him she ruffles his hair. It starts friendly but she does it hard and for a bit too long until he pulls away.

'Ow.'

'Don't be such a baby.' They continue in silence. She can see he is going to sulk and regrets the impulse to tease him, doesn't want the day to be spoiled with cross words. She touches his arm. 'Hey, sorry Jimmy. Didn't mean to be so rough. Race you to the field?' Then she sets off at a run without waiting for an answer. After a hundred yards she turns and sees he is wavering. 'Come on!'

Reluctantly, Jimmy breaks into a loose jog and she waits until he is close before sprinting on. She can hear him speeding up behind her, their feet skidding on the loose stones that litter the track, and feels a rush of pleasurable terror at being chased, losing the notion of where she is, just escaping into something easier and purer. They crash into the gate at the same moment, out of breath from pelting uphill like children. Layla folds in two, gasping and laughing, dragging in air. She tilts her head, intending to catch his eye, but she is facing the sun and can't see his expression.

They catch the horses and groom and tack them up quickly. Layla usually prefers to ride alone but today there is a companionable atmosphere between the two of them. They let loose in a field and she relishes the way the horses match pace, galloping side by side in perfect unison. They stay out for over an hour and she feels able to slough off the stresses of the previous days, the anger and bitter feelings that have raged inside her. It is a relief, this casting away of something she hadn't realised had taken such a grip.

Back at the stables, she slides from Duchess and grins at Jimmy.

'Thanks. I needed that.'

He blushes and she busies herself with untacking the horse and rubbing her down. It feels like he's being weird again. If only things could be simple.

'Layla.' He holds the gate to the field open and watches as she releases Duchess, who kicks up her heels and then rolls in a patch of mud. 'Would you like to go for a drink one night?'

The suggestion floors her. Jimmy is more like a younger brother to her than someone she would date. The reflex to slap him down is strong but she catches sight of the flush on his neck and feels an excruciating beat of embarrassment.

'Ah, Jimmy. I don't really...'

His face clouds over. She can almost see dislike germinating in his eyes. It's shocking. She steps back.

He turns away.

'Jimmy, don't be like that.'

'You're just a cock tease, Layla. That's all you are.'

The vitriol in his words takes her aback. The echo of Stephen. Normally she would retaliate instantly, but something about today when she has let her guard down stalls her and brings tears to her eyes. She says nothing, just watches him walk back down the hill alone. She doesn't know why she bothers.

CHAPTER NINETEEN

CAL

Cal parks at the top of the track on a wide verge and walks down to the stables, narrating the journey for the benefit of the recording. The stable buildings sit halfway down the long hill, offering a wide view of the fields around them. Most of the surrounding paddocks are muddy, churned by horses over the long winter. He counts twenty of them, grazing impossibly short grass.

This is the way she rode on that last journey; these are the last views she saw. Did she look back? Did she have some inkling of what was coming? Did she know?

No one has ever been arrested in connection with Layla's disappearance. The police interviewed Stephen but couldn't make a charge stick against him. In such cases as these, it's usually unlikely that a stranger is involved, but Layla's case is extraordinary. Was there someone watching Layla as she left that day? Did she cross paths with a killer? Perhaps his fixation with Dubois is colouring his views about the rest of the world. For the millionth time, Cal wonders how Detective Foulds is getting on with the information he emailed her.

Pushing the thought away, he squares his shoulders and trudges down to the yard, where an old farmhouse is flanked by stables and newer barns. An iron five-bar gate blocks his path. He remembers images of police cars parked on this verge. There was no gate then.

'Can I help you?'

A woman wearing jodhpurs and a body warmer slides back a stable door, driving the bolt across before she strides towards him. The horse left behind whickers and kicks at the door impatiently.

'Quiet, Star,' the woman calls. She holds a plastic brush in her hand. The horse shakes its head up and down vigorously.

'My daughter has always wanted a horse,' he says, displaying his most unthreatening, winning smile.

'They're not for sale.'

She must be in her late forties. Her skin is ruddy, weathered, fair hair tied back in a bun, strands held in place with a net and clips as if she is about to go into the show ring. He holds out his press card. She squints at it, waits for him to speak.

'Cal Lovett. Don't worry. I'm not here for a pony. I'm making a podcast about the Layla Mackie case.'

The sun breaks out from the cloud cover behind him, striking the woman in the face so that she has to shade her eyes. He sees clearly the distrust for him, this southern journalist at the gate, someone likely to lack sensitivity, determined to blaze in and solve the mystery. But this is what he is good at: changing minds, getting people onside.

'I don't want to disturb you,' he ploughs on. 'But I'm working with her family to try and get some answers and...'

'You're helping Jean and Tam? They know about this?'

She still looks suspicious but he can sense a tiny thaw.

'Yes. I'm just hoping to see where she spent so much time. I know this place was important to her.'

He waits, sees her consider.

'I'd need to check with Jean that what you say is true.'

'It is, I promise. We could call them now?'

She makes no movement, so he gestures to the gate, pulls back the sprung mechanism to join her on the other side.

'All right then. I'm Bridget.'

'Thanks, I really appreciate it, Bridget.'

Cal takes a deep breath of relief.

His feet crunch on large grey stones that line the route down to the grooved concrete outside the stables. Another fast-moving cloud has passed in front of the sun and it is cold in the shadow.

'Were you living here back then?'

She nods.

'Do you remember Layla?'

'I was thirteen. I remember her.'

She sets the plastic brush down in a tray of horse-grooming equipment.

'Just give me a minute.'

She strides towards the house, legs long in her riding boots, leaving him with the grumpy horse. He stretches a hand out but thinks better of it when the creature puts back its ears. Instead, he thinks of Layla and tries to picture her here. He has seen a photograph of her jumping a gaping ditch on the back of a horse, hatless, hair streaming out behind her.

He skirts the yard, peering into empty stables that have sawdust beds a foot high on the floor, raked neatly but still reeking. There's a picture of Margot riding a pony on a beach, taken before he was born. His mother used to keep it on the mantlepiece but after she vanished it was all cleared away.

'I'll show you around if you like.' He has been so absorbed in his thoughts that he hasn't registered Bridget's return. She takes him around the tack room and the hay barn, then shows him the riding school – a large covered sandy arena.

'This was open to the elements back then,' she says, and he pictures Layla schooling horses under an iron sky.

'Will you walk up the hill with me, do a short interview as we go?'

She nods. 'Aye, I suppose so. I've an hour before the kids come back from school.'

He has the strange sensation he sometimes gets from people that she wants to talk to him, that there is something unsaid from those days and his arrival is a relief, a chance to unburden herself. He waits, letting the silence weigh between them.

'I remember that day, you know,' she tells him when they are standing higher up the hill. She runs her hand along a tangled piece of wire, fixing the fence, as if she can't possibly remain still. 'No one ever asked me about it, though.'

He imagines an overlooked teenager, irritated at being ignored.

'Not even the police?'

She shakes her head. Her eyes are fixed on the stables below where two girls are wheeling a barrow through the lower fields, stopping to lift horse dung into it with large forks.

'At first it was the horse everyone was worried about. Dad was furious – he assumed she'd just stayed out too long. She was always doing that.'

'Horses are valuable.'

She laughs and it's a mixture of awe and bitterness that circles them.

'People put up with a lot from Layla. She was an incredible rider and a hard worker, but it was more than that too.'

He waits.

'A sort of power. It sounds silly, but it felt like everyone was under Layla's spell. All she had to do was look at a man and they'd fall at her feet. Like they all wanted her but were a little bit afraid of her.'

'Were you afraid of her?'

She comes back to herself, seems to realise that they are standing on the crest of the hill in the present day.

'Maybe a little.'

'Tell me more about that day.'

'She was supposed to go with Jim – they had to muck out first, but she took off without him. He called her a selfish bitch and worse – said he was going to make her pay. By the time he was done with two people's chores there wasn't really time for him to ride. She still hadn't come back and it was getting dark.'

'Did you see her leave?'

'No. I looked for her, though. We all did. Dad and I drove the roads in the Land Rover. We kept stopping the car and shouting her name. We walked into the fields and listened in case she'd been thrown off and couldn't move.'

She looks at him.

'I was even angry with her. I had to miss a trip to the cinema in Aberdeen that I'd been looking forward to for ages. I didn't realise that while we were bitching about her carelessness…'

She swallows.

He knows these thoughts, these dark imaginings. What was he doing at the exact moment Margot went missing? Did he feel it in some imperceptible way? It seems impossible that he could carry on oblivious at such a seismic moment.

'You couldn't have known.'

'I just wonder. Did she hear us, calling for her?'

'Where did she ride?'

He hopes the change of subject will jog further memories.

'That way. The only way.' She gestures in the direction his car is parked, but Cal notes the hesitation.

'You aren't sure?'

She shrugs. 'Where else could she have gone?'

'Do you have a theory?'

Bridget exhales, as if embarrassed.

'I didn't think at the time. Only really wondered years later. Layla never did what she was supposed to. She used to jump the craziest things: ditches, walls that shouldn't have been possible. She took risks no one else would dream of.'

She points to the trees that sit high above the road – a tangle of pines, some of which seem to have fallen like toothpicks in the wind. He hears an ominous creaking, as if they are alive and in pain. 'I had a fancy that she went in there. But that's mad.'

The wood is overgrown and looks impenetrable, a vertical bank before it.

He steps forward, curious.

'Will you show me?'

They climb the bank and wall. Cal catches his hand on a hidden snarl of barbed wire and he swears, sucks the blood that blooms from his palm. When they are over, they thrash their way through ferns as tall as he is. Bridget is right, this is crazy. But then, in the cool darkness, he can see the impression of what once may have been a path. Large boulders are strewn to its sides, covered with thick moss so bright it almost glows, flanked by foliage. No birds sing.

'Where would this come out?'

'Up near the hotel, maybe. But there are fields that touch it at different points,' she says. 'It could be possible to go in lots of different directions.'

'Did anyone ever tell the police this?'

'I don't know. It seems so unlikely. I'm probably being ridiculous.' She shrugs and he can see she is glad to have shared the burden of the suspicion, however fantastical it seems.

As far as he can tell, everyone worked on the assumption that Layla took a particular route. His mind swirls with thought. What if, all this time, they've been looking in the wrong place?

CHAPTER TWENTY

Jim, the stable boy, now works at a lumber yard near Kintore. Cal drives along the A96 in the direction of Aberdeen. The road appears slashed through the countryside, bypassing villages it must once have weaved through.

It doesn't take long to reach the yard, which is silent, deserted as he wanders into it. Vast bodies of trees are stacked high on one side, sawdust carpeting the ground, eddying in the breeze, older flakes clumped in puddles. There is a shout, no words discernible, though the warning is clear, and he looks up to see a man emerging from a Portacabin, wearing a navy boiler suit that is faded and stained.

'You lost?' The tone of the man's voice, the aggressive way he comes towards Cal, suggests he has no intention of welcoming a stranger.

Cal knows instinctively that he needs to play a different role with this man, that openness and friendliness will not crack through the harsh exterior. He holds firm, uses his height to his advantage.

'Maybe you can help? I'm looking for Jim Campbell.'

'What do you want with him?'

Cal examines the hard angles of the man's face, the strong arms and the cold, dark eyes underneath overhanging brows.

'I'd need to tell him that.'

'I'm Jim.'

Now that it's confirmed, he can see the shadow of the stable boy from the few photographs taken at the time. He wore a flat cap then, jeans with holes in the knees.

'It's about Layla Mackie.'

A brief storm of anger crosses the man's face.

'You polis?'

'Nope, not police. Journalist. I'm doing a podcast on the case.'

Cal extracts a card from his pocket, takes one step forward and holds it out. The man waits a beat then shakes his head, shoves his hands in the boiler suit pockets.

'Can you not let it rest?'

'Layla's family want answers. I'm here with their blessing.'

'The quine is dead. They'll get no more answers than that.'

'What makes you so sure?'

'It's been more than thirty year. Police at the time couldn't find anything. How would you do any better, like?'

Cal squares up a little.

'People remember things differently with time. They don't always want to protect the people they did back then.'

'Seems to me that being killed turns people into saints and no one will speak the truth.'

'You didn't like Layla.'

He is careful to form this as a statement, not a question.

'She was a selfish bitch. Good luck finding anyone to tell you that now, though.'

'You were meant to be with her that day?'

'Aye. Stupid cow left me with all the work.'

'Did you see her go?'

'I shouted after her. She didn't pay ony attention. That was the way she was. Ay doing what she wanted and leaving others to clean up her mess.'

'Did you actually see her ride along the road?'

'She rode right past me.'

'But did you see where she went?'

'There is only one road out.' The man shakes his head as if Cal is dim.

'Could she have taken the horse into the forest?'

'The woods at the top?' He looks surprised for a second, then spits on the floor, glares at Cal while he considers. 'I wouldn't put anything past her.'

'So, it's possible everyone was looking in the wrong place?'

'Maybe.'

'Did you not want to follow her – after she left without you?'

Jim's face turns a beetroot shade and Cal sees the shadows of the kind of anger that comes with rejection. Maybe he liked Layla a little too much back then. Maybe she turned him down.

'I've work to do.'

Cal holds the card out again. 'Can I leave my details? In case you think of anything.'

He knows the man takes it just to get rid of him. Jim folds it over in his palm. It will hit the bin the moment he leaves.

Cal steps back. 'I'll leave you to it.' Then he throws out a final question. 'What do you think happened to her?'

Again, Jim's face takes on a belligerent anger. Cal wonders if he was ever a suspect at the time.

'I think some man she was fucking had enough. That's what I think. It's what everyone thinks. You ask them up at the hotel what she got up to. Maybe someone up there will tell you what she was really like.'

He strides away, leaving Cal alone in the sawdust.

CHAPTER TWENTY-ONE

Cal hates having to plead for funding. That was one of the anticipated consequences of a big-hit series with Dubois – being able to set his own course, budgets flexing to suit him instead of the other way around. It seems so long since that was a primary concern.

'It's not that expensive,' he tells Sarah. In the distance, the hill by the hotel stands purple-grey, wreathed in cloud at the summit.

'But it's happening on a whim.'

'It isn't. Layla didn't go the way they thought she did – she hasn't been seen since then, so something happened to her and the chances that it's someone at the hotel, that her body is hidden in the area, are good.'

Sarah is silent. He waits, hopes.

'We can't stretch to the full amount. What about the family?'

Cal thinks of Jean and Tam – their simple surroundings, the way they live cleaved to the land, eking out an existence on the hillside, missing their daughter. He can't imagine there are bags of gold beneath the mattress.

'They've barely got anything.'

'I could authorise half the figure you're suggesting.'

'Mel has already done us the best deal possible.' Cal knows he is fighting past the point of sense. Sarah is a decisive person; she rarely backtracks and he can hear by the tone of her voice that she's digging in.

He can't work out why it feels so personal this time. When he argues for Layla is he really arguing the case for Margot? Does it matter if he is doing that? Surely the families of the disappeared need someone on their side who understands, who will keep pushing at the doors closed to them.

He isn't going to give up.

'I'll speak to Jean and Tam,' he says.

–

Jean answers the door. The hope that flickers into her eyes when she sees him melts away as he shakes his head.

'No big news, Jean.' He knows to say that quickly. 'But a few small things and I thought it would be good to update you.'

She sags a little, nods. 'I was away to have a fly cup. Come in.'

He stands in the doorway as she takes a mug from the cupboard and pours tea for him, the water steaming as it hits the tea bag. 'No Tam today?'

'He's up at the top field. He's been on about re-fencing that for a while now. Do you want me to fetch him?'

'No need.'

They settle in the conservatory.

'So, one thing that came up. The lady that runs the stables now. She seems to think maybe Layla didn't ride out the way everyone thought.' He sips his tea while Jean digests her confusion.

'But there's only one road in…'

'She said something about the wood at the top? Though it would be hard to get a horse in there.'

Jean looks sceptical but he notices her body language; she's sitting straighter.

'It would be like Layla to find a secret place.'

'Really?'

She smiles and her eyes brim. She pats her pocket for a hankie, wipes her face. In the moments of exposure Cal sees the lines and the age. His own mother's face comes to him – something familiar in their desolation. He presses on.

'I think this gives us another place to search. If she had an accident elsewhere, for example.'

'But after all this time.'

'I'd like to try dogs that are specially trained. I know a lady who can bring her team. I've worked with her before and she's excellent. If there was any trace, I think they'd find it.'

Jean nods. The fateful fragments of hope are back. 'If you think it's worth a try.'

'The only problem is that it does cost a bit to do. It might take a few days to cover the area between the stables and woods, especially if we loop round to the hotel.'

He hates himself as he says the words. It feels like exploitation. He knows desperate people will pay anything for answers – he could be suggesting a clairvoyant.

Jean lifts her chin at his words. 'The hotel?'

'It would be a sensible border to set.'

He sees the thoughts rolling, the determination in the set of her jaw. Her fingers clench the hankie in her lap.

'How much are we talking?'

–

As he leaves the cottage, dusk is falling and he can see the lone figure of Layla's father in the distance. The faint sound of a mallet hitting wood reaches his ears. Clouds press down on them and the scent of rain is in the air. He shivers. Since Dubois, he doubts himself more. He doesn't know what to believe about Layla, what he would feel if a strange man was making half promises to his mother and suggesting she open her wallet to find Margot.

He drives slowly back to the B&B, heart racing when a pheasant makes a suicide dash across the road. Perched on the edge of the bed, he traces a route through the rational arguments. You have to narrow down possibilities, eliminate certain options, that's how you inch closer to the truth. They are adults and he has laid it out truthfully, that is all he can do. Even so, it takes him a long time to fall asleep. The responsibility sits on top of the blankets, weighing so heavily his chest tightens.

Eventually he must sink beneath consciousness, because he dreams. A hot day, sunlight fierce overhead, refracting from water, making his eyes sore. A wriggling maggot on a hook, thick hands over his, helping him cast into deeper water, where grasses overhang the banks and shoals sleep in shade.

In his dream he is seven, maybe eight, his knees raw with the permanent bruises of childhood. He stares and stares at the water but the fish don't bite. It doesn't matter. They eat their sandwiches sitting on tickly grass, thick wedges of ham between doorsteps, melting Penguin biscuits.

In his sleep he settles, relaxes. It's a mirror of a real day, a day with his father *before*. On the bank, he scrambles to his feet, dusts the crumbs from his lap. Across the water, in the distance, he can see lines of cars, rotting and rusting into the earth. Turning to scrap.

CHAPTER TWENTY-TWO

EPISODE THREE: THE WRONG PLACE

The day Layla went missing she seemed distracted. Staff at the hotel reported that she showed up late for her breakfast shift. She yelled at the chef when he remonstrated with her. After she left early, the chef spoke to the hotel's management and a verbal warning about her behaviour was due to be issued the following day. It wasn't needed. Layla never worked there again.

From the hotel, we know she went home and changed her clothes. Her mother heard her come into the cottage and go upstairs. She slammed her wardrobe door against the wall and Jean called up to her, angry about the noise and Layla's lack of care. Those were the last words she spoke to her daughter.

'I've never forgiven myself for that. I was so angry. She was difficult, always had been, but it had been getting worse. Her father was beside himself. Maybe she should have moved out, living with her parents can't have been fun, but... Anyway, I heard her, but I didn't see her. She was only in for ten minutes before she went off to the stables. I wish I could change that. I'd give anything to go back.'

At the stables, Layla was supposed to work through a list of chores with stable hand Jim before riding the horses. Instead, she tacked up the best horse on the block, a young thoroughbred called Ruby. Before Jim could stop her, she'd ridden off without him.

Sue was a regular at the stables at the time. She remembers that afternoon clearly.

'Jim was red mad. He was swearing and saying how he was going to get her back. I think it was worse because he was sweet on her for a while. He asked her out, I think, but she turned him down. He wasn't the only one, though. I saw the way Doug looked at her. We all did.'

In episode one, we detailed the extensive searches that took place on the riding routes near Hightap stables. What we've since discovered is that those searches were likely doomed to fail. In this episode, we'll examine the possibility that Layla took Ruby somewhere else entirely. A path no one has considered before...

CHAPTER TWENTY-THREE

LAYLA, 1986

It's raining but she doesn't care. The cottage manages to be freezing cold and stifling at the same time and she feels trapped. Her parents are looking at her with increasing frustration. What is she going to do? When is she going to attempt to make a home for herself? There has been talk of a job at the stables in the college – helping out on a course she wishes she could do herself. But she doesn't have the grades.

Head down, she walks through the fields in the direction of the hotel. Stephen will be there, hungover from the previous night, and it is something to do.

The rain pelts the grasses, making pools in the track she trudges <u>along</u>. Even when she steps under the cover of the wood, it trickles through the canopy. Tears drip from the mist of bluebells that carpet the woodland floor. She throws back her hood and allows the rain to run down her forehead, frustration boiling inside her.

He doesn't see her at first, the guest. He is running through the trees, kicking up mud, spattered with it. At first, she doesn't realise it is the man from the room service morning, the one for whom normal rules do not seem to apply. She steps into the middle of the path and has time to see his initial irritation at the obstacle change to something else. He halts abruptly, and a smile comes to his face.

'Fancy meeting you here,' he says.

The way his eyes travel across her is intoxicating. She feels relief. He will leave, but for a short period of time she has something to help her forget.

He asks to see the grounds, so she shows him the overgrown pathway to the back of the kitchen garden – walled in with grey stone ten feet high. It is a strange fortress of protected plants in neat rows, a sheltered microclimate. When they reach the edge furthest from the hotel, he stops and quirks an eyebrow at her. She holds his gaze and, before she knows it, her back is pressed against the sodden wall, unfamiliar lips hard against hers, the weight of his body fixing her in place.

A trail of cold drips makes its way down the back of her neck. She opens her eyes and he is watching her, his expression intense. With a thumb, he traces the track of the rain down the side of her face. For a moment, she feels self-conscious, aware of the pointlessness of it all. She wishes she'd made it through the forest to the cottage without stepping into the path of the wolf.

But then the feeling vanishes and they both laugh.

'Well,' he says, taking a step back, rubbing the stubble on his chin.

She feels a sudden urge to walk away. It is safer to reject now, quickly. She flips her hood over her head, raises a hand.

'Bye then.'

–

She dresses carefully for the evening shift, wears more eyeliner than usual, smooths her hair into a ponytail that swings when she walks and hikes her skirt higher than they are allowed.

It doesn't matter, because he isn't there. In the candlelit dining room, there are only older couples sitting silently across from each other beneath vast oil paintings. Night falls outside and she sees the ghost of herself in the long windows, flitting from table to table in the low light.

Her mood deflates. Monotony replaces the excitement she felt at being desired. Not for the first time, she finds herself daunted by the prospect of life continuing in this same way. There has to be more, but she doesn't know how to find it — where to look or how to unlock it. Money is an impenetrable barrier. She needs to train for something, but what can she do? If it wasn't for the horses, she would go mad. All the mucking out, the schooling and the endless tack cleaning is worth it for those moments of freedom. When she's on horseback she has confidence — leaping jumps and ditches that make others quail. If only it spilled over into the rest of her life.

She sticks her head out into the hallway, thinking she might be able to chat to the new receptionist, tap her up for information about people staying at the hotel, but the night porter is already sitting at the desk, frown in place and gaunt suspicion at her appearance.

'What are you needing?' he asks, as if he knows.

'Nothing.' She shrugs. 'Just seeing if Babs was here, like.'

He turns back to his paper.

'Nup.'

She lays the tables in the dining room, hearing the chatter in the kitchen rise now all the guests have moved to the bar or the billiards room. There's a squeal from one of the younger waitresses, and she can picture the sous chefs jesting with them, offering up the puddings and expensive ice cream as they clear the fridges and freezers for the new week.

The kitchen door swings back and the head waitress strides across the room.

'Layla, are you still here? Away with you. The night porter can tidy up these bits. He's little else to do.'

She grabs her coat and bag and scuttles down the creepy back corridor, out into the car park, which is overhung with starlight and the dark silhouette of the hill above. Behind her, the hotel and its hotchpotch of turrets and towers glows with life and luxury. Layla holds her breath and turns on the spot, craning her neck to the constellations and grasping for a sense of herself, a clue of who she is meant to be.

CHAPTER TWENTY-FOUR

LAYLA, 1986

She traces the rim of her wine glass with a wet finger, enjoying the grimace on Stephen's face.

'Cut it out.'

Layla smirks, sighs. Across the bar, a group of his friends are sinking pints, their voices loud and their faces red.

'So, what do you think?'

'Sorry?' She refocuses on Stephen. 'Think about what?'

He frowns. 'About us going on holiday. I was thinking maybe Tenerife for a week? We could ask for the time, anyway. It's not like we work in the same department.'

'But then… they'll all know.'

'About us? They all know already! And anyway, what's wrong with them knowing?'

Layla drains the last inch of warm wine so she doesn't have to answer right away.

'Nothing, that's not what I mean.'

'Well. What *do* you mean?'

She means: I don't know if I want to be with you. I don't always find you that interesting. The sex is good but maybe that's not enough. I make you hurt me and you like to do it. But she can't say any of it. She pushes back the padded stool she's perched on. Picks up his empty glass and hers because she can't help herself, just can't leave it for some other poor sod to clear.

'Another?'

Stephen nods. She goes to the bar without letting any of the thoughts pelting around inside her spill free. Maybe she should go to Tenerife. For a break. But her ambivalence about Stephen isn't the only hesitation. It would cost most of the money she has saved. The escape fund. Is it silly to have an escape fund and nowhere to escape to? Probably. It isn't much, but she likes having it there. In her worst moments she thinks about the trickle of pounds in the account, how they are gradually building.

The barman catches her eye and serves her earlier than he should. His shirt sleeves are rolled back to the elbows and her eyes wander over his strong forearms, something in her brain activated and aroused by the movement, the capability. She glances back and their table is empty. Stephen has joined some of the boys playing pool. He doesn't look at her. He's pissed off. She slides the banknote across the bar then pockets the change and carries the drinks to the table. Sits alone.

He ignores her for another hour, letting the pint warm, untouched, while he hits the pool balls too hard with the cue and they ricochet across the table without finding their mark. She thinks about leaving, but then she catches sight of Doug and Sal coming in through the swing door and weaves her way to them.

She sees the way Sal's eyes narrow, the sourness in her face, but Doug reaches out an arm to draw her in and buys her a drink. He is red-faced and half-cut, always an expansive drunk, though with an occasional cruel side.

'Don't know what we'd do without this one,' he tells the men lined at the bar, turning to his wife with a twinkle. 'Eh, Sal?'

She stays with them, ignoring Stephen, relieved that she has a place in the world, that she is useful, wanted.

It's getting late and she's tired so she crosses to the Ladies where she can splash some water on her face, cool down. When she looks up, Sal is standing over her.

'I think it's time you went,' she says. Her lips are painted bright red; Layla notices the sharp points of dangly earrings.

'Doug asked me to stay for a drink,' she says, injured.

'And now you've outstayed your welcome.' Sal doesn't wait, flips the door so hard that it slaps back and forth behind her.

Layla goes to retrieve her coat. Stephen is at the table, a flushed look on his face.

'Are you not wanting another?'

'No, think I'll get on.'

'You let him buy you a drink.' He raises his chin to where Doug is holding court.

'I work for him.'

'No, Layla, you don't. It's not a job.'

'I do a lot for them.'

'He looks at you funny.'

'Fuck off, Stephen.'

Layla grabs her jacket, her heart stuttering fast at the argument, afraid the people around them will hear, will say something to Doug and Sal.

'Wait. I'll give you a lift.'

'I'm fine.'

'Don't be like that.'

'Like what?'

Radiating animosity, they thread their way through the crowd at the bar – Layla forces herself to smile and wave at Doug and Sal.

'Are you away?' Doug leans in and she feels the hot sweat of beer and breath on her. Layla nods. 'See you in the morning.'

Sal is talking to a woman by the bar. She doesn't turn to say goodbye.

The pub is small and the heat of the bodies means the outside world feels even colder than it should. Rain drives sideways across the car park. She hesitates in the doorway, then feels Stephen's hand sneaking down the back of her jeans.

'Get off.'

She's drunk and smarting still from Sal's words.

'I can't fucking win, can I?'

'What do you mean? Is this about the holiday?'

'No, Layla. It's about everything. Just talk to me. What's going on?'

He tries to touch her cheek and she flinches, then regrets it as she sees rage and despair slide into his eyes. She thinks he might cry but instead he grips her upper arms, hard.

'What's your problem? Why can't you just have a conversation?'

She turns her head away and somehow he ends up pushing her backward so she's against the wall of the pub in the rain. His face is close and the anguish and intensity she sees there frightens her. She doesn't want to mean this much to him, doesn't want to drive him crazy. Yet she keeps doing it, over and over.

'Please, just tell me what's wrong?'

Her arms are pinned. It doesn't hurt, but she can't move, struggles a little trapped against the wet stone, against the feeling of panic. Water runs down her face like tears and she remembers the kitchen garden, this moment a distortion of that one.

Stephen's face comes forward and she kisses him to shut him up, to stop him asking questions she can't answer. She closes her eyes and tries to imagine she's back in the woods, but she can't recapture the scent of the earth and the leaves and his taste. Here there is only beer and smoke, boredom and normality. It isn't enough and she can't explain why.

'Layla...'

'I need you to take me home. I'm up early in the morning.'

He makes her wait while he takes his time finding his keys. The rain pools in the neck of her jacket. Her feet are cold. He drives her home but they don't speak, even when she opens the door and steps into the night. He accelerates away before she pulls her fingers from the handle. Her arm wrenches, making her cry out in pain. She stands on the driveway watching the lights vanish in the distance.

CHAPTER TWENTY-FIVE

CAL

Generally, Cal likes to appear unannounced, but this time he has called ahead and made an appointment. He's even wearing a shirt to help him fit in with the hotel's upper-crust clientele. It feels tight against his neck and he tucks a finger in to try and loosen it, without effect. Stepping in through the large front door, he can smell the woodsmoke from the fireplaces. A dull chatter from a room to the left accompanies the muzak playing in the background.

Cal's dream still reverberates inside him. The images from *then* photographically perfect even now he is awake. The idea of the scrapyard brings him out in a cold sweat, the click of a jigsaw piece into place.

He realises the woman at the desk is staring at him. She wears a neat navy-and-green tartan jacket as well as an expression of irritation, impatience. He feels her gaze on the holdall he carries; the recording equipment lies snugly inside.

'I'm here to see Archie James,' he says, smiling to cover his discomfort, tucking Margot away for later. 'I have an appointment at eleven.'

Before she can answer, a man strides from the shadows further along the grand hallway, his hand already stretched out in front of him. He's wearing a suit that smells of money – you can tell its quality by the sinuous way it slides up his wrist to reveal gold cufflinks. He is polished, aware of his own importance.

'Do call me Archie.'

Cal shakes the insistent hand. 'Cal. Thank you for seeing me.'

'No problem. I'm not sure how I can help to be honest, I only took over five years ago, but very happy to try. I thought we could have coffee in the billiards room.'

Cal follows him along a dark corridor with red walls and a tartan carpet. Paintings line their route: stags pinned to the ground, their necks arched and arrows piercing flesh. When they enter the gloomy billiards room, the results of such endeavours stare down with glassy eyes. Cal shudders, reminded uncannily of Dubois.

A fire has been lit in the room but only recently, and it isn't taking the edge off the chill. Archie chooses an armchair close to the crackling logs and gestures for Cal to take the one further from the flames.

'One of the waitresses will be in shortly with the coffee,' he explains. 'Do you want to record this?'

He straightens his tie and Cal resists the urge to point out that it's audio only.

'If that's all right with you?' He unstraps the bag and takes out the microphones.

'Of course, no problem. Happy to help in any way I can.'

It is tempting to smile at the sense of self-importance, the way Archie James acts as if this is his home instead of a business financed by a luxury hotel group.

As Cal slides the microphone onto his tie, they talk about the hotel's history, the size of the estate and its hunting grounds, now much reduced from previous years. It is a struggle to keep his mind in the here and now.

'I don't mind saying, I'd had my eye on the old place for a while.' Archie chuckles.

The door swings open and a nervous-looking waitress carries a clinking tray across the room. Archie makes no move to help her, it is Cal who drags a side table closer so she can set down the heavy load. She smiles gratefully and he realises that she can't be much older than Chrissie.

'Shall I pour the coffee?'

He is about to say no, they can do it, but Archie speaks first. 'Yes, do.'

The silence while the liquid pours is excruciating – the girl's hand shakes under the strain of the heavy pot.

Archie waves her away without thanks. Cal feels dislike for the man coil inside him. 'The hotel had been in one family for years, had become a bit of a burden over time,' he continues. 'I came in and reinvigorated what was a pretty tired operation, then secured the investment and the main group asked me to stay on and keep things in order.'

'Did you know anything about the Layla Mackie case?'

'Not in detail.' He shifts in his seat, crosses his legs. 'I mean of course I'd heard about it. She worked here, poor girl. Have you made any progress?'

'We're looking at some possibilities.'

'Well, anything we can do to help.'

'There is one thing. I'm hoping to use dogs to search some of the places Layla may have ridden that day. I wondered if you might allow me to search the edge of the hotel grounds while we're at it?'

The man looks at him over the rim of his gilt-edged coffee cup in disbelief.

'You think dogs can find her?'

'Cadaver dogs. If she had an accident and has lain undiscovered then it would bring her family peace to have her remains returned to them.'

Archie pales. 'Of course. I wasn't thinking. I can give you a map of the estate. It's just, the publicity isn't really… ideal.'

'We'll be as discreet as we can of course. And anyway, I'd like to co-ordinate when we do this. It might not go down well with some of the staff.'

'You mean the chef.'

'Stephen, yes. Might be better if it was done while…'

He gives a curt nod. 'We could certainly check when he is on shift for you. Nobody wants a scene.'

'Thank you. I don't want to upset anyone unnecessarily.'

'Naturally.' The owner clears his throat. 'Not that he would be the only one, by all accounts.'

'What do you mean?'

'Oh, nothing. People in this line of business do talk, but I try not to listen to the gossip.'

'And what do they say? In this case?' He is careful to keep his tone neutral.

'I wouldn't like to cast aspersions on the dead, Mr Lovett. I'm sure you understand that.'

'Missing.'

'I'm sorry?' Archie James is only half listening, tugging at his sleeve to check the time on his gleaming watch.

'Missing. Layla hasn't been declared dead.'

'No. Of course.' The silence between them is awkward. 'Well, she may have had one or two male friends on the go. If you know what I mean?'

'Right. I see.'

Archie presses his hands to the arms of the chair, standing to end their interview.

When they reach the front door, he adds, 'Leave your details with the receptionist and I'll be in touch with a convenient time for the search.'

Cal smarts at the imperious tone.

'I will. Thanks for your time.'

He waves from the stairs, leaving Cal stranded in the middle of the opulent hallway. Cal turns on the spot, tries to imagine Layla working here thirty-five years ago – the place clearly hasn't changed in a century. Although he is one tiny step closer, he feels frustrated. Layla is still an enigma, a shifting picture in his mind.

Later that night, Cal walks the fields near the bed and breakfast, watching the dusk settle over the countryside, thoughts of home and Dubois and Margot competing for his attention. Allie hasn't been in touch with him at all. Not even when the episodes have gone out. They've never gone this long without speaking before.

The break from her is both a relief and a torment. He wishes he had someone he could talk to about his theories, about Dubois and the scrapyard. The words from the interview run in circles in his head. *The Woodland Killer. That's what they called me. They don't know the half of it.*

He spent an hour searching online earlier, desperately trying to pin the killer to a location that year. There is nothing. And no word from the police either. Uncertain, he found his childhood home on Google Maps, scrolling closer and closer, dragging and shifting until he found the river, the place he thinks they used to fish. Across the water, the swathe of unmarked land. He almost closed the window, but then, on the satellite view he saw it – what could be lines of cars, piled high and coated in vegetation, rusted and sinking into the earth.

He needs someone to tell him he's wrong, it can't be true. In the absence of a confidante, he walks until it is getting too dark to see.

There is no signal on the hill so he only gets the voicemail when he reaches the road, sees the lights of his home from home. The hotelier is brisk and only lightly apologetic.

'Archie James here. I'm afraid I've spoken to Group about your request and it's policy not to allow the kind of search you mentioned on the property. So sorry to have inconvenienced you, but I'm afraid it won't be possible to accommodate you this time.'

This time? What does he mean *this time*?

Cal swears and kicks at the nearest fence post. He never understands why process and policy stand in the way of humanity. He hates being the one to have to break jobsworth news like this to families. Would Archie 'posh suit' James still be saying no if he had to look Jean Mackie in the eye and tell her it wasn't 'policy'?

He knows this will devastate Jean. She believes in her heart that Stephen killed her daughter. Maybe they can approach the south of the estate and accidentally let one of the dogs slip free. He isn't going to all this trouble to do half a job, he decides. There will be a way to check, even if it means going against Archie James and his 'policy'.

CHAPTER TWENTY-SIX

Mel is a straight-talking, chain-smoking woman in her fifties. He has known her for a decade – she and her dogs Booster and Flight helped search for the body of a five-year-old boy in one of his previous cases. When you have stood ankle deep in snow together for hours, with the best possible outcome being that you find the remains of a child, it is impossible not to form a bond.

It is common for family members to be present at a search – keeping vigil over the proceedings. Sometimes that's all a family has been able to do for their loved one for a long time. He trusts Mel not to say or do the wrong thing in front of relatives. He draws strength from her and her dogs.

Booster is too old to work now, so Mel has brought Flight and Arrow, a younger dog she is training. Tired after a late night of listening to the Dubois recording again, he can't help but smile when he sees canine noses pressed up against the window in her van. His own dog came from Mel. Initial training proved Rocket was more suited to dozing by the fire than plunging through undergrowth in search of bodies.

Mel slams the door and they each raise a hand in greeting. Something taut loosens inside him. She opens the back doors to give the dogs air and he stands by their crates, is rewarded with wagging liveliness, while Mel turns on the spot, surveying the landscape. The woods near the stables are on one side but the moorland opens for miles. She gives a low whistle.

'This is going to be tough.'

'I know.'

'I mean, you did say, but…'

'At least it's not a swamp this time.'

The hillside is thick with heather. If you step off the path you might plunge as far as your waist. He has tried it and knows the ground beneath is uneven and treacherous, some sections boggy and wet. In the distance there are groups of straggly trees – woodland 'islands' in the heather sea. Places only the deer visit.

They spread a map on the bonnet of his car and are choosing routes when another vehicle pulls into the car park. The sky has turned a dark grey and it seems certain the day will be squally. He expects both of Layla's parents to be here but only Jean emerges. She looks nervous as she approaches them, wrapped in a warm fleece and wearing a tall pair of wellies that make her seem even smaller than she is. He tries to reassure her with a smile. The one she gives in return is wobbly.

'No Tam?'

'He couldn't do it,' she tells him. 'He wanted to, but… he's not feeling well.'

Her face is pinched. She is here for the both of them, standing strong because she has no choice. He squeezes her arm and she nods.

'Jean, this is Mel,' he says, walking her to the map.

'Nice to meet you, Jean.' Mel is kind, business-like – and it helps. There's no need to dwell on the details of why they are here, they all know what is at stake.

'We thought we'd search this area this morning.' Mel indicates a section of the map that is marked in red. The woods first. 'We'll do each dog in turn as we want to make sure. Then we'll see how far we get towards the hotel in the afternoon. It will depend on the terrain and how accessible it is.' They all look doubtfully at the inhospitable moorland. 'I've got a GPS here that we'll use so we're sure we've covered it all.'

Mel releases Arrow from his crate and Flight looks mournfully at them.

'All right, girl, your turn later. He needs to run first.'

Jean ruffles the dog's head and they set off together. Despite her fragile appearance, Jean moves at a good pace, picking her way up the path as Mel sends the dog off into the dense heather, tracking his progress by the sight of his tail and the flash of the luminous coat he wears.

Mel keeps up a steady explanation of what Arrow is doing, and Cal sees Jean's face unclench as they move – the raw air opening parts of them, unleashing them from day to day life. After half an hour slogging, they reach the side of the woods – an easier access point than the vertical leap – and pause to drink from their water bottles. He looks back on the fields and roads, sees cattle grazing, a train cutting a path across the landscape.

When they've settled into a rhythm, he records their thoughts, as well as the atmosphere and the tension in this isolated, unforgiving spot. Arrow plunges through the undergrowth as Cal talks to Jean about Layla, asking her to remember the daughter she hasn't seen for thirty-five years.

'We used to bring her up on the hill for picnics,' she tells him. 'She was so wild – always running, always full of energy, like the devil were after her.'

She is quiet after that. They have no idea what devil was after the woman, when her horse came back as if hell itself was on her heels.

After another hour they have covered the woods so decide to loop back down to the car and switch the dogs. He and Mel wade out into the heather and thrash a trail parallel to the path, leaving Jean to walk down alone. As they move away from her, he looks back. She cuts a forlorn figure, her shoulders hunched and her eyes on her feet. He describes her for the tape, feels her loneliness as a twin of the one twisting inside himself.

When they reach the car park, they are hot and sweaty. Arrow has not scented. It is easy to feel discouraged on days like these but he has learned that it is all part of the longer journey, that only by being methodical can they eliminate places and possibilities. He retrieves more layers from the car and a flask of hot tea – it is easy to become chilled when they stop. Jean is tired, he can see the greyness that has descended on her.

'Will you go home?'

She shakes her head.

'I'll maybe sit in the car.'

He and Mel eat quickly, conscious that the day is moving against them.

'You okay?' She studies him for a moment. He is quieter than usual, he knows his mind is freewheeling.

'Yes, sorry,' he says.

Mel shrugs, taking nothing personally. 'Sometimes they just get to you.'

She opens the van door and throws in the sandwich wrappers.

'I might have another job for you soon,' he says. 'Near Birmingham.'

Mel scrutinises him for a moment, nods. 'Any time.'

They switch Arrow into the van and let Flight out. She sets off quickly, her wet nose ever-twitching, eyes bright and her tail high.

A small rain shower passes over, making it hard to talk, so they move in silence for a while, pressing up and into the woods as quickly as they can, then following their 'off-road' track back down. It is quicker without Jean and with less need for recording. There is nothing. Tomorrow they will return and move higher up the hill, over towards further woodland, nearer the hotel.

CHAPTER TWENTY-SEVEN

EPISODE FOUR: DOGS

It is the end of our third day scouring the hillside with cadaver dogs Arrow and Flight. The rain has set in persistently. My feet are squelching in my boots, Gore-Tex being the opposite of helpful when you step into bogs that are deeper than your ankles and water fills your shoes. We have combed the woods near the stables, then the open moorland, and are thrashing our way through the woodland further up and over the hill. We're not saying it yet, but both Mel – the dog handler regular listeners may remember from series two – and I are thinking it's time to give up.

Mel has to leave in the evening and all I can think as I trudge after her, resigned to failure, is how I'm going to tell Layla's parents that the search has come to nothing. I'm so focused that, at first, I don't notice Mel has stopped. In front of us, and just off to the side, Arrow is poised, his body quivering as he stares at a dense thicket of fern and brush. Somewhere nearby there is running water; we can hear it cascading, a stream swollen by the rainfall perhaps. The voice you'll hear next is Mel's.

'He's getting something. I'm tempted to go and see, but if there's any kind of crime scene…'

'Tell me what he's doing.'

'Arrow is trained to stay still and point – see the shape of his body? – when he scents.'

'So, you think he has scented?'

'Oh yes, definitely. It's a very clear signal from this dog. He is inexperienced though, so I'd like to bring Flight back round here, maybe approach from a different direction, and see if she picks up anything independently.'

We make careful notes of the co-ordinates on the GPS and Mel ties a red piece of plastic to a nearby tree so we can find the same place. It is an hour's hike back to the road where the cars are parked and Flight has already worked hard today, so it's a lot to ask her to come out again, but both Mel and I are convinced this is significant. It is already three in the afternoon. We have some time but need to move fast.

I've known Mel long enough to know she is already sure. She trusts her dogs and Arrow's signal was crystal clear. But if we're going to call in the police we need to double check. We talk as we hike back with the second dog.

'Flight! Heel. What would she have been doing out here? It's so far from the stables.'

'I've been wondering that. Not the best terrain to ride a horse. It's in the direction of the hotel she worked at though, so maybe…'

'She could have been meeting someone.'

'It doesn't seem likely, but…'

'Maybe she had an accident.'

'At least then we'll know. Her parents want to know.'

We reach the trees, and the steady dripping of the forest is unnerving. We loop round to approach from the far side. Then Mel lets Flight off her leash and she takes off, zig-zagging ahead of us. We can hear water rushing over stones. We walk behind, cautious, trying not to influence the dog. This part of the wood has what appears to be an old pathway, overgrown but faintly visible. When we come out behind a fallen tree, there is a waterfall maybe thirty feet high, studded with rocks and foaming water, dropping into a deep circular pool. Mel and I have emerged on a piece of *ground that is actually an overhang, the cliff face cut out beneath us.*

'Wow. Did you know this was here?'

'I had no idea. Careful, Mel – it's a bit slippery on the edge there.'

[Barking].

'Flight! Wait, girl.'

Flight's signal isn't the same as Arrow's. Mel trains her dogs for all kinds of situations and Flight uses her voice to alert. We retreat from the falls and track down the path to find her.

'Good girl. Well done, Flight. Sit.'

'It's the same place.'

'Yep. I'd say.'

'So how sure are you now, Mel, knowing these dogs, that this is significant?'

'Oh, I'm sure. A hundred per cent. There's remains in those woods.'

CHAPTER TWENTY-EIGHT

LAYLA, 1986

Layla knows she doesn't have time for exploring, but the day is too perfect to waste, only wisps of cloud lacing clear blue skies. She has ducked through the pine forest on Ruby and cantered across the heathery hill despite knowing Doug would flay her for taking the risk of the horse tripping in a hidden hole. Now the wood ahead is calling to her. She has never been in there before, but it must connect with the hotel estate somehow. She glances at her watch as the horse bounces side to side.

'All right, girl,' she says. 'Maybe just a little further.'

They skirt the edge of the wood, this one older, not filled with pines but with oaks and beech and tangles of undergrowth that look like they haven't ever been cleared. Maybe there won't be a way in. The tumbledown wall has a length of rusted wire at its feet and she can't risk tangling the horse in its barbs. But then a gap opens and she sees what might once have been a narrow track. She casts a glance around, then urges the mare into the green shadows. Ruby halts and snorts, but Layla squeezes her forward, ignoring the sensible voice in her head.

They follow the path deeper and further until there is a rushing in her ears that she can't explain. She should go back, even Doug will be unimpressed if she stays out much longer and Sal will be apoplectic, but she can't bring herself to turn around. A sense of possibility and a deep yearning pull her further, towards the sound.

When they reach the source of the music, she sees water before them, tumbling over perfect green-clad rocks, swishing and swirling into a pool below. Its magic illuminates her for a moment. No one has ever mentioned this place. The paths are so overgrown and old it is as if it's been forgotten. There are standing stones a few miles down the road that attract sightseers, but this? This is better by far. Ruby spooks a little and she slides from the saddle to calm her.

'It's okay Ruby, easy girl, easy.' She digs in her pocket for a pack of polos and peels the paper back to release two of the white rings, one for her and one for the horse. Ruby shakes her head as she crunches, the scent of mint filling the air, then she shoves Layla with her nose, nudging for more, sending her staggering a couple of steps.

'Hey! Greedy... One more and that's it.'

She has to go now. Has to. Layla springs into the saddle and casts a last look at the hidden falls before turning the horse back through the trees. She is desperate to share them, but only with someone who would understand, and she can't think of anyone she knows who would. So she hugs the waterfall woods to herself as a secret. A little piece of something that is hers and hers alone.

CHAPTER TWENTY-NINE

CAL

After marking the trees near the scene and putting in a call to his incredulous contact at Police Scotland, Cal drives to Jean and Tam's house in an exhausted daze, bumping the car down the track in the almost dark. The land is shadowed, but the sunset that followed the rain lingers on the horizon in stripes of orange and indigo. A plane flies overhead, bound for Aberdeen Airport. Nothing seems real. Triumph jostles with sadness.

He doesn't want to go in. Hooking up his equipment with cold, tired fingers feels mercenary, intrusive. But this is what they have all signed up for and the podcast is what makes the search possible, so he tucks any misgivings to the side and leans back into the steep gravel path as he follows it to the cottage door. He will slot his own feelings into a drawer in his mind.

Tam opens the door a few moments after he has knocked. Layla's father has aged visibly in a matter of days. He meets Cal's gaze and his face crumbles.

'Ach, no.'

'We're not sure,' Cal hurries the words out. 'The dogs picked up a scent today, that's all. I don't have proper news for you.'

Tam looks pleadingly at him. Cal's eye catches Jean stepping into the hallway, her hand to her mouth.

'Hi Jean,' he says.

'Have you found her?'

'Maybe.'

Tam recovers himself enough to step back and usher Cal inside. He sways a little as he crosses the threshold, conscious suddenly of the emptiness in his belly and the ache in his legs after days of walking, the tiredness that has sunk into his bones. He wants to be back at the guest house having a hot shower, collapsing into bed.

As before, he goes through to the conservatory, which is warm and bright, the cocoon at the back of the house, though the dark presses at the uncurtained windows. The dog is snoring on the floor and he crouches and tousles its head. His thighs scream with exhaustion.

They all sit. He takes a breath and plunges in, telling them fast, as he would want to be told.

'Today one of the dogs alerted to a particular piece of woodland. We took the second dog to the same area and she did the same thing.' He tries to be gentle, though the news is bleak. 'We don't know if it's Layla, but I have told the police and they'll make a proper search on this basis. I called DI McKenzie just now.'

Jean sits back in her chair, hand pressed to her mouth as if she can hold back the tide of feeling. She looks at her husband.

'Oh Tam.'

He says nothing, his face is grey. He looks out into the darkness, clears his throat. Cal feels how badly he wishes to be alone.

Jean starts to cry softly.

Cal swallows the lump that rises in his throat, the unbidden image of Margot that sidles into his mind. Not now, he can't, not now.

'We don't know what this means yet. But I didn't want you to find out from someone else,' he continues. 'The scene of crime team will go over in the morning. For now, no one knows the location. So... if it is her, she's safe.'

Jean's dry sobs are the only things that break the silence.

'It's hard to think of her there. Overnight. If it is her,' Jean tells him, and he nods, fixing his eyes on hers, trying to give every ounce of his attention – the only thing he has to give. If Layla's body is in that copse, it has lain there nigh on thirty-five years; what's one more night? But Cal can see it is everything. He stretches a hand to Jean's, squeezes tight.

'I'll leave you,' he manages to say, switching off the recording.

–

Cal sits in the car, his throat tight and his hands shaking. Why has Layla affected him so badly? Their pain is too close to his pain, the feelings are merging, magnifying each other.

Afraid of the power of the emotions spinning inside him, he starts the engine, guns the car up the track and away. He heads to the nearby town, stands in line at the chippy and orders a large parcel of fish and chips and a diet coke, focusing on the warm hum of the lights, the sizzle of the fryer, anything but the images of those women nailed to trees, the ones that keep superimposing themselves on the memory of his sister. His left eye is twitching and when he glimpses his reflection in the glass he realises how tense he is, his shoulders knotted and high, changing his silhouette, making him unrecognisable even to himself.

He drives back out towards the hotel, parks near the top of a hill and eats his meal in the car, scoffing the food so quickly he hardly tastes it. Nothing will fill the void. When he's done, he balls up the greasy paper and opens the can of coke. It is now that Margot catches up with him, with the feel of the ring pull against his fingers. His parents never let him have fizzy drinks, but she would buy him a can on a Saturday as a treat, putting her finger to her lips and whispering that it would be their secret.

Tears form at the back of his eyes but they won't fall, blocked by years of deadening. Her absence has followed him through most of his life. What if he had her to call now – to ask advice about Allie and Chrissie? What would she say? Would she be telling him to get home and take care of his family? Would he even be doing this job if she hadn't gone? Whatever he says to Allie, he knows that Margot's disappearance governs his choices. It is an indelible part of him, strands of marble running through rock.

The urge to talk to his daughter overcomes him. He rubs his face to wake himself up and dials her mobile number, a cowardly choice, but if he calls the house phone he might get Allie and he can't cope with confrontation tonight. He feels slightly sick, the chips and grease heavy inside him.

'Hi Dad.'

Her voice is small and flat.

'Hi darling. How are you doing?'

There is a strange beat before she answers.

'Fine.'

Maybe the line is bad, forcing discordant notes between them.

'How's school?'

'The same as it usually is.'

Cal leans his head against the glass, exhaustion felling him. He misses her. He wishes he was there. At home. Safe.

The silence drifts around them. He doesn't know how to break it.

'We found something today. With the dogs.'

'Really? What?' Life finds its way into her voice and he breathes more easily.

'I'm not sure. They alerted.'

Chrissie knows what this means. At home they joke that Rocket alerts to dinner.

'Layla?' She whispers the name.

'I think so.'

It weaves a spell around them both and they stay silent a moment. The silence stretches too far.

'I better go,' she says, sounding so far away. 'I'm sorry, Dad.'

'Night, Chris.'

He holds the phone to his ear even when she has gone, staring at the dark outside the car. Seeing nothing.

CHAPTER THIRTY

Sleep descends on Cal like unconsciousness, merciful and obliterating. When he wakes, the events of the previous day slide in front of him, try to pin him to the bed, but he forces the covers back, stands under the shower, keeps moving.

He drives up to the hotel and calls DI Keith McKenzie, is told a forensics team is being dispatched to the waterfall.

'Can you meet the forensic anthropologist there, make sure she has the right place?'

He doesn't think McKenzie really believes Layla is decaying in the treeline. There is no way he would want Cal to be there unless it was to witness his own mistake. This is a box-ticking exercise for him.

'That's fine,' Cal tells him. 'I'm up at the hotel just now. I'll walk from here. Give them my number.'

He wants to make the walk anyway – to see how easy it is to get to the site from this side. He jogs back to the car and grabs the bag he keeps ready with his recording equipment, takes his jacket, despite the weather's current co-operation. He is starting to believe Aberdeenshire's four seasons in one day reputation, no longer trusts his old squint at the sky approach. He stuffs a bottle of water in the mesh pocket on the outside of the bag, keeps the OS map in his hand and sets off through the woods.

If you know where you are going, the waterfall must only be an hour's hike from the hotel, though the ground is rough underfoot. It takes him longer as he stops to examine the map several times. The paths don't match, so he tries to keep the shape of the woods in mind, the pointed corners where trees meet moor or field. He doesn't see another soul – only the white tails of deer bounding away from him and the rustling and twitching of creatures in the undergrowth. On an ordinary day, this would be a relaxing stroll, but the fact that he is walking towards such sadness overlays everything. He trusts Mel and her dogs implicitly, knows that there is a body in that copse. The only question in his mind is whose.

The sound of the waterfall guides him in until he joins the path he and Mel discovered. Cal pauses on the lip of the cliff overlooking the pool, feels the peculiar urge to dive into the freezing water. He shivers, then follows the path along to where two suited technicians are hovering. They look at him in relief.

'Cal Lovett?'

'Yes.'

It takes him a moment to identify the humans beneath their alien forms. A frowning woman, maybe forties, and a younger man, green about the gills. He raises a hand in greeting, unable to shake theirs as they are already gloved, poised to forge a path into the bushes. Further down the path, a young uniformed officer is shifting from foot to foot.

'Shona Williams and Clifford Duffy,' the woman says. 'Can you direct us? Are we in the right spot?'

He gestures past the red tape tied to the tree.

'The dogs were alerting to those trees there.'

Shona sighs.

'I was afraid you'd say that.' She turns to the younger man. 'Right, Cliff laddie. In you go.'

'Thanks, Shone.'

Despite the grumbling tone, he moves forward with purpose, using a metal probe to carefully lift branches out of the way.

Surprised at being allowed to observe, Cal turns on his microphone. No one has told him not to.

'How are you going to search?' he asks Shona.

'Oh, I'll just stand here and let him do it.' She cackles. 'Or is that not what you meant?'

He likes Shona.

'We'll just take a wee look first and see what's what,' she carries on. 'Then we can make a plan. Possibly involving string.'

Cliff has stepped into the copse, branches pinging up behind him. They can just make out his ghostly form creeping forward. Shona sighs again.

'Maybe I'd better show willing...'

He is left alone on the path while the techs canvass the area; the young officer remaining in the distance. It's too hard to keep his toes on the dust – he edges closer to the trees, pokes his face through. It seems to take ages. He hears Shona calling to Cliff further in, followed by the crack of a branch and some elaborate cursing. The foliage is almost impenetrable. After a while, the shape of a technician appears, weaving its way back, so he darts to the path, tries to look as if he has been there all along.

He doesn't need to ask. Shona's jesting expression has vanished; her face is grave, professional. She meets his eyes.

'This needs to be off the record, okay?'

He nods, makes a show of switching off the microphone. It is better to lose the immediate opportunity for the long-term relationship.

'Could it be her?'

'I can't say for sure...' She hesitates.

'But?'

She glances down the pathway to where the officer is waiting, his back to them.

'There are remains in an advanced state of decomposition. Very advanced. Whether it's her, I can't say, but...'

'You think it could be.'

Something inside him thrills and collapses together.

'I shouldn't be making any comment. At all.'

'This isn't a comment. Promise.'

He holds his hands up in surrender, crosses one finger over his chest.

'An item near the remains suggests... a horse-riding link.'

She stares meaningfully at him. He scans his memory for what item there could be after all this time. The confusion must show on his face but she isn't going to help him with specifics. Fair enough. Then the fog clears.

'The stirrup. There's a stirrup in there.'

She doesn't confirm or deny, just keeps his gaze.

It is quiet. The forest seems to darken around them, holds its breath in reverence.

'Cause of death?'

She shakes her head.

'Now you're just taking the piss.'

CHAPTER THIRTY-ONE

EPISODE FIVE: MISSED AND FOUND

Searchers find the remains in a crevice, protected by rocks on a ledge above the waterfall, as if she sought shelter from the elements. Crime scene technicians take a full day to remove them, combing the foliage for every scattered piece, making painstaking searches on hands and knees for any evidence. I'm not allowed into the treeline or close to the falls, but from the pathway the camera flash is like constant lightning.

The technicians are sombre. One speaks to me briefly.

'The site is isolated so it's not easy to access the remains. On the other hand, a rockfall seems to have protected the body from the elements and the bones haven't suffered as much animal interference as we would expect. I'm hopeful we will be able to reach a conclusion about who the deceased is and what happened to her.'

'It's a woman?'

'When I get the remains to the lab I'll be able to confirm.'

If you're listening to this with disbelief that a body could lie undiscovered so long, believe me, I'd have felt the same. But when you're here in the wild edges beyond field and farming, decidedly off the beaten track, it's far easier to understand. We know that the horse Layla was riding that day came back injured and spooked, so right now we are facing the distinct possibility that Layla had an accident in a place far from home and was unable to summon help.

It does, however, call into question the competence of the police in the original search. Both leading detectives who worked the case have since died so we can't ask them directly about their investigation. It's also worth remembering this was a different time and it was assumed by many that Layla had run away in search of a better life. If the forensic anthropologist confirms what we expect, we'll know that is definitely not what happened.

CHAPTER THIRTY-TWO

The day passes in a blur of anti-climax. He waits with Shona and Cliff until the bones are removed without fanfare or drama, then he is left behind with the police tape drifting in the breeze and the promise not to step across it. More crime scene techs will go over the copse in the afternoon. The knowledge that Jean and Tam may get the closure they need is a relief, but that doesn't eclipse the nagging feeling that Sarah will consider the neat and simple conclusion a narrative disappointment.

He bids goodbye to the boiling pool and the lucid green, the sinister sound of the plunging water sending him into melancholy spirals. Beautiful and bleak together. Forgotten bones in the rocks. Unwillingly, his heart starts to thud as his mind travels to other bones. He imagines officers sitting before his own mother, telling her that Margot has been found. Would she knit her fingers together as Jean did when he gave her the news? Would she try not to cry? He no longer knows her. He is not a good son. He cannot forgive and move on. Margot stands on the rock beside him and as they gaze into the ice-cold water, her red hair is lifted by the breeze. When he looks, the figment vanishes.

Cal hikes back to the hotel. Maybe it is good that his work here will be done. It's easy to see how Layla could have an accident in a remote place like this and not be found. He doesn't have a crime podcast, but Tam and Jean have closure – that's going to have to be enough. Or that's what he keeps trying to tell himself. In the spaces between rationality, he rails against Dubois and the collision course he has been on with himself ever since he sat across from the man. He's spent his whole life trying to stay on an even keel, carefully bottling his feelings about Margot, and in one moment with Dubois everything burst free.

–

When he gets into his car, he sees he has seven missed calls. All in the last hour while he's been gazing into the waterfall. His heart stills. Some of the calls are from Chrissie and two from Allie. Something is wrong, but it isn't his wife or daughter. It can't be. There are text messages and he opens them hurriedly, his fingers clumsy. He hardly notices that the rain has started in earnest. It distorts the windscreen, hiding him from the darkening beyond.

> Your mum had a fall. She's in hospital. Call me. Ax

He stares at the words and then at the windscreen. The worlds he has kept separate keep colliding oddly, each holding equal sway in his brain: Cal and Chris, Layla and Margot. It is jarring to pull himself away from this rainswept hill.

With his thumb he traces the letters on the screen, takes a breath. He is the sole child. There is no one else who will fix this for him. No one to tell him what to do. He calls his wife.

'Al? Got your message. What happened?'

'Someone at social services called. She had a fall but she's okay. Just bruises. She couldn't get up so she was there for a while. Overnight at least, they're not sure. A neighbour noticed she hadn't taken in the post and started knocking.'

'Oh shit. Thank God they did.' Guilt pulses inside him. He has been clueless.

'The neighbours didn't have our number. It might be worth…'

Allie's voice is gentle, but he fills in his own admonishment. He hasn't planned for this. He closes his eyes against the failure, pictures his mother. She is old but has been made older by grief and pain, like Tam and Jean, like most of the parents of the missing or dead people he investigates. Loss adds years, piles age on like a camera adds pounds.

'She needs one of those buttons,' he garbles, but Allie is speaking over him.

'I have the number here for the ward. I called earlier but they want to speak to you. She's insisting they discharge her, apparently. I could drive over there…'

Cal's mind buckles beneath the responsibility.

'No, I should be the one, I'll call them now.'

'Okay.'

'Thanks, Allie. I'm sorry you couldn't contact me.'

The pause, an acknowledgement of the past. He closes his eyes, wishes he could have her arms around him, smell the ever-present oil-paint odour that is so intimately associated with her, has sunk into her skin.

'I'll text you the number now,' she says.

The hospital agrees to keep his mother in overnight for observation. She's asleep and he tells the nurse not to wake her, hears the relief in her voice and reads between the lines: his mother is not an easy patient. He needs to go there, tonight or in the morning at the latest.

Cal's mind flicks to Layla. He can't abandon Jean and Tam. The thoughts curl around him. He has to go to his mother, he sees that, and yet that means hurdling the past, their semi-estrangement. It means revisiting who he once was, just at the worst possible time, when Dubois' words are spreading like a cancer inside him.

As he runs through the things he must do before he leaves, Cal's mind calms, opens a little. Maybe there are opportunities he can take while he is at home. He allows himself to linger on the idea of the scrapyard, the throwaway comment that could mean everything. It wouldn't hurt to take a look, to speak to the owners, pave the way for a proper search.

–

He is standing outside the bed and breakfast the next morning, lifting his bags into the car boot, when he catches sight of a woman standing opposite on a footpath by a stile. Stock still and staring. Then she raises a hand and he smiles, recognising her. Shona. Just without the white crime scene suit. She beckons and he crosses the lane and climbs the stile.

'What brings you here?'

'Don't know what you're talking about. Total coincidence. I love a country walk.' She gestures to the path then tucks her hands into the pockets of an oversized green jacket. 'Shall we take a stroll together? Coincidentally.'

He falls into step beside her, confused but willing to go along with the pretence. There's something about Shona, with her tousled blonde hair and no-nonsense humour, that puts him at ease. When she doesn't immediately speak, he finds the words tumbling out of his own mouth in a way they only really do when he is with his daughter. It must be the isolation loosening his guard.

'I'm leaving actually. Just on my way to say goodbye to Layla's parents. I was hoping I might hear from Detective Inspector McKenzie this morning – it would be nice to give them the confirmation before I go. After all this time.'

'I think they might keep you waiting a bit longer for that news.' She casts a sideways glance at him. 'Heard a few whispers about putting you in your place.'

'Friendly.' Cal hates it when local police officers get territorial. There's no point. They all want the same thing – or they should do.

'Anyway. I probably shouldn't be telling you this, but as I happened to be passing…' she arches a brow '…and you *were* the one who walked those hills and found her after all this time.'

Cal holds his breath. He can hear the emotion in her voice and wonders what it is about Layla that has captured her, what it is that captures all of them.

'You should know the bone analysis showed that our victim had a badly broken leg. Consistent with a fall from a horse and a foot getting caught in the stirrup, but obviously that's speculation after all this time.'

Cal's picture of Layla has merged too much with his memories of Margot. He can't separate the suffering. The thought of it winds him.

'God, I hope she didn't suffer long. She must have been able to crawl to the rocks but no further?'

Shona clears her throat. 'Maybe. But that's not all we found. We think her hyoid was broken.'

'What?' He thinks he knows what this means but he can't get his head around the thoughts fast enough.

'You'd really only see that with neck trauma.'

'Neck trauma?'

Shona shrugs. 'We've been having some... debate, shall we say, about whether that's just animal damage to the corpse and what the cause of death should be.'

Cal comes to a halt on the track. Presses his fingers to his temples.

'What do you think?'

'I was interested in what we found with the remains.' Cal waits, squinting into the sun. She meets his gaze. 'Condoms.'

'She took condoms on a horse ride?'

Shona nods.

'So, you think...'

'It's not my job to think.' She looks back up at him and he notices the way the light catches her blue-grey eyes. He shouldn't be noticing that right now. 'It's possible the hyoid fractured in a fall, or if she got caught in the reins, or it could be post-mortem animal damage, but... it's also a classic strangulation injury.'

Cal stares unseeingly into the distance as he calibrates the meaning of her words. His mind springs back to the lonely, isolated falls, a place far from prying eyes, far from anywhere. If you wanted to be alone with someone it would be the perfect rendezvous.

'You might want to unpack those bags.' Shona is studying his expression.

Cal rubs his head, his mind swirling.

'I can't. I wish I could, but…'

'Things to do.' Her words are light, judgement-free, but inexplicably he wants her to think better of him.

'My mother. She had a fall. She's in hospital down south. I'm the only child, so…'

Shona's hand flies to her mouth. 'I'm so sorry. What are you still doing here? I shouldn't be delaying you.'

'It's okay. They're keeping her in for observation. It's bought me some time.'

She gives a low whistle. 'Ageing parents – it's hard being an only child when it comes to that.'

He doesn't know what brings the truth to his lips. He doesn't talk about Margot. Ever.

'I wasn't always an only child.' Shona tilts her head, waits for him to say more. The words rush free. 'My sister went missing when I was nine. We don't know what happened to her.'

He tries to clear his throat but it makes a strangled sound. She reaches out and rubs his arm. 'I'm sorry, Cal.' Only words, but there is something in the way she says it that reaches inside him.

As they walk back, he marvels that he has told Shona, a woman he hardly knows, the truth he hides from everyone. Perhaps the grief has built so long it can no longer be contained, is spilling out of him, or perhaps it is something about the anthropologist that invites confidence.

'I wish I didn't have to go. Jean and Tam deserve more… now I'm going to have to tell them someone killed Layla and, by the way, I'm off out of here.'

'They'll understand.'

'I know. I just wish I didn't have to let them down.'

'You'll just have to come back, then,' Shona says, simply. She steps in front of him as the track narrows through some trees and the bed and breakfast comes back into view. 'Anyway. You owe me a drink, now.'

Cal's cheeks warm as he falls in behind her.

CHAPTER THIRTY-THREE

LAYLA, 1986

Layla is working a shift she wouldn't usually take – a weekday breakfast that means she's missing an early morning ride through the mists that have fallen over the hills during the night. She's carrying a heavy coffee pot to a table of rowdy oil company executives preparing for a day's shooting on the estate when she sees him.

He turns his head slightly, away from the man he has been speaking to. There is something in his eye that lets her know he is thinking about that moment at the kitchen garden wall, but they are trapped in their different roles. They cannot speak. She blushes, dips her head, then sends one of the other waitresses out with the next pot of coffee, the only power she has.

She volunteers to set the table for lunch in the library, a creepy room at the top of the stairs. She shakes free starched tablecloths, sets gleaming cutlery and shining glassware, trying to still her nerves.

'Are you hiding from me?'

The hoarse whisper makes the hair on the back of her neck prickle. She drops a fork and it clatters to the floorboards, slips down the side of the fire grate.

'Let me,' he says, joining her as she crouches at the fireside to retrieve it. When she stands there is barely a whisper between them. He puts warm hands on her arms and she shivers. 'I've been looking for you.'

Layla finds herself tongue-tied, heat rising in her face. She hates the feeling, shakes her arms from his grip. The certainty in his eyes flickers a little, making her feel calmer.

'I can't talk just now,' she tells him. 'I'm working.'

'How about later, then? Can we meet?'

She looks up at him, almost afraid of the effect he has on her. She longs to pull him towards her and wants to shove him away. 'Why?'

'Because I can't stop thinking about you.' He takes a step back, ducks his head. 'Sorry.'

She knows he's playing at under-confidence because she does it herself. Small darts of excitement fire through her; the day seems less dull. She tosses her hair from her face.

'What time do you finish?'

'Three.'

'Can I buy you a drink?'

She laughs. 'Not here.'

'Somewhere else, then?'

Layla pretends to consider, her heart dancing in her chest. 'Meet me at the foot of the driveway at five.' She wants time to go home, wash the smell of the kitchen from her hair. She wants to make him wait. The thought that she is supposed to meet Stephen to play pool sidles into her mind, but she doesn't care. It's like being hypnotised, shown the world from a different angle.

He steps back towards her, trails a finger down the side of her face and neck until it rests at the top button on her blouse. 'I'll take you for dinner.'

When he leaves, the library floor creaks beneath his feet and the door slams shut.

Layla hides her car down the back of the hotel and walks to the end of the driveway through the woods to meet him. She remembers, too late, that she forgot to tell Stephen she wouldn't be in the pub. It doesn't matter. He'll forgive her, he always does. Maybe things would be better if he didn't. As she crosses the footpath, she hears a crackle in the bushes, but when she turns around there is no one there and she almost laughs at her own jitters, the clandestine thrill.

When it pulls up, the Land Rover Discovery gleams in advertisement of wealth. She swings herself into the passenger seat, noting the rich leather and the new smell of the car. It's immaculate. He appraises her, open about his approval, a twinkle in his eyes that she tries and fails to scowl at.

'Where to,' he asks. 'The local pub?' She thinks of Stephen and the others clustered around the pool table, the floor sticky from their beer, the fruit machines singing in the corner, and shudders. 'Only joking. I have a plan.'

'Do you now?'

He laughs. 'Trust me.'

How could she possibly trust him? She doesn't trust anyone, least of all herself. Now that she is here in this man's perfect car, she can't think of a word to say. There is nothing they have in common. The car underlines that.

'Tell me,' he says into the silence, 'about yourself.'

'What do you want to know?' She tucks her hair behind her ears, catches sight of herself in the mirror and sees how young she looks, hooks her finger under the strands and rearranges them.

'Anything. I don't know anything about you. Besides the fact that you're young and gorgeous and far too good to be waitressing for the likes of Elco Oil.'

Layla stares out at the fields, feeling a prickle of annoyance. She hates her job, but hearing someone else belittle it is different. She thinks of all of the people she works with and experiences an alien protectiveness towards them – they are witty and hardworking; even Chef has redeeming qualities, for fuck's sake. Who is he to look down on them?

'People like you, you mean?'

'Touché.' He smirks and she folds her arms. 'Sorry,' he says. 'I'm genuinely interested.'

'Well. I work at the hotel and I spend the rest of my time at the stables riding horses. That's really all there is to know about me.'

'I doubt that,' he says, shifting gears and slowing on the corner as a tractor goes past. Layla recognises the farmer, sinks in her seat. This was stupid, she thinks, someone will see them. Aberdeenshire is a village when it comes to gossip. Wherever he takes her, there is bound to be someone who knows her.

But there isn't.

Somehow, Oil Man – she cannot yet think of him as John – has a table at the best fish restaurant in the city, twenty miles away from the hotel where she works. It's early, so there is barely a soul there. All Layla has to do is follow the young waitress to a snug corner booth, feeling the presence, the weight of him behind her. She marvels at the foreignness of someone attending to her, shaking her napkin free and passing her a crisp menu. She's rattling with nerves, and she hates that, but here she is at least anonymous, concealed.

He squints across the table at her. 'Too much?'

Layla raises an eyebrow, tries to regain her sense of control. 'How did you get a table here? You only asked me a few hours ago.'

'I come here a lot. They made room.' He slides the bread basket to her, apparently dismissing the thought that someone could say no to him.

'Right.' Layla takes a roll and breaks it absentmindedly, feels it crumble on the tablecloth, soft and yielding. Pleasure at the thought of him making that call drops through her veins, kicks along with the sensation of power. At least she isn't fazed by the cutlery. She's laid enough ridiculous settings in her time. A laugh bubbles to her lips and breaks across the distance between them. He sits back and smiles.

Outside, cold North Sea waves are thrashing the sands, driving their spray into the road. But in here it is cosy and they are cosseted by thick walls and darkness. He chooses the wine and tastes it, while keeping eye contact with her, and when the blood liquid is poured and the waitress is barely two steps away from their table, he leans back and says, 'So, be honest, what are your dreams? For the rest of your life.'

'What makes you think I have any?'

He laughs and takes a long draught of wine. 'Don't you want more?'

It irritates her beyond belief that this man with his wealth and his Rolex watch and his shine of confidence is judging her life. It irritates her even more that he has tapped into her restless desires and is now casually tossing them across a restaurant table at her. She doesn't know how to say this to him without sounding petulant, shrewish.

'Tell me about you,' she says, realising this date was a mistake, almost wishing she was playing pool at the pub. At least Stephen doesn't look down at her. Say whatever else you like, but not that.

–

Two bottles and four courses later, she stands to go to the Ladies and finds she is unsteady on her feet and the nervousness has dissipated. As she concentrates on walking a straight line across the restaurant, she is startled to see the transformation. The whole place is lit by candles and thrumming with chatter. Two women lean conspiratorially across a table, a man scrapes back his chair, forcing her to side step, the richness of smells and the confidence and wealth in the room is staggering. She feels like a moth at a butterfly party, dancing too close to the flame. An older woman eyes her suspiciously as she passes, and she realises the thing that makes her different here isn't her invisible economic status but her youth. She draws her spine straight, allows her hips to swing as she glides. No one knows, she tells herself. No one knows that I shouldn't be here.

–

'What would you do,' he asks over dessert, 'if money were no object?' She snorts. 'You don't like the question.'

'It's just such an irrelevant one,' she says, deciding to be bold, truthful, that there's no point hiding anything from him. 'It's the kind of question you ask if you're rich but is just… pointless… indulgent if you're not.'

'Insulting?'

She meets his gaze over the top of her glass of wine, the world soft, fuzzy and swaying. 'Maybe.'

'Okay.' He looks around the restaurant. She sees his body language change, as if he's pulling away from her. This game is more important to him than she realised. She sighs.

'I'd train as a show jumper. Work at a top stable. Make the Olympics.'

Layla studies the wine glass. She doesn't want to look at him. Her dreams sound childish spoken aloud. She's never told anyone this before.

'So, you're good enough?'

She thinks about being humble. Wonders why she would start now.

'I could be.'

'I'd love to see you riding.'

She laughs.

'I bet you would.'

—

They are too wasted for either to drive, but the restaurant conjures a taxi, so they spend only a moment in the tumult of the beckoning storm before the quiet engulfs them. His hand on her knee, the smell of salt that has followed them in. He leans forward and gives the address of a hotel in the city centre without asking her permission. She idly wonders if he has the false impression that she owes him because he bought her a fancy dinner, but the crackle between them and the soft cloak of alcohol dull the outrage she might feel. She wants to go with him, this strange man with his talk of dreams and his lack of understanding of reality. Regrets are for the morning.

They sit in silence as the car whips them through the orange-lit streets and she holds his hand as they hurry through the hotel's reception, anxious, now they are close, to reach the destination, one that she's thought of since their kiss in the rain against the kitchen garden wall.

By the time they close the door to his room, she is breathing heavily. When his mouth meets hers, she tastes brandy and her head spins so much she almost loses her bearings, has to hold tight to him to stop herself being swept away. He lifts her onto the huge, soft bed and she is vaguely aware that the lights are bright and the curtains wide open, but they are high above the city and he is more considerate than any of the men she's slept with before and so she loses herself in him, drinks in his appreciation until sweat slides between them and a flushed, wanton reflection stares back at her from the mirrored wardrobes. As she sits astride him, she catches her own eye in the glass and she is awed by herself, by the tides of feeling and freedom that are rushing through her.

CHAPTER THIRTY-FOUR

CAL

When she answers the door, Cal can see that Jean has been felled by grief. Red-eyed and drawn, she looks at him hopefully, as if he can make it all better. His heart contracts at the sight. He's done this to her.

'Come in, Cal, come in.'

He swallows and steps into the tumbledown cottage with the peeling frames and the unravelling lives within.

'How are you doing?'

He stands in the kitchen, alarmed at the vagueness he sees in Jean. She seems unable to find the kettle in her own home; her hands flutter from the worktop to her face and back again. He takes her arm, sets her down at the table and navigates his way around the room, though it feels intrusive, making her tea in her own home. A pot of broth is bubbling on the stove, threatening to overflow, and he turns it down slightly, gives it a stir.

'Is Tam here?'

'He was out seeing to the beasts,' she murmurs, twisting her wedding ring on her finger. 'He'll be back in soon.'

'Is there no one else who could sit with you?'

'He'll be back soon...' Her words fade away.

Cal sets down the tea in front of her. He has added a second teaspoon of sugar to the one she usually takes.

'Jean, drink this. You don't look right.'

She sips obediently. Her capacity for conversation seems to have vanished, so he sits opposite, quietly drinking his own tea and waiting.

The door slams open, heralding Tam's return, and they listen to the sound of him pulling off his boots on the wedge by the mat. Cal calls out to him that they are in the kitchen and he appears in the doorway in his socks, holding the frame as if he cannot stand without it.

'What are you doing in *here*?'

He asks the question sharply, looking at Jean, but Cal answers for her, making a joke out of it.

'It's warm in here with the broth.'

'The police were here this morning. Again.'

Cal nods. He has guessed as much. 'Why don't you have a seat, Tam?'

'I'll stay where I am, thank you.' Maybe he intends the words to be as barbed as they sound, maybe not. Cal has the sinking sensation that the anger that has flourished in Tam over the last day or two is about to find a target. 'Did you know?'

'I don't think it's official yet, but I did hear this morning that they'd found something during the examination.' Both sets of eyes hold him. It occurs to him that he hasn't expressly asked permission to record today, though he is doing so. 'They said a bone in Layla's neck was broken.' He finds himself touching his own neck.

Tam nods.

'I still don't understand.' Jean's voice is thready, weak.

'I've explained already,' Tam barks. 'The bobby explained and all.'

Cal stretches a hand to her. He can see she is in shock, her mind desperately trying to protect itself against a thought that has already made it through the barrier.

'Jean,' he says. 'You know it means there is a possibility that her death wasn't an accident.'

The wail that escapes her is so abrupt it hits him between the eyes and sends the cat streaking from the room. Shocked at the sound, Tam steps forward and places one hand on her shoulder. 'Jesus.'

'That chef,' Jean shrieks.

'We don't know that,' Tam says.

'Who else would it be? The police won't do it right. You know they won't.' Jean's face is bloodless. 'It'll be like last time. All that time she's been in that wood. They should have found her.'

'No one thought it was possible to get in there,' Tam reasons.

'Well, they were wrong.' Jean wrings her hands repeatedly. 'Who says it will be any different now?'

'*He's* here, watching them,' Tam says. 'They'll have to.'

They both look at Cal.

'I will be able to do that, yes,' he says. 'Though I have to go home for a little while.'

'When?' Tam's face is clouded with anger that Cal knows, rationally, isn't really meant for him, but it strikes him anyway. He sees his father standing there, thunderous, uncompromising, and he flinches automatically. It has been decades – the man is dead – and still he reacts.

'Today.'

'You're leaving?' He can almost see Jean's relief segueing to panic, like the sky changing mood. His heart contracts. 'Why?'

'My mother had a fall,' he says. 'She's in hospital.'

'Oh, I'm sorry.' Jean reaches for him, rubbing his hand.

The news seems to take the steam from Tam as well. 'Aye, well you'll need to get away.'

Their attempts to conceal their distress make him feel worse than ever.

'I'll be contactable at all times, if you need me. I promise I will be back just as soon as...'

Jean swallows, presses a tissue to her eyes to blot the tears.

'I'm so sorry.' He wants to be the good guy. Leaving them feels like the worst betrayal.

When he shuts the door and steps into the bitterly cold spring air, there are daffodils bobbing their heads at the corner of the building. He hadn't realised the extent to which hope and the battle for truth were holding Jean and Tam upright. As complicated as he knows it is, he is still responsible for knocking them down.

CHAPTER THIRTY-FIVE

Guilt and frustration sit beside Cal on the long drive south, while outside the world transitions from wild hills and twisting cross-country roads to long empty stretches of tarmac. The need to air his fears about Dubois is all encompassing. There is someone he could talk to. Andy. But if he tells his sister's boyfriend what he suspects, it will make it real.

He stops for a bacon sandwich and a coffee in a roadside cafe, dawdles in the shop needlessly, palms sweaty. Here he is oddly free, neither in Aberdeenshire nor home, poised between his reality and Layla's. He wishes he could stay here forever, safe in the anonymity of a service station between the road maps and the boiled sweets.

Back in the car, Cal takes his phone from his pocket, nurses it in his hand. Andy. A day from the past sidles into his mind. A field of wheat or corn, the stalks tall, sweating under a blue sky. Poppies lining the edges like drops of blood. Andy walking the perimeter, peeling off down tracks left by tractors, wading into the maze, peering through the crop. Cal trailing behind, the back of his neck burning in the sun, the only sound the occasional car passing on the melting tarmac.

'I thought maybe here,' Andy muttered when they got back to his car, mouths dry and skin dusty. Not talking to

Cal, not even really talking to himself. 'Not here. Keep looking.'

Cal presses the call button. The moments stretch as he waits for Andy to answer.

'Hello?'

'Andy,' he says, his mouth as dry as that day in the fields. 'It's Cal.'

They don't usually speak this often. A thousand thoughts spin in the silence. Andy is the one to break them, with a creaking whisper.

'Is there news?'

'No, nothing concrete. Just… Oh God, Andy, I don't know. Through work I spoke to someone who seemed to know too much about me, about who I used to be. He said things that made me think maybe he…'

Cal can't say the words. Even starting to articulate his fears aloud makes him doubt himself.

'What did he say? Who?'

Andy's voice is different, confused, perched on the edge of something terrible.

'I don't want it to come as a shock. It's not definite. Just a theory.'

Cal feels unaccountably like this is a mistake, but it's too late. He's started now.

'Just tell me.'

'Marc Dubois. I interviewed Marc Dubois.'

Silence.

Cal waits.

'Andy? Are you still there?'

His voice, when it comes, is a distant echo of the man. 'Marc Dubois. The serial killer?'

'I know it sounds crazy, but…'

'Yeah. Yeah, it does sound pretty nuts.'

Cal doesn't know what he expected. Tears? Sympathy? Some sort of articulation of the maelstrom inside his own head? There is nothing but the exhale of a breath held for decades.

'I don't know if you should be going down that path, mate.'

'No,' Cal says, regretting the impulse to share, 'maybe not, but…'

'I'd better go.'

When the line goes dead, Cal feels even lonelier than ever.

–

The small town where he grew up is forever entwined with Margot's vanishing. When he finished school, he fled its constraints and his history, has rarely returned. Her loss altered the relationship he had with his parents. The pain of not having her there severed them. He has investigated cases where the agony of loss has bound families together, like vines holding up the shells of trees, but his own couldn't take the pressure.

He's been told his mother won't be discharged before four p.m. so he parks near the river, walks along from a bridge downstream. It is hot and hazy; flies skate across the water and there is no breeze to stir the rushes. The banks are middle-of-the-day quiet – the children still in school. He can hear the sound of the motorway in the far distance. The clothes that were perfect in Aberdeenshire are too much – he feels sticky and nauseous. But that is not the only reason for the sickness in the back of his throat, the slavering-dog saliva that fills his mouth.

He crouches by the water in the shade of a footbridge, dips a hand in the flow, lets the liquid run over his wrist, cooling him. The scrapyard is waiting for him, according to his app, only a few hundred metres away. He needs to see the place, and yet he doesn't want to move, is anchored to this peaceful spot. Reluctantly, he stands, makes his way to the hoarding that protects the site.

The old arched entrance to the yard remains in place but the gates are heavily padlocked. Signs proclaim: Danger, Keep Out! Cal shades his eyes and looks up. He strains to read the faded paintwork, make out the letters. *Guthrie Scrap. Cars bought and sold.* Could this be where his beloved sister has been all this time? Did Dubois leave her with the scrap? Memory nudges at him, then retreats.

Only now does he notice the developers' signs attached to the fence. Land acquired. An artist's impression of a river quarter, flats with balconies overlooking the water, imaginary people walking arm in arm, a child on a scooter, fountains and landscaping. They're going to be clearing the land. Cal walks back to the gate, feeling a swooping surge of urgency. He grips the bars with his fists and pushes his face up close, trying to see more, trying to find some answers.

He can see some bare patches of ground where cars have been removed. Further along, the shells of expired vehicles remain in place, newer, shinier machinery frozen above them. The contrast between Layla's resting place and this hellish dump strikes him – no cooling waterfall or dripping moss, only rust and hot metal smarting in the sun. He wishes instantly that he could be back in Aberdeenshire, staring down at the frothing pool, trying to make sense for someone else, not for himself.

Memories of his sister assail him, as if they have been waiting off stage for this moment. He sees her pouring him a glass of milk, tossing her hair back as she handed it to him, lifting him onto a kitchen bar stool and twirling him.

He imagines grasses growing around her, threading through her skull, weaving themselves in her hair. He remembers her eyes, their piercing blue. There were arguments about her going out for drinks with her friends. Though she was an adult, she lived *under our roof*. What if she'd never gone? What if she'd stayed?

Cal sinks, unable to keep himself vertical. He presses his head to the bars separating him from the scrapyard and his cheeks squeeze between the cold metal. And then he is Chris again, crouched on the landing, head pressed between spindles, listening to the voices raised in anger.

Surprise rushes from him in a groan, takes the power from his legs. He didn't think he had any memories left to mine. He crouches on the ground and presses his head to his knees, wishing he could blot out the pain. The sun strikes the back of his neck and, finally, mercifully, he cries.

CHAPTER THIRTY-SIX

When he reaches the hospital, she has already gone.

His mother, awkward to the last.

'She wouldn't wait for the discharge papers,' a nurse tells him. Her steel stare softens a little when he rolls his eyes and apologises for her. Now he is late and wrong-footed, a child once more. He should have come straight here, should have predicted this. He jogs to the car in the heat, flustered and exhausted, drives through streets that feel simultaneously familiar and alien.

His mother opens the door: startlingly the same and different. Her hair is white and, though neatly waved, it is thinner than it used to be. As always, she is wearing powder and a fuchsia-coloured lipstick, but a little of the colour has bled into the wrinkles around her mouth. He bends and hugs her, wondering if she feels as awkward as he does. This will be the first night he has spent in his childhood home for over a decade.

They sit at the kitchen table; he cradles a cup of too-milky tea, nibbles at one of the plain biscuits she has placed on a plate. It makes him sad that this is all she affords herself. She has a generous pension and savings, but hardly anything in the house has changed. It's like stepping back in time. There is a fine line between simplicity and claustrophobia.

'You should have waited for the discharge,' he tells her.
'I could have driven you back, then.'

Magpie eyes fix on him.

'I wanted to be at home.'

'I know, Mum, I do.'

She doesn't say anything.

'It's her birthday tomorrow,' Cal says.

He doesn't know why he says it. Maybe because Margot is so close to the surface of his thoughts, maybe to get a reaction. The words stick like dust in his throat. He can feel himself closing in, shutting down.

'Didn't know if you'd make it,' she says, sniffing.

And she's right. Without the fall, he'd be in Scotland.

'I'll get some flowers.'

He wishes his sister could have a proper memorial: a floral outpouring, tributes, perhaps an ivory-coloured coffin decked in pinks with crowds of people following the hearse. She deserved all those things. Maybe now, if his suspicions are correct, it will be possible. But it's all too late. He has only a hazy recollection of her friends, no way of contacting them, of gathering them together, of remembering.

'I thought I'd go and see the police,' he tries. 'Get them to take another look at her case.'

His mother raises her gaze to him. Piercing blue desolation. He cannot bear it any longer.

'Just going to take my bag upstairs,' he says, leaving his cup half drunk.

–

He wants to treat her to dinner but she won't have it.

'I've defrosted chops,' she tells him, and it's final. Everything in this house runs to order. Disorder, chaos, spontaneity are dangerous elements. Margot was all of these things. His parents blamed themselves for the indulgence ever after. Life froze, time froze and the house is testament to it.

He peels the potatoes for her, suffering the tuts that illustrate that the wedges of skin he peels are too thick, the pinch of salt he tosses into the pan excessive. He has bought a bottle of wine and he ignores all protests, pours generous glasses into goblets from the glass cabinet after washing the dust from them.

'These were wedding presents,' she says sadly, as if they are wasting them by using them now.

What are you waiting for, Mum? He wants to shout at her. *Life is short. Use the fucking glasses for Christ's sake.* But he doesn't yell, because they don't yell any more. You don't yell at someone whose daughter disappeared, do you? Instead, you let it all fester, turn to ice beneath the surface.

He keeps her glass topped up so neither of them knows how much they are drinking, and after a while her cheeks are flushed and she doesn't remember to tidy the strands of her hair that slip forward. The white waves frame her face in a softer way, her eyes dance a little; he feels the lurching loss of the mother he might have had.

'Will Allie be coming tomorrow? To go to your sister's bench?'

He shakes his head and in the purse of his mother's lips he sees the disapproval she holds for her daughter-in-law.

'All these years,' she mutters.

'It isn't Allie's fault,' he says. And it isn't. He has never allowed her or Chrissie to come with him, no matter what they say. It's an annual argument. But how does he tell his mother that he doesn't want his wife or daughter near this house, this history? That they are perfect and this, all of it, is broken.

'It's just going to be us, Mum. Like normal. That's better, isn't it?'

She shrugs but makes no comment.

He stands and clears plates, stacks them beside the sink while he runs hot water to clean them. There is no dishwasher, of course.

'Where are you working at the moment?'

He is surprised at the interest.

'In Scotland. Aberdeenshire.'

She waits, watching him, so he continues.

'A missing girl. We found the body, we think.'

She bares her teeth a little and he sees they are stained with red wine.

'Missing. Like her. Like Margot.'

'That's right.'

'I don't know how her family can bear to have it all raked over.'

The plate Cal is holding slides from his fingers into the suds with a plunk, spraying foam up into his face. He reaches for a tea towel, wipes the bubbles away, playing for time, finding that his fingers are trembling. All of a sudden, he is a little boy again. If he hadn't drunk so much, if she hadn't, then they wouldn't be having this conversation. He spreads his hands, leans on the surface for strength, fails to bite back his thoughts.

'They want answers, Mum. Don't you?'

He waits for a reply, turning to face her when none is forthcoming. His mother has left the room. Her chair stands at an angle, napkin neatly folded and inserted in its wooden handcuff. He doesn't even know if she heard him.

CHAPTER THIRTY-SEVEN

Cal opens his eyes, frowns at the stippled paint on the ceiling, wondering briefly where he is before he remembers he is in his old room and his life is imploding. Oh, yes. He closes his eyes again, wishing he could delay the return to reality, but his phone is buzzing and he reaches for it, rubbing his face to wake himself.

When he sees the messages, the links to headlines, Cal's stomach drops and his skin goes cold. He can't grasp the words he's reading.

He clicks on the link and stares at a posed shot of Andy, his arms folded, Margot's bench in the background and a stricken expression on his face. *Police explore new evidence sicko killed my Margot.*

His Margot? There's a shot of her too, with Andy, smiling into the camera. Only it's a smaller picture. Cal feels rage compete with bewilderment. Margot. In the news. His names – new and old. Complete exposure.

It never for one minute occurred to him that Andy would betray his confidence. How *could* he? After everything. If he needed money, Cal would have given him money.

Below it all, in a box at the bottom, there is a picture of Cal. It's the one on the production company's website, a decade old, now printed alongside a rehashed bio.

'Shit.'

Until now Margot has been his secret pain. No one cares about the personal life of the podcaster when they are listening to true crime, so it hasn't been hard to hide it. Since he changed his name when he left home, he hasn't had to do anything, lie to anyone. He has never wanted his personal experiences to get in the way, hasn't wanted them to be relevant. He isn't the story, he's the conduit. Not any more…

He's Christopher Longacre again, the boy with the missing sister and the broken parents, the million questions destined never to be answered.

—

The doorbell goes and the noise is insistent. He remembers where he is, who he's with. Cal stumbles from the bed and drags his jeans and T-shirt on. But by the time he gets to the stairs, it is too late. His mother stares up at him, horror in her eyes. He can see she has lost even more of herself, like a dandelion clock shedding seeds in the wind, a bitter kind of vitality that he hadn't appreciated was there.

'There are reporters out there,' she says as he descends, her voice almost pleading. 'Asking questions about her, about Margot.'

'What did you say?'

'Nothing.' She shakes her head, starts to move towards the kitchen as if she's in a trance. 'I don't want to talk to anyone.'

'I'll speak to them, Mum, I'll get them to leave.'

She whips round, tears in her eyes. 'I don't want you to say anything to them. Don't talk to them.'

He follows her through and stands helpless in the doorway, guilt tearing shreds off him. His mother can't stay still – she's wiping shining surfaces, reordering perfectly lined spice jars. Cal's mind flits to Jean.

'Mum,' he tries gently. 'It's my fault. Andy talked to the papers because of something I told him. About someone I interviewed. Marc Dubois. I'm sorry. I'm so sorry.'

He isn't sure how much she knows about the serial killer. She doesn't watch the news, not since back then. Stories about missing people blindside her and she prefers to live in ignorance and memory. Her hand is shaking as she pauses in her cleaning, stares out of the window at the neat lawn.

'Why is he doing this? I just want to be left alone. Is that too much to ask?'

'But, Mum, maybe now it's out there again, it could help – jog someone's memory, help us find out what happened after all this time.'

'No! No, Cal. I don't want it. Raking over your sister's life.'

The room around him shrinks a little. He fixes his attention on the cuckoo clock that has been on the wall since his childhood. It hasn't worked for decades, like everything in the house it is paralysed, waiting for Margot to come back and life to start again.

'Don't you want to know?'

'She's been gone so long, Christopher. Your father is dead. It isn't going to bring her back. It's all too late.' Her voice is shrill – almost panicked.

'It's not too late, Mum.'

But the look she gives him tells him that she doesn't agree.

'Margot's gone,' she says. 'It won't bring her back. All of this… digging and pushing,' she becomes tearful, 'won't bring her back.'

Cal makes a noise of frustration, holds his hair off his forehead, exhausted by it all. 'I know it's hard, Mum, but I still think I should speak to the police. It's out there. I want to help.'

She stares at him, anguish colouring her grey. This is the moment he relents, backs down, plays the part of the good son. A moment from the past flickers back again, that same feeling of pressing his head between the spindles on the landing, looking down on it all. He can hear the sound of a hand striking flesh.

Neither of them moves. There are footsteps on the path and then the letterbox flaps, making her jump. The person retreats. There is a faint beeping of a reversing van in the street. Life continuing as normal, while inside the terraced house everything is being cracked open.

–

Cal tells the reporters to go away, offers his card, promises to contact them if anything happens. Anything to get them away before it's time to go to Margot's bench. It works and he retreats upstairs, taming his hair with gel after taking an anaemic shower in the bath he used as a child, the same stains stretching from the overflow like fingers scratching the enamel.

As he stares at the elongated shapes, he drifts backwards in time, remembers pressing small toes on those same patterns, lying in the bath with his ears underwater, sounds from downstairs distorted and distant. Matey bubble bath on the side, Margot pouring a carefully measured capful. He can almost smell it, see her hand swirling the water.

He's getting dressed when he hears the doorbell. Anger at the reporters presses into him but then he hears the voice and shock hits. It's her. Margot.

His mother's voice rises and he rushes down the stairs, nauseous with memory. When he reaches the bottom, heart thudding, he is shocked to see his daughter, clutching a bunch of irises. He is so glad to see her and yet so stunned by the trick his mind has played. The confluence almost brings him to tears.

He pushes past his mother, folds his arms around Chrissie, squeezes her tightly, gathering himself and his thoughts as he does. Then he looks over her shoulder to the empty street.

'Where's Mum? She can park right there if she wants to...'

Chrissie's face drops a fraction.

'She isn't here. It's just me. I came on the train.'

He musters a smile from somewhere, masks the disappointment.

'Why didn't you call?'

She looks sheepish.

'I didn't want you to tell me not to come.'

'Come in off the doorstep,' his mother barks. 'All the neighbours will be watching you.'

There is no one on the street now, no one cares, but her antipathy to spectacle is learned. She knows what it is like to be the subject of endless speculation.

As he follows Chrissie down the hall, he wonders at the irises in her hand. How did she know those were the perfect choice? Margot loved purple; perhaps he told Allie that once, though he doesn't remember doing so.

Then another thought sneaks into his head...

'Christina, does Mum know you're here?'

He can tell by the set of her shoulders that the answer to that question is no.

—

Cal makes phone calls while his mum makes toast and drinks in the sight of the granddaughter she has barely seen. He hears her telling Chrissie she is too thin. The first call is to school to inform them that Chrissie is sick today and won't be coming in. The second, more dreaded one, is to Allie. He takes a couple of deep breaths before spilling the news, emphasising how unplanned it was from his perspective.

'She did what? Did you put her up to this?'

He tries for a soothing tone, not willing to fight with her today.

'I had no idea, honestly. When I saw her, I thought it might have been your idea,' he says.

She sounds awkward. 'After all these years of trying, I'd given up. I didn't think…'

'I know. I'm sorry, Al.' He stumbles over the words, realising how much damage he has done in the name of protection. 'I just wanted you to know she's here. I've called school. We'll have her back on the four o'clock train. Sorry.'

'You don't have to apologise, Cal. You didn't know she was coming.'

Allie is gone before he can tell her that's not why he's sorry. He thinks about calling her back, hesitates. Then the phone vibrates in his hand and he rushes to connect. But it isn't her. It's Sarah.

'Cal,' she says, and her voice is quiet, not the usual brusque disapproval. 'I've just seen the newspapers. Is it true? About your sister?'

His time-worn instinct is to conceal, to change the subject, but it's too late for that.

'Yes,' he says. 'It's true. I'm sorry, Sarah, it wasn't supposed to come out like this. Her stupid ex-boyfriend. If I'd had any idea, I never would have talked to him.'

'Margot,' she says the word softly. 'The name he gave you.'

'I should have told you.'

And he waits for the storm to hit him, the recriminations and repercussions. But that's not what happens.

'I'm sorry,' she says. 'I'm so sorry. We have time. I'll square it with the advertisers. Take all the time you need.'

He's both relieved and thrown by her sensitivity. Forced to reconsider his antipathy. It's only later he remembers he didn't call Allie back.

–

The weather is again hot and hazy. They drive to the green space where Margot's memorial bench is located. Cast into the sultry day, their progress feels glacial. At one point, his mother stumbles on the uneven ground and Chrissie takes her arm. The sight of his daughter holding up her grandmother fixes a lump in his throat.

They retrace the steps they have taken so many times, but he cannot connect properly with his memories of his sister. Everything feels awful and strange. More so than in previous years. Dubois has poisoned it all. Andy has made everything worse. As he wipes the sweat from his forehead his mind drifts only a few miles away, to a river where the wildflowers mingle with hunks of unwanted metal. Flashes of crime scene photographs, the pain Dubois inflicted.

They lay their blooms on the bench beneath the plaque, but don't sit down, instead forming a semicircle around it. The bright sun bleaches the scene like they're fading into the past. Cal feels he should say something but he doesn't know what. It's a struggle not to break down and cry. He notices a jogger look curiously at their little tableau before averting his eyes and sprinting on when he sees the flowers.

His mother dabs at her eyes with a handkerchief she has clutched in her fist since they left the house. Chrissie strokes her back and he watches the swirl of her hand, feels the tight burn of the sun on his neck.

'Do you want a moment alone, Mum?' he asks. She nods and he and Chrissie retreat to the edge of the pond. They turn their backs to give her privacy and he feels Chrissie's fingers lace through his own. He squeezes tightly, bewildered at the realisation that this year is so much worse than the one before it. Fifty-four. She should have been fifty-four years old. Grief hasn't acted in a straight line: it refuses to obey the rule that time should heal. Cal finds he misses Margot more the older he gets, not less.

There is such anger and confusion welling up inside him, no sense of peace or acceptance. Her loss and the mystery around it truly is a life sentence.

Finding Margot has been the ultimate goal for most of his life. His father died before they achieved it and he doesn't want his mother to die with the same unanswered questions. He needs to talk to the police again. He needs to make them see. Layla has changed everything for him. Injected a dark hope. She proves it isn't too late. Not ever.

CHAPTER THIRTY-EIGHT

His mother is tired, absent. On the drive home she sits quietly in the back next to Chrissie, staring out of the window with glazed eyes. He watches her in the mirror, worried at her withdrawal, twitching with the responsibility of what this means and the overwhelming desire to flee to Scotland and Layla, where he can make a difference, where it doesn't feel like he's drowning.

At home, she grasps the back of a chair and sways a little, looks up at him.

'I need to go to bed. I'm worn out.'

She never goes to bed in the middle of the day. Not even back then.

'I'll help you up the stairs, Gran.' Chrissie takes over. 'Dad can make you a cup of tea.'

His mother nods, sets her heavy beige handbag on the chair. It is a structured beast with a golden clasp that clunks shut. The handles stay upright for a moment, then drop individually as if they are alive.

'Not too weak, mind,' she tells him. 'He always makes it too weak,' he hears her grumble as the two of them climb the stairs. Chrissie's cheerful tones are so much stronger in comparison; it is as if his mother is fading away. He rubs his forehead, sighs and fills the kettle. Dark anxiety is pattering in his mind. He hasn't had a chance to talk to her properly about Dubois. There is never the right moment in their relationship. For anything.

He hears Chrissie going into the bathroom upstairs and her movement brings him back to himself.

By the time he has made the tea and taken it upstairs, his mother is asleep. Her features have sunk, her cheeks are hollows. She breathes so quietly, so infrequently, he is afraid she might be dead. The poetry of going on her daughter's birthday. In a way it would be a relief. But her chest heaves and she draws enough air into her lungs to keep going. He sets the tea on the bedside table and closes the door softly behind him.

–

They have some time before Chrissie's train so he leaves a note for his mother; they walk to the station and he buys her an iced coffee. They sit at a metal table on the concourse, pigeons at their feet, a wind whispering through and stirring the litter. Cal is jittery: everywhere he looks, he thinks he sees reporters watching them.

He forces his attention back to Christina, watches her sucking coffee through a thick green straw. Now that he's properly focused on her he can see she is pale, her features tight.

'How are you?' She peers at him, waiting for the answer. He should be asking her that question. He forces a smile, shrugs a little. The truth is that he feels rattled, further from acceptance than ever. Something nudges at him but he isn't sure what.

He is struck once more by how haunting it is looking at Chrissie sometimes, the resemblance with Margot uncanny, the love so similar. Maybe that's all it is.

She takes another sip of the coffee, making the ice cubes tinkle.

'Are you okay?' he asks.

'Of course.' She swivels to the side, trying to hide her face, and he sees with shock that there are tears in her eyes. He notes again the pinched look that is so different to the easiness of even a year ago. This isn't about her aunt or the emotions of the day.

'Sweetheart,' he says; the water going still, revealing the world beneath. 'What's going on?'

He stays motionless, letting excruciating silence sit between them. It takes every ounce of restraint he has just to wait, give her time.

'There's this boy at school...' She tails off. He's never seen this grey fear in her before and it sends his stomach plunging.

'You're being bullied?'

She half nods, half shrugs.

'He liked me. He asked me out and we went on a few dates...'

'Okay.' The graveness of her expression makes him afraid.

She swallows. 'I said I'd rather be friends, but he's started all these rumours about me, shown people... things.'

He leans forward. 'What things?'

Chrissie looks at him. Her eyes pleading, her cheeks flaring with sudden heat.

'It's really hard to say, Dad.' A sob escapes and Cal waits. Something inside him drums a warning. She takes a breath and looks at her hands. 'He has pictures of me.'

'Pictures?' He's playing for time. He knows what she means. Cold spreads through him.

She looks at him, her eyes begging him not to make her say it.

'I shouldn't have sent them. I wasn't thinking. I'm so sorry, Dad.'

'No!' He grips her hands in his. 'No, Chrissie. You have nothing to be sorry about. Nothing. What he's doing, sending pictures of you. That's illegal.'

She shakes her head. 'He hasn't sent them. He's too clever for that. He just lets them see his phone. Everyone has seen them.' Tears trail down her cheeks. 'He's really popular. He turned everyone against me. No one speaks to me any more. They all hate me.'

'How long has this been going on, Chris?'

Tears travel down her cheeks.

'Since Christmas.'

'Christmas? Does Mum know?'

She shakes her head. He feels red rage, helplessness. He tries to remember everything Allie has ever shouted at him when he tries to wade in and fix things, grips the chair to stop himself from springing up.

'It's really good that you're telling me now, sweetheart.'

'I just don't think I can carry on, Dad. I'm so miserable. I don't want… to be here.' She tilts her chin up and he sees the combination of misery and last-ditch determination. 'I've thought about, I've…'

Cal's chest tightens and his heart thumps. He looks at his beautiful daughter, her face framed by those auburn curls that he used to twist round his finger and watch bounce back into shape when she was small. But things don't always bounce back. He knows that. He has spoken to so many parents who regretted missing the signs, waited until it was too late, until things were irretrievable.

'What sort of thoughts have you had?' Cal makes his voice soft and low, entreating her, somehow knowing that this is the chance, the window. He can feel it in the hairs on his arms, how everything hangs on now. 'You can tell me.'

Chrissie looks at him, tear stained, as if not sure she can trust him. Then her shoulders drop in defeat and she rolls up the sleeve of the floaty blouse she is wearing, the emerald green that sets off her hair and reminds him so much of his sister. He sees dozens of scars. Some red and angry, others silvery and ghost-like. There are so many. So very many. Cal's heart crumples.

'I've decided,' she says quietly, without drama. 'I'm not going back to school.'

Oh shit, exams in a few weeks, he thinks, *what will Allie say?* But above all he thinks, *No. You are bloody well not going back.*

'We could stay here,' he says. 'Call Mum?'

Chrissie shakes her head wildly, tears in her eyes. 'I want to go home, Dad, please. I want Rocket.'

'Right,' he says. 'Come on. I'm driving you.'

–

Chrissie falls asleep on the journey back. He wonders if the people he interviews feel this wiped out afterwards, if he would feel the same if he let the bottled-up thoughts fly free. He drives while his girl sleeps, feeling a fierce combination of failure and protectiveness. He doesn't know what he is going to say to his wife but this can't go on. Chrissie is one of life's sunshine copers. Or she used to be. He explained to his mother that he is needed. Guilt at abandoning her throbs in his chest – she looked so vulnerable, only just woken from her sleep.

Chrissie showed him her phone, and before they left, he scrolled through the messages, horrified. The things the kids say, the links they have sent her under cover of false concern, the sheer volume of it all. Anorexia, self-harm encouragement: the slow drip of toxicity and mental abuse. He grips the wheel, breathes deeply to calm himself. He wants to break this boy apart. He hates him in a way he has never hated anyone. Anyone.

They pass through familiar streets, bathed in the orange glow of evening sun. Pubs thrumming with pre-summer drinkers, people spilled onto every available patch of grass, staking claim to shade and air. After winding out of town, he turns down the track to their house and he feels Chrissie stirring and then tensing beside him, the sight of the weathered clapboard bringing them both back to reality.

'What's Mum going to say?' she whispers, and Cal squeezes her hand.

'Let me worry about that.'

When they step from the car, the golden shape of Rocket barrels from the porch. Within seconds he is whipping circles round them in excitement.

Chrissie crouches and buries her face in his fur.

The front door opens and Allie stands motionless, shock in her eyes. He realises, too late, that he has blindsided her. She was expecting Chrissie, not the pair of them. He should have texted first. He raises a hand in greeting, looking around as he does so, panicked. Is *he* here? Allie registers him straining to see into the house behind her and a cloud of sadness forms on her face. There's no one there. They all remain in place, fixed for a moment like the characters of a play. Even the dog is still.

'I might take Rocket to the lake,' their daughter mumbles, breaking the spell.

He nods and they watch as she strides away, her head down.

There is a moment of silence before Allie speaks, tiredness seeping from her.

'Cal,' she says, 'what are you doing here?'

CHAPTER THIRTY-NINE

LAYLA, 1986

He seems to like surprising her.

She's back in the library, absorbed in memories of their date, doesn't notice him enter the room until a hand snakes down the back of her skirt and lips touch her neck. She feels small under his touch, controlled in a way that's both dangerous and delicious. He smells expensive, powerful, intoxicating.

'Hello, gorgeous.'

She flushes under his gaze, liking the feeling of nervousness that runs through her. 'What are you doing here?'

'I had a meeting this morning – persuaded them a civilised lunch was in order.'

He kisses her and she lets herself fold into him, the proximity to the corridor, the chance of being discovered, prickling her neck, heightening her senses. She tastes bitter coffee on his breath. He pulls away.

'I have to get back to them. What time do you get off shift?'

'Not until three. I might be able to get away a bit early...'

She can't possibly sneak away, but it's like being caught in a spell – the scent of him whisks her back to the hotel room, the tantalising glimpse she had of something else. The risks she has to take to feel that hope once more are worth it. Since that night, she's felt more restless, more trapped than ever before. Being near him makes her alive to possibility.

So, at two thirty, she walks into the empty staffroom, liberates her bag and coat from the pegs and walks out the back door without saying a word. No one sees her go. She runs down the path until she is out of sight, her chest hammering with fear that she'll be called back. She can't miss this chance to see him. The sky is growing dark, filled with storm clouds that close over the hotel like night. She flips her hood up, feeling the first few drops striking it.

He's there, against their wall, leaning on the ancient stone. He lunges, grabs for her and she thinks maybe she'll drown in him and be happy. The sensation is over-powering; it sweeps her away.

Breathing heavily, he casts a glance up at the sky, touches the top button of her regulation blouse. 'It's going to pour. We need shelter.'

Before she can think through what she's doing, Layla takes him by the hand and leads him to the place she shouldn't.

They slip in through the unlocked door, just as light-ning flashes in the sky and the dull growl of thunder bounces off the hillside above.

'We'll have to be quick,' she whispers, though Stephen will be in the hotel kitchen for at least another hour. The cottage is eerily quiet; they stand in the hallway staring at each other. Layla slips her coat from her shoulders and steps out of her shoes. Another shock of lightning illuminates the corridor and she sees his face clearly for a second, frightening in its intensity. He steps forward and finds her.

By the time they reach the top of the stairs, she is barely dressed. Layla feels a spasm of regret for what she is about to do, take him to Stephen's bed, an unforgivable betrayal. But it doesn't come to that because they don't make it that far. He fucks her on the tiny landing. In each brief stunning moment of light, she can see the legs of the bed through the open door, the shadows of Stephen's possessions, the shape of the chair.

Then he flips her onto her back and she sees only John. He fills the air above her and she is consumed, lit from within and she can't, just can't, settle for anything else after this. She didn't realise – she thinks as she gasps for breath – she didn't know that life could be so real, that everything could be switched to a level so rich in colour and feeling. She has been sleepwalking. She tips her head back, and the skylight above frames purple sky, as bruised as the heather on the hills.

The storm is passing by the time they gather their clothes. Stepping into her skirt, she tucks in the now-crumpled shirt, pulls the zipper and smooths the front. Out of the corner of her eye, she watches John slide his arms into his suit sleeves, tug the cuffs into position below them. He catches sight of her watching him, studies her for a moment. She feels vacant with tiredness, floored by changing perspective.

'I'll go first, shall I?' He is impatient, ready to be away.

He doesn't kiss her, simply raises a hand and slips from the door into the world that is wet and new. His mind already elsewhere. She wonders if he thinks of her – does she float into his thoughts, can he smell her? The sky is clearing, the rain has stopped. She watches him stride away, then she steps out onto the large stone step and pulls the door shut behind her.

She hears words of greeting, gruff, brief, stares in horror as John and Stephen cross paths ahead of her. Stephen sees her on the step; his expression freezes for a moment, she is sure. Fear and panic stir themselves together. Her hair is down, she must look dishevelled, can he tell what they have been doing? How has the time fast-forwarded like this? She flips her hood up, then down again. Lingers too long, has to stay where she is.

He stops at the gate and stares at her. A thousand calculations run between them. 'You waiting for me?'

She shrugs. 'I was. Time's getting on though.'

'Who's that?' He gestures after John.

Layla repeats her shrug, though her heart stutters inside her. 'Some guest. Took a wrong turn.'

'Did he now?'

'See you later.' She squeezes past him and he reaches for her, pulls her in for a kiss. She turns her cheek at the last moment and it sears with heat as he plants his lips on the side of her face.

'Layla…'

'Got to run.'

She walks as quickly as she dares, feels the water from the potholed road seeping into her shoes, making her toes wet. She can't look back. She knows what is written on her face.

CHAPTER FORTY

LAYLA, 1986

Her hair is still wet from the shower when she rushes through the kitchen door.

'What time do you call this?' Chef shouts from behind the hotplate, but she can tell from his expression that he's in a good mood.

In the staffroom, Layla scrapes her damp hair back into a bun, tidies the strands that fall in her face and slicks on some lip gloss, the taste cherry-sweet and sickly. Piles of freshly pressed dishtowels sit in cellophane packaging and she has to squeeze between them. She slides her feet into heeled work shoes, doesn't notice Stephen until he grips her arm so tightly she cries out.

'Where have you been?' His face is red, accusing.

'Nowhere.' Despite herself, Layla is unnerved. It's only Stephen. She can weave him round her fingers and hold him up to the light. But there is something untethered in his eyes that she hasn't seen before. 'Ow. You're hurting me.'

He looks down at his fingers as if they belong to someone else, releases her.

'Can I see you later?'

The thought of his hands on her makes her feel queasy. She thinks of John, how it feels that she would be cheating on him, how that shift of loyalty has occurred without her realising. Everything turning on its axis.

'I don't know what time I'll be finishing.'

'Hasn't stopped you before.' She flinches when his hand slams into the wall next to her. 'Damn it, Layla. What the fuck's wrong with you?'

Afraid to meet his gaze, she can barely answer past the lump in her throat. 'I don't know what you mean.' He makes a growling sound of frustration, his hand still pressed against the wall, knuckles red. 'I'm late, Stephen.' Layla holds her breath as she ducks under his arm and twists away.

She skids into the kitchen. The heat hits her full in the face, bright lights illuminating everything so that she is momentarily disorientated. As she gathers herself by wiping the spotless serving station, she senses Chef watching her, registering Stephen thumping in close behind. The older man stays uncharacteristically quiet, but there is a thickness in the atmosphere. Layla grabs a notepad from the side and flees to the calm of the dining room.

All evening, as she takes orders, pours wine, offers the bread basket, her mind springs unwillingly back to the look on Stephen's face, the distortion of anger that lay beneath the surface. She feels foolish, realising that Stephen cares far more for her than she does for him. She needs to tell him it's over.

She is aware of him as she flits in and out of the swing doors. His head bent over the sauces and meats, a look of furious intensity on his face. There is no banter between the serving staff and the kitchen this evening. Only Chef's watchful gaze.

'Service!' Plates set down and whisked into another world. *Service, service, service.*

Eventually, the last couple moves from the dining table to the drawing room and Layla carries through their coffees and a little plate of petits fours. From the hallway, she can see the moon high above the trees, turning the lawns platinum.

Back in the kitchen, Chef is wiping down the stations, inspecting the fridges, all the jobs he usually leaves for the more junior members of the team. Layla cranes to see if Stephen is there. She needs to speak to him, set him straight.

'I've sent him home.' She startles, swivels to find Chef looking at her. 'Leave him tonight.'

'I need to talk to him.'

Chef shakes his head. 'Not tonight. Leave it tonight.'

Layla's instinct is to tell him to fuck off and keep his nose out of it. She can taste the words at the back of her throat. But something in his eyes stops her. Chef is doing this for Stephen, but there is something else. Something he sees and she doesn't and it frightens her.

CHAPTER FORTY-ONE

CAL

Allie stands above him on the porch, so close and yet he sees her through a distant lens. Their marriage is shipwrecked and unless they pull it off the rocks soon it is going to be unsalvageable.

'You came home?' She crosses her arms over her body and looks at the ground, concealing the mixture of apprehension and hope that's too plain in her eyes. 'I can't believe what Andy did, Cal. I'm sorry. Is your mum okay?'

'I don't know.' He wishes he could shrug off the unease that has stuck to his skin. 'She's Mum.' He can feel Allie trying to understand. 'But that's not why I'm here right now. We need to talk about Chrissie.'

Allie frowns. 'Chrissie? What's wrong?'

He looks around. In the far distance a tractor is lifting bales. There is no sign of another living soul, yet he feels exposed standing in the dust.

'Let's talk inside.'

It is Allie who opens the bottle of wine. He waits for her to pour two glasses and hand one to him, for a split-second an exhausted co-conspirator rather than a sparring partner. She smells of turpentine and sunshine.

She cries when he tells her about the pictures, about the scars on their daughter's arms.

'How long?'

'Christmas,' he says. 'She didn't say much. She just showed me some messages. They're horrible.'

'Have you seen?'

'The pictures?' He shudders. 'No, she's deleted them from her phone. She says the kid isn't forwarding them. Just "accidentally" letting other people see.'

'I should have known something was really wrong.' She swipes at the tears, furiously. 'How come I didn't know?'

'It's not just you. I didn't know either.'

'But I'm the one who's here all the time. I should have known.'

'I was there at the right moment,' he says. 'It could have been either of us she told.'

Allie sucks breaths in and takes another swig of her wine, eyes closed.

'Thank God she told you.'

Cal is silent – feeling their joint failure. He knows that they have not been focused on their daughter. But they have never needed to supervise her that closely. She is the sensible one to their chaotic lives.

'What do we do?' She looks at him, helpless.

'She can't go back to that school,' he says. 'It isn't worth it.'

'She's got her exams.'

He shrugs.

'She can still take the exams. It's only revision and her art portfolio to finish. She can do that here. We can find her another school, a college for next year. I'll make some calls.'

Allie frowns in confusion and he sees hope kindling. 'So, are you finished with the podcast? Now that you've found it was an accident?'

Cal hesitates. His conversation with Shona feels a million years ago. So much has happened since then.

'It wasn't an accident. They haven't released the information yet, but it was murder. I'm going back.'

There is a cold beat of sadness. When she speaks again, Allie's tone is gentle but laden with resignation.

'If you're going back, you can't be here for Chrissie.'

Cal feels like he's drowning. He sees how the absence matters.

'I'll ditch the podcast.'

'You don't mean that.'

He nods, shoving all the practicalities and impossibilities to one side. 'I'll talk to Sarah.'

'There was a moment when you could have done that, Cal, but it isn't now. Not now you've found Layla was murdered. You owe Jean and Tam.'

She knows their names. She's been listening. He realises that he has been thinking of Allie as selfish when the truth is more complex than that. Then he thinks of the man in her studio, his fingers tangled in her hair. He looks at her, helpless. Everything around him is falling apart.

'I'll push back the gallery date,' she says. 'It's fine, honestly. You have so much to be dealing with…'

'No, you can't do that.'

They both know that the gallery offer is a once-in-a-career opportunity.

Their eyes meet as the same realisation dawns over them.

'So we both cancel,' Allie says softly.

Cal nods. 'She's more important.'

'Did either of you think to ask me what I want?'

Chrissie stands on the threshold looking mutinous, her face a thundercloud of misery and anger.

'Of course, love, we only want what's best...'

Chrissie's face convulses in response to her mother.

'You never listen,' she says, turning on her heel, ready to slam her way out. 'Why would you start now?'

'Wait.' He feels stuck between daughter and wife, more used to being the target of frustration than the voice of reason. 'What *do* you want, Chrissie? Tell us.'

She tips her chin up. 'I don't want to do my A-levels...'

'What?'

'I want to try podcasting, like Dad. I don't need A-levels. I just need a microphone.'

He cringes at the paraphrasing of things he has said in the past.

Allie makes a stricken noise in her throat and sets her glass down awkwardly on the table. Wine slops over the side.

'Your future shouldn't be ruined by this, Christina. What we need to do is go into school and sort this boy out. He's the one who shouldn't be going on to do his A-levels.'

'No! That'll make it all worse.'

Exasperation bursts from Allie.

'But you can't just give up on your life. It doesn't work like that.'

'You don't get it, Mum,' Chrissie almost screams. 'I knew you wouldn't get it. That's why I told Dad.'

Cal thinks, *Fuck*.

Allie crosses the room, stretching her arms to their daughter, trying to hold her, but Chrissie shakes free and thunders away from them.

'Chrissie, come back. We're only trying to help.' She rushes to follow.

'Wait, wait, wait.' Cal strides to the doorway and stops in front of her, forming a human barricade against a formidable wall of emotion. 'Don't go up there, Al, give it a minute.'

Her chest is heaving, her face red. Tears spill from her eyes.

'Oh God, Cal. Our little girl. I just want to make it better.'

She lets him put his arms around her, sobs into his shoulder.

'We will,' he says, stroking her back. 'We'll think of something. She'll be okay.'

He wishes he believed it.

CHAPTER FORTY-TWO

Chrissie refuses to come down for dinner. After they've eaten, Cal checks on her to find she is asleep, her face wan and her legs pulled up to her chest. He stretches a blanket over her then tiptoes away.

When he gets back downstairs, Allie has gone out to her studio. He is unable to settle, in limbo in the house that should be his home, so he winds his way through shadows and long grasses to find her. Light glows from the viewing panel in the studio door and he is reminded of that day: the moment he saw.

Allie isn't painting. She perches on the edge of an old armchair, her head in her hands.

'I needed to get out of the house,' she says, and he nods.

Now that he's here, he doesn't know what to say. Around them, her canvas creations sit silent, great flashes of colour and bursts of inspiration.

'How did it go, today, with your mother, at the bench? I didn't have a chance to ask you properly.'

'Pretty awful. Andy's little revelation was badly timed.'

'I'm sorry. Where would he get such a ridiculous idea? Marc Dubois? Honestly. If there was "evidence" you would know.'

Cal walks to the full-length window and stares at his reflection in the dusk-darkened glass, so she won't see the guilt crossing his face. He should have told her before.

'Allie, there's something I... Dubois. When I interviewed him, he knew my real name.'

'What?'

There is a long pause while she waits for words he doesn't have. While she realises that he's kept this secret from her.

'I think maybe he...' His hands shake and his voice breaks on the words. Through tears, he registers the shock on her face. She steps towards him, stretches out a hand but doesn't make contact. 'It's driving me mad.' He shakes his head, turning back to the window, to the darkness outside. 'What if it was him? What if he hurt Margot?'

He feels her there, close behind him, but she still doesn't touch him. The divide between them has widened. He has seen it happening, has watched her pulling away and felt powerless to stop it. Their relationship now hangs on only one thread.

When Allie speaks he can tell she has drawn everything together inside herself. Her voice is soothing.

'He was a crazy, evil man, Cal. He'd say anything to hurt someone. He'd enjoy it, remember that. But if you really think it's possible, you should talk to the police.'

'I have.'

Another pause as she digests the level of secrecy.

'And?'

Cal sighs. 'They've said they'll look into it. But they sounded sceptical. I've been thinking about looking into it myself, into what could have happened to her.'

Allie exhales. 'Cal, are you sure you're the right person to do that?'

He prickles at the question, pivots to look at her.

'What do you mean?'

'Nothing.' Allie's cheeks colour, circles of rose appear like blotches of paint. 'You're good at it, I know you are, but it would be difficult to be unbiased, dispassionate.'

She's right. Cal swallows the bile that rises at the thought of pawing through his sister's past. The people he would have to speak to and the truths he would need to confront. He still feels like a lost child when it comes to Margot. Would he be able to see it all from an adult's perspective? It feels forever distorted and confused in his mind.

'Someone has to, Allie.'

'I just think maybe you need to look after yourself. It's been so long, Cal. What if there aren't answers? What if they're not the ones you want?'

As if a layer has been stripped away between them, Allie touches his back. He turns, and the smell of her shampoo, the paint she uses, the washing powder, her skin – it all hits him at once in a wave of nostalgia and pain. There is such familiarity and love there, buried deep beneath everything they have said and done. They stay there, holding tight, holding each other up.

Before he really knows what is happening, Cal is turning his head to hers. Their lips find each other's – the sensations painfully familiar, like a memory of the people they used to be. He isn't even sure he wants to be doing this, but their movements are automatic, he can feel his body taking over, rising to meet her.

'Allie,' he whispers.

'Shhhh.' She kisses him harder, her eyes shut, grips him tight.

He slides his hand beneath her top, groans at the feel of her skin, heat rushing through him, better judgement vanishing.

They break apart to pull their clothes off, breathing hard, the movements urgent. Allie's gaze is fierce. She pushes him to the chair and a tin of pencils crashes from the arm to the floor as she kneels over him, her hair falling onto his face. She slides herself onto him and Cal forces the image of that other man away, grips her hard to pull himself deeper. Their movements are violent, raw. His anger at her mixes with desire.

She grinds into him, her eyes dark and movements frantic. As they come, Cal cries out. Allie collapses onto his chest, her breasts slick with sweat, gasping. The scent of oil paint tangles with the smell of sex. They stay there, fused together, while their breathing returns to normal.

Eventually, Allie pushes back, lifts herself off and away. She turns her back to Cal, gathers her underwear.

'I'm so sorry, Cal.'

'What do you mean, you're sorry? That was…'

She spins to face him and he is shocked to see the tears in her eyes. 'No, Cal. It wasn't. I just don't…'

He's suddenly conscious that he is naked, soft. They are no longer on the same page. He wants to get dressed, but dread pins him to the chair.

'Is it about *him*?' He nods towards the place he saw them.

Allie shakes her head. 'No. He was a moment of madness, that's all. I'm so ashamed.' She rubs her face and when she speaks again, her voice is spilling over with regret. 'It really isn't about anyone else. You know that. You feel it too. You didn't talk to me, Cal. You talked to Andy and the police but you haven't spoken to me.'

And she's right.

The last thread breaks.

'Allie…'

Cal's sadness whispers into the studio, but before he can say anything more, his phone vibrates in his jeans on the floor. Allie reaches out.

'It's fine. I'll leave it.'

'It could be your mum,' she says, passing him the jeans.

There are too many ongoing crises to ignore the call.

He withdraws the handset from the pocket and stares at the phone. It isn't his mother. It's an Aberdeen number.

'Cal?' The voice is thin, tremulous.

'Jean? Yes, it's me.' He presses the phone hard to his ear to hear her properly, his eyes drawn to the bright canvas in the corner. Allie is pulling her shirt over her head; he feels a desperate wave of tiredness overtake him. Jean sounds frightened.

'It's Tam,' she says. 'He's in the Royal Infirmary in Aberdeen. He's had a heart attack. I don't know why I'm calling. I don't know what to do.'

He pictures her in the lonely cottage on the hill; the dark descending around her. Inexplicably, he thinks of the pink wafers, the weathered dog permanently placed at Tam's feet. A tidal wave of responsibility breaks over him.

CHAPTER FORTY-THREE

The moon is a faded arc above the cornfields. Cal knows the pathways through them to the lake intimately, remembers walking at night with a sleeping baby strapped to him to give Allie some rest. Rocket snuffles at the hedgerows, staying closer than he usually would, as if he knows that everything is broken.

Tam is out of immediate danger. A friend of Jean's has promised to take her into the hospital in the morning as she's too shaken to drive. Cal knows, logically, that he cannot be held responsible for the weakness in somebody else's heart. And yet he also knows that the timing is not coincidental.

Stepping onto the lake shore, he listens to the quiet sound of water touching pebbles and withdrawing. It is calming, but just for a moment he longs to be back in that dripping Aberdeenshire forest, the pounding waterfall underlining his thoughts. Maybe there, he could work out what to do. There are too many competing crises in his head. Chrissie, Margot, Layla, Allie. His marriage is over, he sees that now. He wishes he could work out the moment it failed, the crucial mistake he made. He wishes he had someone to ask for advice.

Oddly, the person who springs into his mind is Shona. He has her number. He pulls his phone from his pocket, looks at the last message she sent. It is late, but he could send a text. He starts to type the words, longing for some no-nonsense advice, some levity. But he deletes the message, shakes his head.

'Shit,' he tells the moon slivers on the lake.

He calls for the dog and turns for home, aware that he is in danger of making a complicated situation a thousand times worse.

Allie is in the kitchen. He sees her from a distance: the lights in the house frame her as if she is living art, clutching a cup to her chest and staring out into the darkness. Her melancholy is beautiful. The knowledge that they have lost each other spears him.

By the time he makes it inside, she is back at the kitchen table, a pan of hot chocolate steaming on the hob. Rocket takes himself straight to his bed in the utility room, flopping down with his head on his paws.

'Chrissie didn't want one,' she says, sadly. 'Help yourself.'

He fills his favourite mug with the velvet drink. How long will this be his mug, his house, his life? He has no idea what she wants or intends. It's too soon to even contemplate.

'So.' He clears his throat, suddenly sure of what he is going to say, even if the idea is ridiculous. 'I've had a thought.'

Allie diverts her gaze from the mug in front of her, watching him warily through the tendrils of steam.

'Hear me out and if it's a stupid idea then we forget I said it.'

'Okay.'

'What if I took Chrissie with me?'

She stares at him.

'Took her with you?'

'To Scotland.'

'To Scotland,' she echoes. He can't tell what she's thinking. She shakes her head a little as if to dislodge a ringing in her ears. 'What?'

He leans forward, suddenly captivated by his own idea.

'It would only be for a couple of weeks. She'd have to take all her revision with her and work all day. There's a desk in my room in the B&B and literally nothing else to do. It's in the middle of nowhere. I can keep an eye on her. She's been banging on about being a podcaster and not needing exams. Maybe she needs to see how it all works, that it's not at all glamorous. It will put her off, give you a break, and then she'll know she needs to get some more education.'

Allie laughs.

'Stupid idea?'

'Really stupid idea. But…' There is something wistful and afraid in her voice.

He ploughs on.

'She doesn't want us to fight the school. She isn't going to go back there with those kids. Let's just get her out of there, make sure she does the best she can in her exams, without that useless place.'

She looks at him and the tiredness and tears in her eyes make his heart throb with loss.

'I'm her mother. I should be able to help her fix this.'

'Allie.' He reaches for her hand and squeezes. 'You are helping her. Your parents would have made you go back there, you know they would.'

She nods, as they both picture the military convention she rebelled against.

'I just wish she could turn to me. I'm failing her.'

'She's being a teenager, challenging you. It's natural. It's just hit at the worst possible moment because she needs us, too.'

'She would have to knuckle down. She still has sketches to do for her portfolio and piles of English and history revision. Maths, past papers... she's worked so hard. She doesn't deserve this.'

'We'll take it all. I'll call the school and guilt them into giving us anything we need.'

'We should call them anyway. Give them hell.'

'Yes.'

'It's all happening so fast.'

She lays her head on the table. Her curls fall onto the surface. He remembers wanting to push his fingers into the perfect spirals. It saddens him that he no longer feels that desire.

'Allie? What do you think?'

She lifts her chin and he sees the pain in her eyes.

'I think I need to let her go.'

CHAPTER FORTY-FOUR

'Thanks for coming in and talking to us, Mr Lovett. It's good to see you.'

'No problem.' He doesn't think she means it. There's a copy of the *Sun* on the table between them. Cal can see Andy's treacherous face on the fold.

He uses the plastic stirrer to agitate the insipid machine coffee they've put in front of him. Surely if anyone deserves a decent cup of coffee it's victims and the bereaved, but no, the same crappy vending machine coffee seems to exist as standard in every police station he's ever visited. Perhaps it's designed for the perpetrators.

Usually he comes to these places as an independent reporter; today it's hard to connect with the thought that he's here for his sister. Snapshots stutter from memory, more strange unleashed fragments. An earring catching the light, her tights drying on the radiator, the bow of her lips as she slicked on red lipstick. Somewhere in the background, raised voices and the wire of tension sit like sickness. He pushes those thoughts away, but they push back. Her laugh echoes and he clears his throat to dislodge her.

'I'm sorry for your loss.' Detective Foulds in the flesh. She's older than he expected, eyes creased in sympathy. He nods, wishing they would get on with it so he can stop his mind spinning.

She smooths out the paper, looks up at him. *Foulds unfolds*, he finds himself thinking, hysterically.

'I didn't have anything to do with that.'

'No?'

'Well. I did tell Andy about my interview with Dubois, but I never expected him to do this.' Cal lets the disgust show in his voice. 'I had no idea it was coming out. He didn't even have the decency to tell me what he'd done.'

Foulds sighs.

'The thing is, Mr Lovett…'

'Cal.'

'The thing is, Cal. We have looked into your suggestion, and I'm afraid we just can't find any evidence that Marc Dubois was in any way linked with your sister.'

'But, you have the recording, the letter he sent me. He makes reference to a scrapyard. There's one only a mile from our house. I went to take a look and I think you need to search it. She could be in there.'

Foulds holds up her hand to get him to stop.

'You went to take a look?'

'I didn't go in…'

The detectives look sympathetic but he feels hot and unsteady; the look in their eyes tells him he is overstepping.

'You need to leave this to us now.'

He nods, feeling he is trapped behind glass trying to get their attention. Foulds shifts in her seat. Cal pictures the tight-packed cube of a crushed car, swallows saliva.

'We will look into all the information,' she tells him. 'After this,' her gaze lands on the paper, 'we are under additional pressure.'

Good, he wants to shout.

'So we'd like to ask some questions about your sister, if that's all right with you?'

He nods. The back of his neck prickles with sweat.

'I was only nine when she went missing...'

'I know.' The detective is gentle. 'Do you remember how she was at the time?'

Again, his memory spirals. Her long legs up on the coffee table. Short skirt. A sharp voice. *Margot, get your feet down.*

'She had a job at an office in town. She had lots of friends. I remember her getting ready, going out a lot. She was a good sister. Fun.'

'Boyfriend, Andrew Cameron?'

'Yes, Andy.'

'How did they get on?'

'Well. They were happy.'

'Was it serious? Did he come round for dinner, stay over?'

Foulds leans forward.

'No. My parents... our parents wouldn't have been okay with that. I don't think.' How does he know that? Does he know it for sure? 'She never brought him home.'

The detectives exchange a look.

'Were they strict?'

Cal feels that odd falling sensation inside. 'They were okay when I was a teenager, but I remember it being different with Margot.' They weren't the husks of people they later became is what he doesn't say. They still cared.

'Did she get on with them?'

His memory flickers once more and he's kneeling on the landing in the darkness, gripping the spindles as they argue in the brightly lit hallway below. Margot's crimson lips as she spits words he can't remember now. Then the dark horrible feeling, the pictures spooling on so fast he can't really see them. He swallows, shakes his head.

'As well as teenagers and parents ever do.' But he falters on the words and he wonders if they notice.

'What about friends? Do you remember anyone in particular? Any names?'

He shakes his head. 'She kept them separate. Surely, from the old case file…?' The detective inclines her head, makes a note on the piece of paper in front of her. Cal can't see what it says. 'I can ask my mother, Andy.'

They focus on him now.

'You still speak to him? Even though you were only nine. And she never brought him home?'

Cal shuffles his fingers, pauses to think what this could mean. Has he missed something fundamental? 'He's never got over it,' he tells them eventually. 'We speak every year. On her birthday. Other times. She would have been fifty-four. This week.'

The detectives look at each other.

'Do you remember what car he drove? There was a car mentioned at the time, a Vauxhall that a witness said your sister got into. Do you remember anything about that?'

Again, Cal shakes his head, pierced by the knowledge that he has hidden from these details. Yes, he was too young to take them in when they happened, but he has avoided researching them later. Surely, they can't think that Andy…? Even though he hates him for cashing in, he knows Andy just wants to help. He can't let them think that.

'He loved her,' he says. 'He was there for me, afterwards. When no one else was.'

'Do you remember how your parents seemed, after Margot vanished?'

The second detective has been silent until now, but now he finds himself pinned by intense brown eyes, amber flecks at their core. She is kind, but her question makes him feel exposed, afraid.

'They were devastated,' he says, afraid to step across the gap, to bring life to the darkest, most hidden thoughts he didn't really even know he had. 'Of course they were.'

But as he shifts uncomfortably on his seat, Cal's thoughts flit back through the years. To raised voices and slammed doors. He accepted all of that, back then, as normal teenager–parent volatility. It was all he ever knew. But now he has a teenager of his own, and when he looks back it is from a different angle. Would he behave that way with Chrissie? Never; the thought makes him shudder. But times were different back then. You can't judge them by today's standards, can you?

CHAPTER FORTY-FIVE

Spat into the warm air outside the police station, Cal hesitates, unsure where to go now, what to do.

Preoccupied, he takes an indirect series of loops through the streets, like the child he used to be, reluctant to return to the bleakness of home, kicking a twig or a pebble, taking his time before entering the marked house and absorbing its heaviness. He is exhausted by the interview, the emotion, the memory.

The untamed green space that houses Margot's bench is only a mile or so away, maybe there he can think properly, compose his thoughts before facing his mother. He sets off in that direction, but as he turns the corner, he can see in the distance that a man is already sitting on it, hunched over, swirls of cigarette smoke haloing him. Disappointment hits him; he will have to sit elsewhere, or wait for the person to move.

But as he draws closer, he realises that the person sitting there is remembering her too.

Cal is only metres away when Andy looks up, eyes red-rimmed, face stubbled and drawn. He feels a sweep of rage chased by despair.

'Didn't expect to see you here.'

It's strange to see the flicker of reluctance, fear even, in Andy's face. But Cal feels the fight falling away. The search for Margot has always been their uniting cause and if Andy's fucked up along the way, can he blame him?

Wordlessly, Andy shuffles along to make room for him and stubs out his cigarette. They sit either side of the plaque. Cal waits for an apology that doesn't come.

'What the hell were you thinking?' he says eventually, gets only the briefest shrug in return.

'Why didn't you tell me, Andy?'

'I *wasn't* thinking. When you told me, I just… There's a bloke down the pub who's a snapper. He said I should talk to his mate. I needed some cash. It got out of hand, I guess.'

On the pond, a duck is plunging beneath the water and springing back up some distance away, shaking the drops from its feathers. Cal sighs.

'I've just come from the police station. You've certainly put the pressure on. So maybe it's not a bad thing. But Christ, Andy, I had to explain to my boss, my family. I could have done with a heads-up.'

'What did the police say?'

His voice is unsteady. Something is off-kilter. Cal wonders if he's been drinking. Maybe the police have been pursuing their theory about the car. He thinks Andy did drive a Vauxhall back then. The other man rubs his hands on his trousers, which are threadbare and dirty. Unease germinates inside him.

'Have *you* spoken to them yet?'

'No. Not yet.' Andy stares at the pond, hunched forward so that Cal can hardly see his face.

'Are you all right? You seem…'

Andy clears his throat and the sound is phlegm-filled, disturbing.

'What did they say? Did they ask about me?'

Cal pulls away a little. 'What's going on, Andy?'

The older man rocks in his seated position. 'They're going to think it was me.' The words on their own would be easy to dismiss, but such intense agitation sets an alarm off.

'Andy,' he says, dread seeping through him. 'Why would they think that?'

'I saw her.' The words are almost whispered. Cal hears them, but he can't take them in.

'What?'

'I saw her that night.'

'I thought...'

'I lied.'

'But she left before you got there. When you came to pick her up, she was gone.' He repeats the story he has always known. The truth his life is based upon. There is a singing sound inside his head.

Andy shakes his head slowly.

'Nah, mate,' he says. 'That's not what happened.'

Cal takes in tiny sips of air, afraid if he moves he will break the spell and Andy will clam up forever.

'What happened, then?' he says carefully, making it sound as if the facts are incidental.

Andy buries his head in his hands. 'I found her on the road outside yours. She'd had this row with your dad. It was over me, partly.' Cal swallows down the rising memories, his dad's anger. 'I got angry. Said she needed to stand up to him. Oh Christ.'

Again, the coughing. Blackness crowds into the edge of Cal's vision. He grips the arm of the bench. When Andy takes his hands from his mouth, they are shaking.

'I'm sorry,' he says, over and over. 'I'm sorry.'

'Tell me.'

'I got mad at her. I stopped the car. Told her if she wasn't going to stick up for me then we were over.' He groans. 'I told her to get out.'

Slices of memory cut into Cal's brain. He can't think quickly enough.

'Where?'

'On one of the country roads.'

'What? You just left her?'

'I wasn't thinking.'

Cal feels an intense urge to punch him. His hands curl into fists automatically, heat spreads through him. But he needs the information more than revenge, for now.

'What happened after that?'

'I don't know. That was the last time I saw her.' Andy buries his head in his hands and his body shakes with sobs. 'It's all my fault.'

Cal feels winded, his chest heavy, something stuck in his throat.

'Are you sure that's all that happened?'

Andy jerks his head up. 'I swear, Cal, I never hurt her. Never. I would never.'

He stares at him, previously solid facts drifting on a changing ocean.

'Why didn't you say anything? Back then? It could have helped.' Cal's voice has risen so much that a woman walking a dog by the pond swivels to look.

'I'm sorry.' Andy reaches his arm along the bench, touches the plaque that bears her name.

Cal can't sit there any longer. Not with this man. He left her and she stumbled into the path of a monster.

'All this time. I trusted you.'

Racked with coughs, Andy buries his head again. Cal doesn't wait for him to lift it. He didn't think Margot's loss could possibly hurt any more, but as he strides away, he realises he was mistaken. Things can always get worse.

CHAPTER FORTY-SIX

Cal gets home late, finds the house silent and reproachful. They have plans to leave early and though he is tired, it is a relief. In the morning Allie fusses, making too much toast, pressing sandwiches on them, a flask. When she asks Chrissie if she's been to the toilet, their daughter snaps.

'I'm not five, Mum. Back off.'

Allie tries to laugh it off, but the notes fall flat and they all sink into uncomfortable silence. Cal drains his coffee cup.

'Right,' he says, standing. 'We should get on the road if we're going to manage the drive in one day.' He looks from his wife to his daughter; the hostility between them is palpable. 'I'll put the bags in the boot.'

Outside, the skies are heavy with rain and a pre-thunder closeness. The dog pads by his side, forlorn. It looks strange to Cal, Chrissie's bag next to his, her ruck-sack in the front footwell.

The door flips and then Chrissie is beside him, bending to hug the dog.

Allie stands on the porch. Cal can't bear the sight of how alone she looks. He takes the steps, pulls her into his arms and they squeeze tight. Just for a moment. The feeling of finality knocks the breath from him. By the time he is at the car door again, Allie has gone inside.

The journey north passes in a blur. They talk about nothing, then eat the sandwiches far too early. Eventually, Chrissie plugs in her earphones and falls asleep, head against the door, her face drained of life.

While she sleeps, Cal finally has time to confront the dead weight of dread he has been carrying around since Andy's revelation. His career relies upon people divulging secrets they have kept for decades, but still he didn't see it coming. Andy has been a constant since Cal was nine years old. He trusted him because Margot trusted him.

When Chrissie is browsing at a service station, he makes the call from the car park, listening to the traffic while he waits to be put through to Detective Foulds.

'Mr Lovett?'

'Thanks for speaking to me.'

'Not at all.'

'I spoke to Andy yesterday. He told me some things and I thought you should know.'

'Right...'

'He did see Margot that night. He said that he picked her up and they argued and he left her by the side of the road.'

'Which road?'

'I don't know. Somewhere in the countryside.'

'We will investigate every angle, Mr Lovett, I assure you.'

'I think he drove a Vauxhall. You asked me, before, if he drove a Vauxhall? I think he did.'

There is a beat of silence.

'Mr Lovett...'

'That would fit, wouldn't it? If Dubois found her? If he followed her or offered her a lift, or...'

'Cal.' Her voice is gentle, and he knows she is managing him as he has managed others. 'Leave this with me. We will explore every possibility, I promise you. We will do our best to get you the answers you deserve.'

When he looks up, Chrissie is standing by the car, scanning the tarmac for him. He waves from the verge. She grins and holds up a bulging bag of pick 'n' mix.

He takes a deep breath and pockets his phone.

—

By the time they reach the bed and breakfast, it is dark. Marilena greets them like old friends, wrapping his daughter in a tight hug and then leading her to a little room in the eaves, just along from Cal's.

'I'll bring her a hot chocolate,' she announces, beaming at Cal. 'And some cookies.'

'She's never made me hot chocolate,' he whispers when Marilena has gone.

Chrissie sinks onto the bed and smiles weakly. 'You're not as pretty as I am, Dad.'

It's good: Chrissie needs to be spoiled, looked after. She needs to come back out of her shell and find the world a less hostile place, a place worth being part of. Maybe one day Cal can do the same.

CHAPTER FORTY-SEVEN

They are due at the hospital to meet Jean at ten. Marilena plies them with full breakfasts and multiple cups of coffee so that Chrissie just has time to grab her revision, sketchbook and pencils before they go.

At the hospital, he leaves her working in the canteen and makes his way through the maze of corridors, following markings on the floor. On the ward, Cal stands lost for a moment, scanning the beds. At first he doesn't recognise Tam, wouldn't have found him if Jean wasn't sitting at the bedside, an empty chair waiting across from her.

The old man at the end of the ward has his grandchildren visiting – a boisterous toddler launches himself onto the bed and the child's mother shushes them. Cal's shoes squeak on the floor as he walks and Jean looks up. She seems small here, out of place.

'How are you doing, Tam?'

The old man watches him from beneath bushy brows.

It is Jean who answers: 'They say he can come home in a day or two.'

'Nothing wrong with me,' Tam growls. Jean rolls her eyes and gestures for Cal to take the chair on the other side of the bed.

'I'm sorry I had to leave before.'

'Your name was Longacre,' Tam says, eventually. 'Not Lovett.'

'I should have told you.'

Jean shrugs. 'Why would you?' But Cal knows more is owed.

'I don't find it easy to talk about her. You'll know that.' Tam grunts; Cal senses a fractional easing in his body language. 'But I'll answer any questions you have. You both deserve that. It takes bravery to speak out like you have. Margot, my sister, would have said I'm a coward.'

'Is that why you do it, like?' Jean tilts her head.

'The podcast?'

'Aye.'

'I think it must be. But I can't imagine life if Margot hadn't disappeared. It changed everything. You can't go back.'

Others might probe, but they sit in a silence that is filled with mutual understanding. Cal feels the ultimate gift they are offering is privacy.

'I've always thought that if I'd understood her a bit better, Layla would still be here,' Jean says. Tam's attention jerks to her.

'It's not your fault,' Cal says.

'Maybe not.'

'Ach, Jean.' Tam rests his hand on top of hers, shakes it a little. She looks gratefully at him.

'I thought finding her would help,' Tam says, turning to Cal.

Jean hands him a tissue from the box on the side and Cal studies his hands for a moment. How diabolical that he wants what they have. 'And it doesn't?'

'It just raises more questions.' Jean sounds so very tired.

'We're not there yet,' Cal says. 'Maybe this is the worst bit. We know she died, she isn't coming back. But we don't know exactly what happened, you don't have any justice.'

Both sets of eyes fix on his.

'Someone needs to talk.' Cal feels grim responsibility pushing him down. 'I don't know if I can make that happen. But I'm going to try.'

–

Tam falls asleep, so Jean walks through the endless corridors with Cal, keen to meet his daughter. They find Chrissie in a corner by the window, her head bent, her focus on her work. She looks beautiful, independent, like a university student, her fingers wound round a cooling cup of tea as she reads a textbook. He feels a rush of awe and pride.

'Jean,' he says, 'this is my daughter, Chrissie.'

Chrissie smiles shyly as Jean slides in opposite her. Cal can see they are both nervous, so he heads to the counter for tea and cakes, leaving them to work it out. He takes his time choosing and when he looks back from the till, the sketchbook is swivelled towards Jean, who is examining the drawings, her face more animated than Cal has seen before.

He exhales a long-trapped breath of worry. For Chrissie, for Jean, for everyone. The sight of them together gives him hope. Not everything is dark. There is still light to be found in the shade. Strength in the most unlikely connections.

CHAPTER FORTY-EIGHT

They drive back out of the city. Chrissie watches the sky from the window. Her presence soothes Cal. He is glad he has the chance to show her this place. He wants to share the hillside and the falls, the wilderness where Layla cantered into oblivion, because he thinks his daughter is one of the few people who will understand the indelible mark it has made on him.

He glances over at her. She's thinned, insubstantial even, like you could see through her. He wants to fix that, too.

'How's the school work going?'

'I'm making good progress,' she says. 'Promise.'

'Take a break and come for a walk with me, then.'

He stops at a petrol station. Chrissie chooses bright sunflowers, then he drives up into the foothills, near to the hotel and the riding stables. They leave the car beside standing stones – pink granite slabs that glitter in the light. From here, they can see for miles, fields folding out in front of them.

'That's where she was riding when she vanished.' He draws a line across the moorland with his finger. 'She went into those woods.'

'And no one saw her again?'

He shakes his head. 'No.'

'Just like Auntie Margot.'

The spectre of her jolts into his mind. He swallows, trying to stave off the images that come to him so easily: feet cut to ribbons, clothes discarded, skin torn. He hopes the detectives are making good on their promise to invest-igate.

He feels the burden as they walk, the weight of two missing women and not enough answers between them. When they reach the falls, Chrissie gasps.

'You'd never know this was here!'

'I know. Lots of local people don't even really know.'

She lays the sunflowers at the head of the falls, near the crack in the rock where Layla was wedged. The bright yellow stands out against the cool dark trees, a flash of life. A testament to one. Chrissie scrambles down the rocks to the pool and he watches as she closes her eyes, turns her face to the spray. Just for a moment, he glimpses contentment. In an instant it's gone, but the snapshot is powerful.

She climbs back up, using her hands to help herself over the slippery stone. 'What about Layla? What's next?'

'I think she was meeting someone here. But no one has ever come forward to admit to it. I need to go through my notes tonight.'

In truth, the events of the past few days haven't allowed him much time for practicalities. Now he's here, he needs to refocus and make the time count. He's made promises.

–

They are almost back at the car when Shona calls.

'Hello stranger,' she says. 'I heard a rumour you were back.'

'Your sources are good.'

'I'd make an excellent journalist. Apart from the writing bit. Always get Cliff to do the reports.'

Cal laughs. He is aware of Chrissie standing only a few metres away, scanning the landscape with her artist's concentration.

'Anyway, on that note, I have a tip for you. Get hold of the evening paper. The police have made a statement.'

'Really?'

'They've confirmed it's a murder enquiry. Local hacks were invited but I wondered if you might have been missed off the list.'

'NFI,' Cal confirms. Not fucking invited.

'Ah well, we can't all be popular.'

He smiles, despite the frustration at being left out.

'The *Express* have done a huge piece on it,' she says. 'With a big picture of the chef she was seeing.'

'Thanks Shona, appreciate the heads-up. Definitely owe you a drink now.'

'Several.'

He's about to say goodbye, but she hesitates and he waits.

'I saw the papers, Cal. I'm so sorry about your sister.'

A lump makes its way to the centre of his throat. His voice has to wobble past it. 'Thank you.'

When he hangs up, Chrissie looks at him quizzically. 'Who was that?'

He clears his throat.

'A friend – a forensic anthropologist who's working the case. She's helping me with the podcast. They've just announced they're treating Layla's death as murder.'

Chrissie glances back at the woods in the distance.

'That's a bit late.'

'Better late than never, I suppose. Let me just search for these articles online, then we can head back.'

On the small phone screen, Cal scrolls through the piece – a hatchet job on Stephen. The photograph they have used seems to have been taken with a long lens on the hotel estate. The chef looks bulky, threatening. He sighs.

'Not good?'

'I don't think Layla's ex-boyfriend is going to like it. I was hoping he'd come round, talk to me, but now…'

It turns out that Cal is wrong. By the time they reach the bed and breakfast he has a text. Three terse words.

I'll talk now.

CHAPTER FORTY-NINE

LAYLA, 1986

They are grooming Duke and Oliver, two of the eventing horses, early in the morning, first light streaking the horizon. Anticipation flutters inside Layla, her fingers feel clumsy as she picks Oliver's feet and brushes his legs. She takes a deep breath. They are on their own so now is as good a time as any.

'Doug, can I ask you something?'

'Ask away.' He doesn't break the momentum of the large brush sweeps he is making. He sounds less patient than normal, but she's started asking now.

'I was wondering if I might be able to come and work for you?'

He moves his attention to brushing Duke's tail. It is knotted and tangled.

'What do you call this? A holiday?'

'No, I mean, I'm thinking of studying. Doing something with horses at the college. I thought maybe I could give up the hotel and work here instead. For you... and Sal.'

'That sounds like the kind of job that wants paying.'

He laughs, and it's a dismissive sound, derisive even, as if there is nothing further from possible. Layla has plucked up the courage so she forces herself forward even though her voice sounds small and her belief that this is obviously a good deal for him as well as her is evaporating.

'Well, yes, but I could give more lessons for you, maybe compete some of the horses more seriously...'

'No. I don't think so.'

'But...'

Doug throws the brush into the grooming box and pulls on the end of Duke's lead rope to release it from the twine looped over the fence. He turns away and the horse follows, then he changes his mind and swivels back. He comes right up to Layla until his face is closer than comfortable. On the surface his voice is reasonable, but beneath it she senses menace, a line crossed.

'Sal was right. Look, I don't know what role you think you play here. Maybe us letting you in the kitchen has given you the wrong impression. You're lucky we let you ride the horses. We're happy for you to do that in your free time. That's all. Got it?'

'Yes.' The word squeaks out, small and pathetic.

The fierceness of his response astounds her. It seems out of proportion to the question. She thinks back to Sal's face in the Ladies at the pub, wonders what she's said to Doug.

'Good.'

He strides away, tugging Duke and his unexpected anger behind him.

Layla feels tears welling with the shock of his reaction. Was what she was asking so unreasonable? She has never seen Doug like that, felt that coiled resentment. Now she feels foolish. She buries her head in Oliver's side, frantically brushing the hair she has already groomed and trying desperately not to make a sound. It doesn't matter. By the time she leads the mare to the field, Doug has closed the gate and retreated to the house. She hears the door bang behind him.

She releases the horse and leans on the gate, watching as he canters around the field. Tears sneak down her cheeks. Maybe she's been overstepping for a long time. Thinking she was different to the others. She feels a hot rush of shame. When the tears stop, she wipes her eyes and tucks her hair into her hood, makes her way to the tack room and fills the kettle from the tap in the yard. She doesn't have time to go inside for breakfast anyway.

–

In her pocket is a little scrap of paper from her waitress pad. She shouldn't have done it, she knows, but she couldn't resist taking John's number. It was just sitting there in the book at work, waiting for her. So easy to steal a glance at the reservations. She's been carrying it around since then. Just in case.

She wasn't going to use it. Just wanted to have it. But now, smarting from Doug's reaction, she needs another way to make some changes. It's asking for help, yes, but it's what she needs to do to make her own way. And John is mad about her. He tells her all the time.

She holds the fragile piece of paper up to the light, nervous now that she intends to use it. He believes in her, has somehow seen through the circumstances of her life to the true person she is, the yearning she has.

A woman answers.

'Hello?'

Layla is thrown, can't speak for a moment.

'Hello? John Knowles' office. Can I help you?' A note of frustration, of irritation, a sense of business and import-ance leaks down the line to her.

'Could I speak to John, please?'

Her voice sounds young, fragile even to herself. Doubt creeps in and she thinks about hanging up, but she has done it now.

'Can I ask who's calling?'

'Layla, tell him it's Layla.'

There is a pause.

'Can I say what this is regarding?'

Uncertainty distils inside her. 'No. He'll know.'

Another excruciating pause.

'Hold the line, please.'

She waits so long Layla thinks maybe they have forgotten her, that she should hang up. Outside, the light is lowering, she can see from her window the horizon streaked with indigo. She is acutely aware that the horses are in that direction, just over the brow of the hill, but she cannot go to them, cannot escape the feeling that she has misplaced herself. She drifts into thoughts of self-recrimination so deep that when she does hear his voice in her ear, it is a shock.

The tone is an even greater shock. None of the indulgence or allure she expected. Another sharp douse of cold water.

'What the fuck do you think you're doing, Layla? I'm at work. You can't call here.'

'Sorry. I need to see you.' She hears the whine in her voice. The loss of control is alien. He sighs and his annoyance stretches from his office to her bedroom.

'I'll meet you by the garden. Nine.'

He is gone before she can reply.

CHAPTER FIFTY

LAYLA, 1986

She is early, scurrying through the woods to the back of the kitchen garden, the scent of crushed garlic in her nostrils. Waiting makes her jumpy; night murmurings push her closer to the edge, and she drums her fingers on her thigh, scanning the treeline.

John has money, influence. He could be her chance to make something of herself. But the coldness in his voice when they spoke earlier has nagged at her, wound its way around her schemes. Perhaps she caught him off guard, that's all.

Another thought creeps in before she can help herself. If he isn't going to help her because he desires her, because she means something to him, then maybe he will help her for other reasons. Maybe she's going to have to grab her ticket out of here another way. She doesn't want to make that threat, but she will if she has to. She's the one in control here. He has more to lose.

He is late. She strains to see, until a darker shade of night detaches itself from the shadows and he is there, overwhelming her with his scent and presence. She feels smaller than usual, the bulk of him looming over her.

'You can't call my work.'

He sounds far angrier than she imagined.

'I missed you,' she says, keeping her voice light. 'Don't be silly. I'll make it up to you.'

His lips meet hers but more in punishment than affection. She is wrong-footed by the unexpected force, staggers then makes herself yield to him, runs her hands teasingly along his waistline to his trousers. She feels for the zip, but before she can tug it down, he thrusts a hand out and grips her throat.

'You're not listening to me.'

'I'm sorry,' she whispers, frightened by the strength in his fingers, the pressure on her neck. The sudden snap in him.

'Don't. Phone. My. Work. Ever.' He hisses the words in her face and tears come unwillingly from her eyes. Everything is different. She tries to reach for him but he shoves her backward, presses her against the stone, rough and angry. 'Do you understand?'

She nods, crying harder now, panic rising until he releases her and she gasps in enough air. He puts his hands to her face, wipes the tears away with his thumbs. When she tries to touch her neck, he holds her arms tight to her sides.

'Don't make a fuss. It's okay.'

And she knows it has to be.

His hands are rough, his grip tight, but he sounds recognisable again, malleable, like maybe she can feel her way back to him. She is newly aware of the dark and the isolation. No one knows she is here in the woods. So she presses her mouth against his, slides her way forward until she is inside his coat with him. She knows what she has to do to show she is sorry.

Afterwards, he is still panting when he rises from the wet ground.

She is sore, confused. It was different.

'Will you get home okay?'

'Yes.'

This is not the time to ask for a favour.

CHAPTER FIFTY-ONE

CAL

The chef fidgets with an unlit cigarette, puts one ankle on his other knee. Takes it off again and shuffles in his seat, looking anywhere but at Cal. There aren't any lights on in the cottage, which is gloomy with its thick walls and small windows, built to keep out the weather.

'Go ahead.' Cal nods at the cigarette. 'Don't let me stop you.'

'I'm trying to give up. Doctor's orders.'

Cal can tell by the smell in the cottage that it isn't really working. Takeaway boxes and ready-meal plastic litter the surfaces. He's shocked that a chef is creating masterpieces for the hotel guests and then eating such crap at home.

'So, tell me about you and Layla.'

'What do you want to know?'

'How long had you been seeing each other?'

Stephen shrugs. 'A year? I don't even know if we were "seeing each other" officially. Layla was hard to… pin down.' His fingers tighten into fists, release again. He lays the crumpled fag on the side.

'How so?' Cal tries to make his voice soft, non-confrontational.

'We'd arrange to meet, but she wouldn't show up. Sometimes she was all over me, sometimes she wouldn't let me near her. She drove me fucking crazy, you know?'

Cal nods, waits.

'Just before she… went missing. We were supposed to be going away together for a week. I'd booked the time, looked into flights. But she just changed her mind, got really angry that people would know we were together.'

'Was it a secret?'

'That's the thing. Everyone knew. We weren't boyfriend and girlfriend as such, but everyone knew.'

'Do you remember when you last saw her?'

Stephen nods. 'It was on a shift. She left after lunch and I had a load of cheesecakes to make for the next day. I asked her if she was going to the pub later.'

'The Bridge Inn?'

'Yes. But she just shrugged and said maybe. So, I didn't think it was strange when she didn't show up. I was playing pool. People started to talk about a horse coming back and the rider being missing. Some of the folk in the pub went to help look. I didn't know it was Layla until later on, though. I stayed put.'

He shakes his head at his past self.

'You didn't realise it was her?'

Cal allows the disbelief to sound in his voice.

Stephen's eyes slide away from his.

'Maybe I suspected. But I was pissed off with her. About the holiday.'

Cal knows the fact that Stephen sat drinking beer while others searched the roads and fields for Layla is one of the reasons many think he's guilty. But it's not evidence.

Stephen shifts his legs again, crossing the other one. There is something he isn't saying.

'Her mum thinks you used to hit her.'

'Fuck. Her mum has it in for me. I never.' Stephen's voice rises, both feet hit the ground. He leans forward, his tone urgent, eyes fearful. 'Not really. Once, twice, I mean, Layla… shit.' Cal waits, uneasy at the echoes of Dubois' rationale. 'She'd blow hot and cold, she just drove me to it, you know?' The desperation snakes through his voice. 'She did it on purpose. You know what I think? I think sometimes she only wanted me mad. That's what I think. But kill her? Make her disappear, like you're saying?'

Cal holds his hands up. 'That's not what I'm saying.'

'Why not? It's what everyone else says. I see the way they all look at me. Feel the way they stop talking when I go in the pub. Not that I bother much now. I used to have pals, a life outside this shit hole.' He gestures towards the five-star luxury hotel hidden through the trees, far enough away to be another world. 'They all think I did it. There's nothing I can do to prove it to them. Nothing. Layla ruined my life. I wish I'd never met her.'

He drops his head into his hands, pressing the palms against his eyes as if trying to hold in the memories. Cal lets him breathe through it without saying anything, wondering what other images he is trying to press away. When Stephen lifts his head, his eyes are red. 'I loved her. I really did love her.'

His discomfort at revealing his emotions is palpable. Cal tries not to think of Andy, doesn't want to draw comparisons.

'Shall I get you some water?'

'Aye, thanks.'

He finds a glass that looks clean enough. Stephen takes it with shaking hands and sets its beside the crushed cigarette.

'What do you think happened to her, Stephen? How do you think she ended up in the woods?'

The chef won't look at him, stares at his fingers, knotting them together.

'Did you meet her there that day?'

Stephen huffs air from his lungs. '*I* didn't, no.'

'You mean she was seeing someone else?'

There is a long pause while the man appears to calibrate, capitulate.

'Aye. I think so.'

It's Cal's turn to lean forward. 'Do you know who he was?'

Stephen shakes his head. 'No. But I think he was older, had money.' When he meets Cal's gaze there is pain in his eyes, humiliation. 'She brought him here, once, I think. To fuck him. When I was working.'

'Why didn't you tell the police this? Back then?'

'I dunno.'

'Is it because they would have thought…'

Stephen's head jerks back, as if he has suddenly remembered where he is, what he is saying and to whom. Cal sees pain, confusion, then a hardening.

'I think you should go now.'

He stands abruptly and the space shrinks.

'Hang on…'

'No. You're just the same.'

'I'm not the same as anything, Stephen. I'm just trying to find out what happened to her. You want the same thing.'

'It's a fit-up. That's what it is. Now fuck off.'

Cal can see he has pushed far enough. He takes himself to the front door, sensing Stephen at his heels, an intimidating presence. He can't help but wonder if the chef was this volatile back then, or if this is the result of recent developments. He turns on the step to say more, but the door slams so hard a chip of wood falls from the frame to the floor. He glances around at the trees. Nothing moves.

CHAPTER FIFTY-TWO

When he gets back, Chrissie is working at the desk in his room. He drops his bag of equipment on the floor and she startles. He notices her fingers drifting from her phone, the nervousness in her expression. It makes him feel jittery too.

'Everything okay?'

She nods.

'Sure?'

Chrissie bites her lip. 'I can't stop looking at the posts, the messages.'

Cal perches on the end of the bed.

'Maybe delete the apps?'

'I tried. It isn't working. I can't stop myself logging into the main sites.'

'Give me your phone?' He means it as a joke, but Chrissie looks from him to the handset.

'Maybe for a day or two. Just to see.'

So, he knows it's bad. He keeps his tone light as she passes him the phone. 'Yep, no problem.'

His eye falls to the desk. She has been working on a small etching on a piece of leather. Cal is grateful for the chance to change the subject.

'That's beautiful.'

'It's just a study – there's seven of them – part of a bigger piece I'm working on.' She stares at the little piece of leather for a moment, seeming lost as she turns it in her hands.

'What's the theme?'

'Seven deadly sins.'

'What's that one? No, wait… anger?'

The leather is etched with a harsh yet beautiful explosion of spiky lines. Fury seems to jump from them. She nods and he sees the ghost of pain cross her face.

'You hungry? Maybe we need to go and commit the sin of gluttony at the pub?'

Is he doing the right thing jollying her out of her down moments? Should he be trying to talk her through it instead? Allie would know. He watches Chrissie shake off the thoughts as she rises and slips her feet into her shoes.

Over plates of fish and chips, without her phone to distract her, Chrissie seems to relax a little; colour graces her cheeks.

'How did it go with Stephen?'

'Strange. He's so tightly wound. It's not hard to imagine him losing his cool. But he seems to think Layla was seeing someone else when she went missing. The place her body was found does have the feel of an assignation. I'm just not sure it fits him.'

'So, who else could she have been seeing?'

'That's the million-dollar question. She was restless apparently, bored. She didn't have a life outside the community really, though. Didn't go to college, university, spent all her spare time horse riding. How would she have met someone and kept it a secret? It doesn't make sense… unless it was someone local who was married, maybe.'

'What about the hotel?'

'I have a staff list from the time, I'm checking those names out.'

'And the guests?'

He stares at Chrissie, feeling pieces slot into place.

'Of course...'

'She didn't need to go and meet people, did she?' Chrissie says, simply.

'They were coming here. All the time.'

CHAPTER FIFTY-THREE

He doesn't want to go back to the lumber yard but something the stable hand, Jim, said has been nagging at him so he forces himself to drive along the A96 in the direction of Aberdeen, heavy grey clouds pressing in on him from above. He mulls Chrissie's insight, daunted by the task of unpicking Layla's final weeks and days. There is always a moment in an investigation when it feels too big, too endless, too hopeless. Even though he recognises this stage, it doesn't help the feelings of despair. Jean and Tam are depending on him.

The man is out in the yard this time, wearing the same stained boiler suit as he cuts logs. The squeal of the saw slices through the air and sawdust flies like sparks around him. Cal waits, sure Jim knows he is here and is ignoring him. The scowl on the man's face makes him wonder again if he was the one who hated Layla enough to strangle her and leave her body on the hill, despite the seemingly watertight alibi that he was with Doug at the stables.

When the saw shuts off, he steps forward, filled with irritation.

'Jim. Have you got a minute?'

He waves the microphone as a signal he is recording and Jim's scowl deepens.

'Turn that thing off.'

'I just have a couple of questions.'

'I'm not interested.'

'It's something you said last time. When you called Layla a whore.'

Jim stops in his tracks. Even he can hear the accusation. 'I didnae say that.'

'You did.'

He spins round. 'Well, it's true.'

'You said to ask them at the hotel. What did you mean? That she was seeing one of the chefs?'

He snorts. Cal knows he is on the right track.

'She didn't limit it to the staff.'

'How do you know?'

'I'd like you to leave.'

'Just tell me and I'll go.'

He spits on the sawdust and Cal marvels at the depth of hatred that lingers for someone he hasn't seen in over three decades.

'I saw her.'

'Where? When?'

'Being picked up in a posh car from the end of the drive at the hotel. A Discovery that had never been over a pothole in its life.' Jim sneers.

'When was this?'

He shrugs. 'Around the time she disappeared.'

'And you didn't think to mention it to the police?'

Jim's eyes glitter. 'Must have slipped my mind.' He steps back. 'You should leave.'

'Wait. Did you see anything of the man in the car?' Cal watches Jim's footsteps falter slightly, a sense of unease creep into his expression. He knows there is something. 'You didn't like her, I get it. She wasn't a saint. But Tam and Jean, her parents. They're good people. They don't deserve this. They need to know.'

'I don't want to be involved.'

'The quickest way to get rid of me is to tell me what you know.'

'Fine. But turn that thing off.'

Cal makes a show of switching off the recorder.

'He was older. Old enough to be her father. Bit of grey in his hair, posh shirt. That's all I saw. I wasn't spying.'

'Would you recognise him, if I found him?'

'Fucked if I know.'

He watches Jim stride towards the Portacabin and slam the door.

Cal stares at the silent saw, its teeth sharp, the wood bleeding sap onto the earth below.

CHAPTER FIFTY-FOUR

Chrissie is settling in. When he gets back, Cal finds her in the kitchen, chatting to Marilena over tea and biscuits. He stands in the doorway, watching them at the old farmhouse table, which is bleached by years of use. The lines on her face have already relaxed and the tightness in her shoulders is less pronounced. He is disconnected from his mother, his marriage is wrecked, but at least Chrissie is okay. He can cope as long as she is.

'Hi, Dad.' She grins when she sees him and brandishes a textbook. 'I'm not skiving. Marilena has been testing me.'

'Are you sure she isn't getting in the way?' he asks, worried that they are taking advantage.

'I love having her here.' Marilena flicks him with the tea towel.

'I have to go and interview someone else now. Chrissie, you could come if you like?'

'I have some sketches to do – then I thought I might walk across the fields and try some landscapes if that's okay.'

'Of course it is. I'll see you later.'

As he retreats down the hallway, he realises she still hasn't asked for her phone back.

–

He parks outside a neat, grey-harled box on an estate at the edge of Inverurie. The views behind it show fields of ploughed stubble, the twist of a river through the flats. He sees Irene at the side of the house, carrying a basket of washing, a bag of pegs balanced on top of the load.

'Hi Irene. Do you have a minute?' He waves a paper bag. 'I brought butteries.'

'You're learning. Are you going to hang my washing for me too?'

She cackles. He can picture her behind the bar – her sense of humour and sparky conversation putting people at their ease. But at the same time there is a no-nonsense air about her. He wouldn't want to chance his luck.

'If that's what it takes.'

'Come on back. I'll get this on the line and then make you a tea to go with those.'

The back lawn glows with the effortless green that all the gardens here enjoy, the turf damp and springy. Irene whips sheets from the basket and hangs them so they flap and billow in the wind. Cal hands her pegs and peers anxiously at the sky – another pewter day that threatens rain at any moment. She catches his gaze.

'It'll be dry in no time.'

He settles in the kitchen at the back of the house. A tortoiseshell cat twists around his feet. He takes in the details of the room to describe later. It's immaculate, laminate shining, sink clean and sparkling.

'Sorry about her.' Irene shoos the cat away. 'Nina. She's needy.'

'It's okay.' Cal scratches the cat's soft head, smooths her flank as she devours the attention. 'I like cats.'

Irene puts his tea down in front of him, then takes the chair opposite. She waits for Cal to take the lead.

'I wanted to ask you if there was anyone Layla was seeing at the hotel besides Stephen. Someone mentioned a guest?'

She shifts in her chair. 'There was always talk about that lassie. You never knew what was true and what just came from her rubbing folk up the wrong way.'

'So, was there someone, maybe?'

Irene stares out of the window to where the washing is dancing on the line. He waits, sensing again the conflict she feels. How memory shifts and turns and plays with your allegiances and your notion of what's right and wrong. He knows this himself. She turns back to him and he sees tears in her eyes.

'When she was just missing it seemed... wrong to pass on the gossip. Back then, it might have affected how hard people looked for her, you know?' He nods. 'But now, to think of her lying out there all that time... I can't help but wonder if we'd spoken up more, whether...'

'She would have died right away, Irene. By the time the horse came back most likely. There's no way anything you said could have saved her.'

He thinks of the way her neck was snapped. The stirrup nearby.

'I'd be lying if I said it hasn't weighed on me since we heard. I didn't expect her to be found so close after such a long time.' She sighs. 'Maybe she did have something with a guest. I can't be sure, but...'

'What makes you think it's possible?'

'I was stacking some extra crates of drinks in the corridor one night. She came down the staff stairs and it was late – too late for her to be there, so that's why I noticed. She'd been crying and she just looked, you know... like something was going on.'

'Did she see you?'

'Yes, but she didn't take me on. She went out the back door and I went back to my bottles. Layla wasn't one to want comfort when she was upset. I'd never seen her cry before that. Not after, either. I noticed, though, after that, couldn't help it. We were serving a private oil lunch about that time. One of the men at the lunch was watching her. Couldn't take his eyes off her. She was all red and coy.'

'She was pretty. That can't have been unusual.'

'Yes, but the way she was ignoring him was different. She liked to flirt. It was good for tips. I just came away with the sense that she knew him. Somehow.'

'Can you tell me anything about the man?'

'Not much. Salt and pepper hair, maybe late forties. Nice-ish looking.'

'Don't suppose you remember the oil company?'

She shook her head slowly. 'Goodness, what were they called? They were in all the time back then, before the market crashed – shooting days, dinners, lunches.' She rubbed her temples for a moment. 'It might come back to me.'

'Maybe the hotel has records. Thanks Irene. You've been such a help.'

She looks awkward.

'I meant to say. I saw you. In the paper.'

Cal nods vigorously, wanting to spare her – and himself – the discomfort of saying it.

'I'm sorry,' she says.

'That means a lot. Thank you.'

It's strange. He's hidden the truth of his past his whole life, so convinced he'd be tearing himself open every time he mentioned it. Only it's not like that at all. Every time someone acknowledges her, it releases the squeeze, ever so slightly. Margot deserves to be remembered.

CHAPTER FIFTY-FIVE

Cal isn't dressed the part this time. The woman at the hotel reception frowns at his T-shirt and jeans.

'I was hoping to speak to Archie?'

Her lips pinch.

'I will check if Mr James is available.'

There's a younger woman sitting behind the desk doing some paperwork – she smiles conspiratorially at him while the first woman mutters down the phone. Archie is there a moment later, the smile on his face dented only slightly by the inconvenience Cal sees in his eyes. He doesn't care. They do the obligatory handshake, but Cal isn't offered coffee or taken through to the billiard room this time. He half expects to be told to use the tradesmen's entrance. He's experienced this before. People will tell you that they want to help but they don't always mean it.

'So, how can we assist?'

'I wondered if you might have any records from that time – of bookings and events. Maybe starting with the month Layla vanished?'

'Records? For the hotel?'

'We're investigating the possibility that she may have met someone here. A guest.'

Archie rubs his chin, looks regretful, though Cal can't shake the feeling that it's a charade.

'We're on a completely different system now, sorry. None of the old information has been kept.'

'Nothing?'

'No. Sorry not to be able to help.' He shrugs, not seeming in the least bit sorry as far as Cal is concerned.

'What about the old guest comment books?' They swivel to look at the young woman holding a sheaf of paperwork. 'Sorry.' She flushes. 'I couldn't help over-hearing. All the old guest sign-in and comment books are up in the library. Might be worth a try? You never know...'

Archie's eyes narrow briefly. 'What a splendid idea, Ellie.'

'Thank you.' Cal tries to transmit his utter gratitude to Ellie, though he has the feeling that she has enjoyed getting one over on old Archie as much as he has.

'I can take you up there,' she says, her gaze flicking to her boss. 'If that helps?'

'Yes, yes.' Archie waves her through, addressing Cal as he passes. 'If you're sure this is necessary.'

Cal is already following Ellie towards the staircase. 'It's very helpful, thank you.'

The library is small and ancient, sloping wooden floor-boards and what must be the original shelves. It seems to be used as a function room now, though today the tables are bare and the room is cold.

'Thank you,' he says again.

'It's no worry.' Ellie grins, leading him to a shelf full of visitor books. 'I sometimes like to have a nosy. The ones from the bedrooms are best but the main ones do have a lot of names in them.'

She selects one from the middle of the shelf and flicks it to the opening page. 'It's just a question of finding the right era. Which year are you looking for?'

'She went missing in 1986.'

They pull books from the shelves, comparing the start and end dates until eventually Cal holds the two volumes that cross the period he's most interested in.

'I think there might be some old desk diaries in the cupboard too. I can take a look?'

'Would you?'

He helps her pull papers and books from one of the low cupboards. Incredibly, there they are, labelled by year.

'Could I take them away with me, do you think?' He makes a face at her; they both know Archie would insist they stay on the premises.

Ellie grimaces. 'Promise you'll bring them back?'

He nods, tracing his finger across his chest. 'Cross my heart.'

'Well, he didn't say anything about not taking them… so we could just assume?'

'I don't want to get you into trouble.'

Ellie laughs. 'I'll just act dumb. It's how I'm usually treated here so it won't be a stretch for them to believe it.'

Cal hugs the books to his chest. 'I can't tell you how much I appreciate this.'

'I've listened to the first episodes.' Her jovial expression vanishes. 'I'm the age she was back then. I've been imagining her working here. Someone must know what happened to her.'

Cal scuttles from the hotel like a rat with a piece of cheese, afraid Archie will come after the precious books and demand he reads them on the premises. But as soon as he is clear of the estate, he pulls over and calls Irene.

'I've got the guest books from the hotel for the year Layla went missing. If I bring them over, will you take a look at the names, see if anything jogs your memory?'

'No problem. You coming now? I'll put the kettle on.'

The route to Irene's house takes Cal past the road to the stables. He can see a woman in a field with a horse. For a moment he imagines it is Layla. Her lonely figure casts a melancholy image. He can only hope he is getting closer, that the answer is in reach.

CHAPTER FIFTY-SIX

EPISODE SIX: OIL MAN

We're sitting in a sunlit kitchen that belongs to Irene – an old colleague of Layla's. Irene's cat Nina is washing her paws in a beam of light on the floor. On the table in front of us is a box of old reservation diaries. The books are a mess of scribbles, decades-old phone numbers and bookings scrawled in their pages, crossed out, amended. But we now believe Layla could have been in some sort of relationship with a regular visitor to the hotel, so we're poring over these volumes in the hope we can help Irene remember.

We start on the day Layla went missing and work back from there to see if anything jogs Irene's memory. It's a shame this wasn't done thirty-five years ago, but it's too late to go back and change how the police investigation was handled, and it's a miracle we've been able to find these. Luckily, the old names begin to trigger memories.

'I mind on this wedding. They were a total nightmare. The best man was wasted, threw up in the bar and then slated the mother of the bride in the speech. Pure carnage.'

'How about this one? North Sea Extractions?'

'Maybe. But I don't think that's the one I remember.'

We spend all morning flicking through the pages. I'm about to suggest we give up, but then Irene spots something.

'That rings a bell. That company.'

'Is there a person's name?'

'Not there, no. But here they are again. This one has two names.'

We're not going to reveal any of these names at the moment, not until we're sure there is a connection with Layla. However, once we see it, it's easy to find one of the two men's names, repeated frequently. It's possible this is unrelated: Irene says some oil companies did use the hotel a lot for business meetings and lunches. This was right before the oil market crashed and entertaining came to a halt. However, she's sure this company was the one holding a particular lunch she remembers, where Layla seemed to know one of the executives. Could this be the lead we're looking for?

Once we've made a note of all the visits in the months leading up to Layla's disappearance, we decide to check the weeks after she went missing. I turn back to the date Layla vanished. We immediately spot something that seems too much of a coincidence:

'Hang on. He was there that day.'

'Really? I wasn't working that day.'

'We didn't see it before because we didn't have the name. There, look…'

'What does this mean?'

We move forward through the pages, scanning in silence. Then. There it is. A week after Layla disappeared, we find a scored-out event.

'Look, Irene. Here, again. They were due in. I think it says lunch and shooting but it's hard to tell. It's been scribbled out.'

We keep going, turning the pages until we reach the end of the book. What we now know, after all this time, is that once Layla vanished, the oil man didn't come back.

CHAPTER FIFTY-SEVEN

Cal parks on a narrow road only a stone's throw from the River Dee. He watches the house through a gap in the trees – a significant departure from the small cottage on the exposed hillside in which Layla lived. Here, the rich green lawns are tamed, striped from careful mowing, and the grey stones of the imposing house glow in the post-rain light.

Something inside him hums with the feeling that he is on the right track. Though John Knowles has retired from the oil company and moved his influence to the golf course, it was not hard to find him online. Chairman of the club, house on Deeside, fishing rights, river views. Balmoral just down the road.

He sits for two hours before he sees movement. There will only be one chance to ambush him. If he fails, then Knowles will be forewarned and the advantage lost. Eventually, his patience pays off: a man he recognises from photographs crosses the gravel driveway to a gleaming Land Rover Discovery – the same type of car as the one Layla was seen getting into – followed by two spaniels, tails wagging, tongues hanging. The man opens the boot and then squints up at the sky, encourages the dogs into the back. He is tall, in decent shape for his seventies, with grey hair.

Cal sets off down the gravel driveway, warmed by the sun creeping from behind the clouds, adjusting his microphone. Knowles must hear the crunch of his feet, because he turns to face him, the car key dangling from his hand.

'John Knowles?'

The man frowns, his face papered with confident caution. 'Can I help you?'

'My name's Cal Lovett. I'm making a podcast about someone I think you used to know.'

John Knowles stares back at him. Doesn't rush to fill the silence, though Cal is sure he sees a twitch in the man's jaw, a hardening on his face, the disappearance of blood from the skin.

'Can you guess who that might be?'

'I really don't have time for games, Mr Lovett. You're on private property. If some old business associate has got himself mixed up in something untoward that's really his affair.'

It's like that, then, Cal thinks.

'Affair. Interesting choice of word. Have you thought about Layla much, over the years?'

There is a long, slow moment when John Knowles looks at Cal, back at the house and then at Cal again. He can see him trying to calibrate what Cal might know, how to react.

'Have you seen the news, recently? It might not have made it to you; it is an old case, after all.'

Knowles steps towards the car. 'This really isn't a good time.'

'I know about you and Layla.'

John Knowles turns sharply. 'I think you should leave.'

'They haven't released the exact details of where she was found, though. Not yet.'

'I don't know what you think this has to do with me.'

'You used to attend meetings at the hotel. Frequently.'

Knowles looks at him; his face seems greyer, his expression less sure.

'Along with hundreds of other people in my line of business.'

'But they didn't suddenly stop going there.'

'I don't know what you're talking about.' He glances back at the house again.

Cal takes the leap of assumption.

'I know about the waterfall. Did something happen there, John? Did she want something from you that you weren't prepared to give?' The man's skin ghosts beneath his expensive skiing tan. 'Is there somewhere else we could talk? Somewhere more private?'

These are not his usual methods, but the painful energy trapped inside him, the need to act instead of think, pushes him on.

'I don't have anything to say.'

'I just think it would be better if you put across your side of the story.'

'What do you mean, side? I don't have a *side*. When I left Layla at the waterfall, she was fine. More than fine.'

Bingo.

'You must have seen she was missing. If that's true, why didn't you come forward? You must realise it doesn't look good.'

He finds himself glancing at the man's hands as he speaks, wondering what they might have done. Did Layla know what was happening to her?

Words stream from Knowles in a sudden rush. 'Look, I assumed she'd had an accident on the horse. Then the papers suggested she might have run away and I just... I couldn't be seen to be involved with an investigation like that. Layla was a lovely girl, but we weren't going to be...'

'Serious?'

'Exactly.'

'Did she know that?'

Knowles sighs and rubs his head. 'Layla was smart, realistic. I offered her an out and she said she wanted it. She knew what we had wasn't going to be forever.'

'But now they've found her – it seems pretty clear she died there, at the waterfall.'

Confusion furrows the man's brow. He is a good actor, Cal can admit. If you didn't know he was the last one to see Layla alive then you'd almost believe him.

'She can't have done.'

'Could you take me through that day? It would really help.'

John looks shiftily at the house and Cal watches the indecision on his brow cloud into something blunt and unyielding. When he returns his gaze, the hope Cal felt for co-operation ices over.

'No. I want you to leave. Now.'

'Mr Knowles...'

But, without another word, the man climbs into his gleaming car, slams the door and accelerates away from Cal, leaving him alone on the raked gravel.

CHAPTER FIFTY-EIGHT

Cal emails pictures of the extracts from the hotel visitor records to the police, reiterates the testimonies he has that Layla was involved with someone. He waits for news that they have questioned John Knowles, but instead Jean calls to tell him that they have taken Stephen in for questioning. There is a high note in her voice: he can hear the adrenaline and hope, and yet can't give in to it.

He has a horrible feeling the police are using the affair as evidence to mount a case against the chef, and increasingly he finds he can't believe the man killed Layla and left her there all this time, so close to the place he lives and works. He doesn't seem cold and controlled enough to be able to tolerate the reminders, the presence, the drift on the breeze.

DI McKenzie refuses to take his calls and the days roll forward. Stephen is released without charge. Cal lines up his notes, writes and rewrites the script for the next episode, splicing together thoughts and comments from the main players, skirting the edges of what he thinks is the truth but cannot explicitly say, hoping the listeners will draw their own conclusions.

Perhaps it is time for him to pack up and leave, monitor the situation from home, but Cal finds he cannot abandon his post yet. Besides, Chrissie is happy here. Watercolours of the Aberdeenshire landscape hang from every curtain rail. He isn't sure if they are part of her course or not; he doesn't want to ask in case they aren't. He finds himself awed by her unleashed talent, in a similar way he'd been when he met Allie and saw the way she made sense of the world, translating its complexity to paper in a way that makes him feel it, understand it.

The primal washes of greens and greys reflect the countryside around them. She's captured the breadth and depth of the sky, the sense that here you can breathe more freely, that you are smaller, dwarfed by the landscape instead of dominating it. He isn't surprised it has inspired Chrissie – he feels a deep, almost religious connection to these hills, woods and fields.

Every time he thinks of home, the anticipation of the decisions that must be made, the dismantling of his marriage, overwhelms him. He liked his old life, cannot comprehend the thought that it is over and they will have to move to a new phase.

And then there is Margot. He sees her in his dreams, clawing her way from the earth, begging to be found. Are the police doing anything to prove the theory he feels in his bones, the dreaded suspicion that wakes him in the early hours, clammy and breathless, heart churning? The thought of contacting them again drains and paralyses him. So instead he fiddles with the paperwork and the editing, takes long walks with Chrissie that leave his boots caked in mud and his clothes sodden but do little to still the drumming in his brain.

–

He meets Shona for lunch one day, to discuss the episode and any progress being made.

They have barely sat down when his phone starts ringing. It is an unregistered number. He looks at Shona apologetically.

'I should probably take this.'

'Fine, I'll talk to the bread basket.' She lifts a roll and brandishes it at him, makes a show of plunging her face into it in despair. He laughs. It's refreshing that she really doesn't mind.

He's still laughing when he answers, so the voice on the other end of the line takes a moment to register with him and when it does it cuts the laughter like a knife.

'Mr Lovett. It's Detective Foulds.'

'Cal,' he says automatically.

'Are you somewhere we can talk?'

He looks around the cafe, which is full and humming with sound. His whole world stills. Is this the moment? 'Hold on.' He signals to Shona and rises from the table clutching the phone. 'It's about Margot. I need to go outside.'

Sympathy fills her eyes and she nods, gestures for him to go.

'Sorry, what were you saying?' He wishes he had brought his coat out with him: a stiff wind ruffles his hair and he turns his back to it, shelters against the building. Bloody weather.

'I'm sorry to call like this, but we wanted to tell you as soon as we were sure.'

Cal stares at the rich grass in front of him. Each individual blade. He feels his sister's memory like a rush of blood.

'Okay. What have you found?'

'The first thing I should say is that we've taken your accusations about Marc Dubois very seriously. I've put two of my best officers on it and they've been very thorough.'

A small seed of concern shudders inside him. *Come on*, he wants to shout, *get on with it*.

'And?'

'And we are one hundred per cent certain that Marc Dubois did not kill your sister.'

'What?' His voice fails to make a mark on the air, only the slightest squeak.

'We are sure that he was in fact in Ireland at the time.'

'Ireland?' Cal echoes. 'That can't be right. There is no record of him being in Ireland.'

'I can assure you that we've been very careful. We have photographs of him at a country fair the day after your sister went missing. We've had those verified and checked and we are certain he was there.' She pauses. 'We believe he may have attacked some women and girls during that time, but that is confidential for the time being so I must ask you not to repeat it.'

Margot's face flashes into his mind, the clearest image he's ever had. Her face is regretful, sad. Shaken, he pulls himself back to now. To the present outrage.

'You have to be wrong.'

'I can send you the images. We've looked into transportation and there is no way he could have abducted Margot and made it to the fair. We have triple checked everything. I know this may not be a comfort right now, but you've helped us. There are new lines of enquiry, families who may find the answers they need.'

Just not him. Not his family.

The air rushes from Cal. He drops into a crouch as his head spins, the blood rises skywards. Memory floods into his mind and saliva into his mouth. He is there again, in the anonymous room with the swollen version of a myth in front of him. *We're all stuck in the scrapyards of our lives.* He's going to be sick.

It doesn't make any sense. Why else would the notorious killer break his silence for a little-known journalist? Bare his soul? He knew. Cal was sure he knew. A groan flows from him onto the cold earth, a bleak pain. He can hear the detective's voice at the end of the line like it's beneath water, clouded by distance. Cal can't find his way back to the surface. Then, a hand on his back, someone taking the phone.

'He'll call you back. Cal, breathe. It's okay. I've got you.'

Shona's arms are around him, both of them crouched stupidly on the ground. He keeps gasping for air like a beached fish. Thoughts overwhelm him, he can't catch any of them long enough to make sense.

'Sorry.' He keeps saying the word over and over, embarrassed, sorry that Shona has to deal with the breakdown of a man she doesn't even know.

'It's fine. Just catch your breath. You've had a shock.'

He worries that the people in the cafe will be watching from the long glass windows, then he realises his mind is latching on to these tiny details because it can't fathom the bigger truth.

If it wasn't Dubois, then what does that mean? He thinks of that last terrible night, of his father's anger and of Andy's confession, but he cannot process the logical steps. He sucks long breaths of air into his lungs before he turns his head to the side, looks at Shona. Her blue eyes are crinkled with concern.

'I think I can stand up now.'

'Can we do it slowly? My knees have seized.' She smiles, though her eyes are filled with worry.

They ease upwards until they stand facing each other, locked in this awful moment, her hands on his arms, pinning him to the earth in case he spins away on the breeze.

'It wasn't him. It wasn't Dubois.' He can barely manage to say the name.

'Let's get inside. You need a hot drink.'

Numb, he follows her back in, his gaze fixed on the floor and his cheeks burning with the feeling of being watched, though when he looks up everyone appears to be focused on their own conversations or spooning soup into their mouths, tearing bread. Shona deposits him at the table and goes to the counter, comes back with a large pot of tea and two pieces of cake.

'Coffee cake or lemon drizzle?'

He eyes the enormous wedges. 'Either. They both look good.'

'Fine, let's split them.' She hands him a fork. 'Take a bite. Now.'

Cal does as he's told, feels the sugar hit his system. She presses a cup of tea into his hands and he realises they are cold and he is shaking.

'I told the detective you'd call back, later,' she says. Then she waits. She doesn't press him and he thinks disloyally that it wouldn't be the case if Allie was here.

'What the tabloid story didn't say was that I interviewed Dubois right before he died.'

Shona grimaces.

He shakes his head. 'I know. He never gave interviews. Ever. Made a big deal about being a fan of the podcast, having done his research on me. I was... flattered? Is that the right word? But then he… knew things. He knew my real name, he wrote to me, he made me think it was him. Why would he do that? I read all of these horrible details, looked at pictures of his victims, all the time thinking…'

'It sounds as if he knew what he was doing,' Shona says gently.

Cal looks at her in disbelief, still trying to join the dots of the deception.

'I fell for it,' he says eventually, still struggling to believe it.

'Because you're not a monster,' she says.

He takes another sip of the tea, feels the heat returning to his face, his bones.

'Why can't I get my head around this?'

'I think you're asking too much of yourself.'

Cal takes another bite of cake but it crumbles tastelessly in his mouth and he sets the fork down. His hands tremble so he presses his cold fingers between his legs.

'She had an argument with my dad that night. He didn't want her to go out. I think… he hit her.' Cal puts his head in his hands. 'I didn't remember before. He was in the house and I saw him hit her. No wonder she ran out.'

Shona's voice is quiet, tentative. 'And if she was upset, she'd have been more vulnerable, I guess.'

Cal feels tears snaking down his cheeks. He wipes them away, shakes his head.

'That's not all. I found out the other day that Margot's boyfriend did see her that night. They had an argument and he left her by the road in the middle of nowhere. All this time and he kept that to himself when it could have helped. I thought I knew him. Turns out I don't know him at all. Christ, he used to take me on days out to look for her body. What if he did something to her and it was all an act? What does that make me?'

'You were a child. It wasn't your fault. It isn't now.'

Cal fixes his gaze on hers, holding himself afloat with her rational strength, but in his head he revisits the years, the distant relationship he had with his parents, the closeness he has always felt to Andy. What does any of it mean?

'You don't need to solve this now.' Shona reaches for his hand and he struggles like a drowning man for the surface.

It is only when they walk out to the car park, emptied of its lunchtime rush, long into the afternoon, that he remembers the purpose of the lunch.

'I haven't asked. Is there any news on Layla?'

She steps back towards him and he can see from her expression that there is.

'I don't know – after the call you've just had...'

'It's fine, Shona. What do you have?'

'DNA,' she says. 'Fibres with two profiles aside from hers, but we don't know whose. They aren't on the system. It's a bloody miracle we got them to be honest. Keith McKenzie is calling the stable boy in for testing, the boyfriend has been asked too.'

Cal takes a breath, uses it to anchor himself back in Layla's history, the developments he hasn't even told her parents yet. 'I have another name.' He likes the way she tilts her head towards him in interest. He feels the inexplicable urge to reach out and touch her so he clasps his fingers behind his back in case they decide to act without his permission.

'Who's that, then?'

'She was seeing someone, one of the guests. He lives on Deeside.'

A raise of the eyebrows.

'You really should tell McKenzie.'

'I have tried, but he's ignoring me.'

Shona snorts. 'Typical.' Then: 'You don't happen to have any of his DNA I suppose?'

'Not on me, no.'

'Shame.'

Her car is closer and by the time he reaches his, she is twenty metres away. 'Shona,' he calls.

'Yes?'

'What would happen if I could get it?'

She waits and he thinks she will leave without answering.

'It wouldn't be admissible.'

He shakes his head, dislodging the notion. 'No.'

She shrugs. 'But at least you'd know.'

He watches her go, a hand raised briefly, the blur of her face and a sense of loss, like something inside him is slipping away and waking up all at the same time.

CHAPTER FIFTY-NINE

Marilena has taken Chrissie shopping in the local town. The farmhouse is mercifully quiet. Cal takes the stairs slowly, using his phone to check his email, to see if there is news.

Detective Foulds has emailed him as she promised. He swings open the door to his room and sits in the sunlight that falls through the high window, downloads several files, feeling waves of exhaustion, the relentless fate of those left in the dark. There is still a possibility, he thinks. Maybe he will see something in the pictures that they haven't.

He clicks on the images first, colour photographs in 1980s definition – a man at a fair on a busy street, thick hair to his shoulders, curling a little and highlighted by the sun, the smile on his familiar face belying the devastation he would wreak. It is him. Undeniably.

In one of the images, Dubois clasps a mini-skirted girl to his side. Cal wonders, with a dropping sensation in his gut, if she grew to be a woman or if she is one of the new lines of investigation. Behind them, a banner on scaffolding proclaims the Puck Fair open.

He stares at the photographs for ages, pores over each tiny detail, magnifying them until the sense is lost in the pixels. He can't find anything.

Cal pictures Margot by the side of a dark road, stumbling into the path of something worse than the evening's arguments. His mouth floods with saliva at the thought that it wasn't Dubois. Someone else has to be responsible for whatever happened to her that night. It is torture imagining the possibilities. His sister. Loved. Missed.

He can see why the police are certain. Who knows where this will lead, which missing women and girls can be laid to rest? Just not his. Not yet. Not now.

Cal's hands shake as he closes the attachments, composes a reply to the detective, fails to compose himself. When he is done, he sets his phone on the desk. Stupefied by the heat of the sun through the attic window, he stares at it for a moment, trying to comprehend the information, the rewriting of his history.

Then he scrapes back the chair and reaches for his keys. He has to get out, he can't breathe inside.

–

Cal parks in the place where they co-ordinated the search, strides up the same pathway, driving his feet into the ground, following the grooves that water has carved in the path as it runs from the hills. His feet drum a rhythm as he goes. *Margot, Margot, Margot.*

He always loved the delicacy of his sister's name. It is a further tragedy that the word became taboo in their house. Her memory hovered around them when she didn't come home. It made the air thick, filled the silences around the dinner table as the days turned to weeks then months. It whispered in his ears at bedtime and when he woke in the morning. But they never said her name, just *her* or *she*, because they all knew who they meant, and every time they heard it, cuts reopened in their hearts, wounds that barely had a chance to close over.

It wasn't Dubois. Then who? A terrible thought sneaks into his head. Does his mother know? Has she known all this time? Where is his sister? Will he ever know the answer to that question? Cal powers upwards, thighs screaming and breath heaving. When he reaches a turn in the path and the toe of his boot hits a rock, he stumbles, falls to his knees.

'Fuck you!' He shouts the words to the trees, the heather, the grey rocks slashed with gold. 'Fuck you Dubois, you fucking arse-wipe.'

Disbelief still sears through him. He can't even cry. Only a dry sob as he pushes himself up from the path and ploughs across open ground. There is only one person he can really talk to about this. One person who was there at the same time. But he doesn't know if she's ever going to speak.

He sinks onto a rock by the path, miles of empty countryside around him. Maybe it's time to try.

He dials her number and the wind whips around his ears.

'Hello?' The voice, frail and questioning, grates on him.

'Mum. It's me.' She isn't used to social calls from him, so she waits, instinctively knowing there is more. 'The detectives called me today. The ones looking into Margot. They say it wasn't him. It wasn't Dubois.'

A long exhale of breath precedes her sharp tone.

'Well, that's good.'

'Is it, though? Is it, Mum? At least then we'd know for sure. We could bury her.'

She makes a tsking noise that irritates him even more. She never held him, he realises suddenly and with a desperate sadness. After Margot went, she never held him while he cried. The dark thoughts creep back in.

He looks up at the clouds scudding across the sky, gathers himself.

'Do you already know, Mum? What happened.'

'What are you talking about? How could I possibly know?'

'I don't know,' he says, miserably, backtracking, afraid now to know the answer to his question.

Her confusion and upset floats into his mind, muttering from the other end of the phone, before words explode from her – emotion pent up inside for decades.

'Why do you hate me so much, Cal? My own son? What have I ever done?' Cal. Not Christopher. She called him Cal.

'I don't hate you, Mum, I just...'

'What? Spit it out. I don't know how many years I have left in me.'

Cal takes in more shuddering breaths, stares at the lump of pinkish stone that glitters in the light.

'Was it Dad?' he croaks, finally, tears spilling down his cheeks.

A sharp intake of breath.

'No. No, not your dad. He was devastated, he could never...'

'You never suspected him?'

'Not once.'

'But he hit her.' Cal sobs, nine years old once more and at the top of the stairs. 'I saw him hit her.'

'Is this what you've thought? All this time?'

The wonder in her voice.

289

'I just thought, if it was Dubois, then…'

'Then it couldn't have been your father.' Understanding clicks between them. Cal tries to stop crying but he can't.

'It wasn't him, I promise you. He loved her. He was too heavy-handed, and he lived with that for the rest of his life. He blamed himself. If he hadn't hit her, would she have gone out? He never forgave himself. *I* have never forgiven myself.'

Cal remembers the silences, the void, the greyness that never left his father's eyes. But his mother isn't finished. It's like he's woken something in her.

'But we never understood why you stayed close to that man.'

She spits venom into the words.

'Who? Andy?'

'It must have been him. Your father and I were sure of it. All this time and you kept in touch with him.'

'You never liked him.'

'He wasn't good enough for her.'

'I didn't know you thought that,' he says. 'I was only a kid. I didn't have anyone else. I didn't think it was him, but then he went to the papers and… now I don't know.'

There is a long silence. He can't be sure, but he thinks his mother is crying too.

'It ruined everything,' she whispers eventually. 'Took everything from us. Not just Margot.'

Hearing her say her daughter's name is so beautiful and painful.

'You still have me, Mum,' he says. 'And Chrissie.'

'Do I, though?'

'You will,' he says. 'I'll make it different. I'm sorry.'

Cal looks up and in the distance sees two horses galloping across a field below, tails raised. Tears still fill his voice. 'All this doubting people, suspecting. Are we ever going to know?'

'I think maybe I'll go to my grave without the answer,' she says. 'I only hope she's waiting for me.'

—

Cal retraces his steps down the hill, wrung out and tear stained. He makes it back to the empty bed and breakfast but his mind is broken. He cannot think what to do. When will Chrissie be back? Struck by overwhelming exhaustion, he retreats to the bed, draws back the covers and crawls beneath them. *Only for a moment*, he tells himself. Then he'll get up, make a cup of tea. But he has no choice in the matter: his eyes are heavy and his body tends towards oblivion, like he is sinking through sand.

CHAPTER SIXTY

Cal's body shuts down for the rest of the day and all of the night. When he wakes it is light and he feels fragile and hungry, like he's been ill. He showers, then staggers stiff-limbed and ravenous to the kitchen, where Chrissie laughs at his dazed expression.

'Epic sleep, Dad. Way to go!'

Marilena slides a plate of cooked breakfast in front of him, studying him as he thanks her. 'Eat,' she says. 'You will fade away.'

It isn't hard. He feels washed out, in need of sustenance. He wonders how his mother is doing, feels the alien desire to call and check in. Maybe he will, he can imagine it now.

-

He needs to keep a brave face for Chrissie; his energy, the sadness he feels over Margot, needs to go somewhere. If he could just find the tiniest ledge of control to cling to. Then he realises that there is somewhere he can direct his efforts. The next episode release date is looming and his conversation with Shona floats over him until it forces an idea. It's good journalistic practice to offer a right of reply.

He makes the call, his hand trembling a little with adrenaline.

'I've got nothing to say to you.' Knowles' voice is low and angry.

'It's just, if you were going to be named in the next episode…' He lets the thought hang there. The lawyers have said he can't name Knowles on such inconclusive evidence but technically he hasn't said he will; he's just leaving a gap in which the man can make his own assumptions. He could feel bad about this subterfuge, but then he thinks of Layla, of Jean and Tam sitting at their small kitchen table laid for two, and he contrasts it with the grand home on the banks of the Dee.

'I didn't do anything to Layla.' Knowles speaks as if his teeth are gritted.

'I'm not saying you did.' Cal uses his most reasonable voice. 'But you saw her on the last day she was alive, and I think it looks bad if you don't make some sort of comment, however brief.'

'I see.'

'Look,' Cal says, into the crack of hope. 'It would look better if you made a statement. Get out in front of it. I'm not trying to cause trouble for you.'

The words slide from his lips and he buries the knowledge that that is exactly what he is trying to do.

—

Cal drives to the cafe Knowles has selected and parks on a side street. Chrissie has insisted on being along for the ride. She is watching him. He feels her eyes on him constantly, assessing, worrying.

'I could sit at another table,' she tries, though the request is half-hearted. He has already said an absolute 'no' to her coming in.

'You're staying in the car. No arguments.'

She sighs and flops back against the passenger seat. The glimpse of the sulky teenager is an utter relief.

Cal chooses a table tucked into the back in an alcove, away from the window. He glances at his watch. Knowles is late. Is this a false promise, a delaying tactic? It wouldn't be the first time, but he'd thought maybe there was a chance. Some tiny chink of emotion on the man's face when he first mentioned Layla's name makes Cal think Knowles was more attached to Layla than he has admitted – that he has regrets. After thirty minutes, he reaches into his pocket for his wallet but stops abruptly. He's there: crossing the street, head down and shoulders hunched.

Cal orders coffee for them both. John Knowles seems older and smaller, the Lord of the Manor less impressive out of his own environment.

'So.' He lays his hands on the table. Cal notes the wedding ring – a shining band of gold. 'I have never spoken to anyone about this. But I had absolutely nothing to do with Layla's death.'

'Tell me how you knew her.'

'We met at the hotel – she brought a breakfast tray to my room and then I bumped into her when I was running in the grounds. I won't lie. I was away from home a lot back then; my first marriage was pretty much over. Layla was very beautiful. More than that, she had something... magnetic about her.'

'Go on.'

'We saw each other whenever I was passing that way – only over a few months, but long enough.' He shrugs. 'I know it seems like I was taking advantage of her. It really wasn't like that. Layla was wild – and I mean that in a good way.' His eyes flash with memories Cal can only imagine. 'She wouldn't do anything she didn't want to.'

'What happened that day at the waterfall?'

'I wanted to see her. We couldn't meet in the open – too many people watching, she wouldn't take the risk.' He shrugs. 'I didn't mind, really. All the sneaking around was… exciting. So, we agreed to meet at the waterfall.'

'And?'

'She rode in and we spent some time together.' He looks meaningfully at Cal and an image of tangled limbs and cold water assails him. 'I had a meeting to get back for. I left her there after we dressed. She was untying the horse from a tree when I looked back. That's the last time I saw her.'

Disbelief rolls through Cal. People tell themselves stories all the time. They use them to make sense of the world. What had Layla demanded that he wasn't willing to give? What had he done to ensure her silence? Wasn't it so much more likely that in that isolated spot he'd lost his temper, put his hands to her throat to quiet her, silenced her forever?

'So, who strangled her?'

'I don't know.' Knowles won't meet his eye and his fingers tighten on the cup. 'I didn't see anyone else.'

Cal thanks him, the words tying knots in his tongue on their way out of his mouth. He is hyper-aware of the crockery on the table, the waitresses hovering nearby.

Knowles smiles tightly. 'I trust we can consider this business concluded,' he says as he stands, dismissing the conversation as well as Layla's importance, her right to justice. 'It was a long time ago and raking through it all won't bring her back.' Cal tilts his head, neither confirming not denying this fact. 'I raise a lot of money, you know. For charity. I do a lot of good.'

The self-righteousness takes his breath away. Cal knows all about his Rotary Club activities, the huge donations he makes, as if a few good deeds can cancel out a terrible past.

'These things,' Cal says, his face turned up to the man, his fingers clasped around his own mug. 'They come back to haunt you.'

Knowles makes no acknowledgement. The door swings and he is gone. Cal glances around, then quickly extracts the evidence bag from his pocket. He tips the mug into the bag and seals it on his lap, all the while waiting for someone to challenge him. Relieved that the precious evidence makes it into his rucksack, he gathers his things and deposits a ten-pound note on the table.

He feels a twinge of guilt at the underhand tactics. This is not the way he likes to work. But Jean and Tam deserve to know. He is not going home without answers.

–

He calls Shona from the car park outside her building and a few minutes later she emerges from a side door, hair pinned with a biro and wearing a white lab coat.

'You did it.'

He holds out the bag.

'Are you sure about this?'

Their fingers touch as she reaches for it. Cal feels a tiny shock of static, like he's been stung.

'Let me worry about that.'

Her eyes meet his and he knows she felt it too.

CHAPTER SIXTY-ONE

EPISODE SEVEN: ARRESTED

'She was alive when I left her there.'

At the falls in the woods, the water crashes off the hills, ice cold and transparent, dropping thirty feet to a deep pool studded with rocks. Unknown even to many locals, it's a dramatic and melancholy spot, though perhaps it is made so by the knowledge of what occurred here.

We now know that this beautiful clearing in the woods was where Layla had arranged to meet John Knowles that day. Knowles, a wealthy Deeside man who made his money in Aberdeen's hitherto thriving oil industry, was a regular visitor to the hotel in which Layla worked – a popular location for meetings and shooting events. During one of these visits to the hotel, the two crossed paths and began a relationship in secret. Layla's then-boyfriend chef Stephen says he knew nothing of this, though he suspected Layla was seeing someone else:

'She was distant in those last months, didn't want to meet up as much. I knew she was seeing someone. Once, I thought I caught sight of her with a guest on a path in the estate, but I was never sure.'

As we reported earlier in the series, cadaver dogs found Layla's remains only a few metres from the waterfall, finally ending the decades-long search for answers. In the process of making this podcast, Layla's parents Jean and Tam Mackie have been through the wringer. The shock of finding their daughter, knowing for sure she had been murdered and her body abandoned, has taken its toll. A few weeks ago, Tam was hospitalised for a heart attack – it's no coincidence this happened while we were recording this podcast, raking through painful events.

Fortunately, Tam is now at home making a recovery.

'It's been so long.' That's Tam – speaking from a chair that looks out on the hills in which his daughter vanished thirty-five years ago, only a few miles from where her body was found. 'I just want to know what happened to her before I die.'

Jean – a small woman whose diminutive stature belies her strength – is sitting next to her husband.

'We want to put her to rest. That's all we ever really wanted. We can do that now.'

They can do that because this week John Knowles, now in his seventies, was arrested and charged with Layla's murder after police took a DNA sample that matched one found on Layla's remains.

In this episode, we explain how chance comments led to the discovery of a relationship that had been hidden so long and ask, how did police miss vital clues at the time of Layla's death?

CHAPTER SIXTY-TWO

Cal pauses the playback of the recording. He has finished the final episode and it is scheduled to go out this evening. Sarah is delighted with the recent turn of events. It is rare to have such a neat end to a true crime series; national paper stories are planned for tomorrow, features in Sunday's supplements. He has everything he wanted. Except one thing. He slips his headphones off, frowns at the rain outside the window.

'You okay, Dad?' Chrissie looks up from the corner armchair, setting her textbook on her blanket-covered lap, her feet nestled beneath her. It is cold today.

He nods. Chews his lip.

'Fine, love, thanks.'

But that isn't true. Something is nudging at his brain, a feeling of apprehension and discomfort. It's hard to disentangle it from his renewed grief over Margot, which sweeps in without warning, a harsh weather front. He has refused to talk to Andy. He no longer knows what to trust, what to believe.

He shakes his head to dislodge the creeping feeling of unease. Tonight is a celebration of a sort – they are meeting for some drinks in the local pub after the podcast airs. Shona will be there, Irene, Jean and Tam may pop in, though he isn't sure – the news of Knowles' arrest, dispelling their mistaken belief that Stephen was the killer, has floored them. He knows how they feel. He keeps turning his own memories over in his mind, trying to create a plausible theory, failing.

Tomorrow there will be a memorial for Layla in the woods so at least he will see them then. The minister from the local chapel will say a few words and Cal hopes this will be a helpful release for Tam and Jean. The funeral will follow later, but they were adamant that they wanted to have Cal at this ceremony and so it has been arranged before he and Chrissie leave for home.

He turns his attention back to the transcript, running over the key moments. There are frustrations, the second DNA profile for one. He had expected it to match Stephen's profile, but so far Shona hasn't been able to get the result she needs and Stephen has been asked for a second sample. He hopes tonight's episode will mean the chef can live his life again, hold his head high.

Ultimately, the police are happy that they've got their man. Knowles is in the inside of a police cell, instead of lunching on Deeside and enjoying the golf course. There is no way of taking back the last thirty-five years of freedom but his fall from grace offers some satisfaction.

In the early evening, he and Chrissie go downstairs to listen to the podcast in Marilena's kitchen. She has invited some friends over and the atmosphere is mercurial and expectant. Cal feels eyes on him, watching for his reactions.

He nurses a cold glass of wine, lets Chrissie have a small glass and picks at the bowls of crisps Marilena has laid out. He is fond of her, so grateful for the way she has drawn Chrissie into her home and offered no-nonsense comfort. The transformation in his daughter is incredible. He looks at her now, chatting to these women, her skin glowing, the shadows from beneath her eyes gone, and he knows it was right to bring her here, to take her away from the pain. He hopes the break will be enough, that when she is back in her own environment, she will be able to start a new school, a new life, without the past hanging over her.

He has spoken to Allie. She's going to stay in the house for now, keep things normal for Chrissie. He's so often on the road, but he thinks he might stay with his mother for a little while, just to give them space. Deep down, they both know this is it. All that is left is to soften the landing.

When there is a squeal of excitement and he hears his own voice from the speaker, Cal shudders and slips out of the back door into the garden. He knows every word, can't bring himself to witness other reactions. There is a bench at the foot of Marilena's garden that overlooks the fields and he makes his way there, perches on the damp slats. The long grasses around it make him think of the scrapyard.

He is in a thoughtful mood but determined not to give in to sadness this evening. He sips his glass of wine in a silent toast to the victims and manages to hold them in his mind together: those found and those still lost. It bothers him that so much time is spent on their killers. He knows he is part of that problem.

'What are you hiding from?' He startles and Shona laughs. 'Your daughter said I'd find you out here. Do you want some privacy?'

Cal shakes his head.

'Not from you.'

She picks her way across the lawn, a glass of wine in one hand and a bottle in the other.

He steals a glance at her as she sits next to him and refills his glass. She looks different – her hair is styled, she's wearing lipstick. He notices but it doesn't matter. He likes her either way. She touches her glass to his.

'Tough few months?'

'That's for sure.'

He meets her eyes and he can see the questions he has, reflected in her.

'You're leaving after the memorial, then?'

He nods. How can he explain to her that everything inside him is crying out to him to stay? That just sitting next to her makes him feel calmer than he can remember feeling for most of his adult life.

But then, he can see that he doesn't need to explain. They understand each other perfectly. They sit a hair's breadth apart and stare out at the hills. He feels comforted.

'I need to come back and climb some of these,' he says.

'These are small fry. You need to go a bit further west, into the Highlands, out to Skye. It'll take your breath away.'

'I'd like that.' He takes a slurp of his wine and forces the courage upwards. 'Things are bit complicated in my life at the moment. But if I were to come back, in a few months, would you be up for going there with me?'

She smiles and he finds himself bewitched by the creases at the side of her eyes, unable to look away from her.

She shrugs. 'I daresay.'

He nudges her, laughing. 'That will have to do.'

CHAPTER SIXTY-THREE

LAYLA, 1986

Layla guides Ruby through the trees, her body warm from the gallop across the hill. The horse twists beneath her as they edge closer and, from her vantage point, she sees John framed by the water tumbling down the rocks, his back to her as he stares at the spray. The horse whickers when she dismounts and he turns then, studies her seriously, raises a hand. She is so relieved the tension between them has passed.

There is something about this place that calls darkness and secrecy to mind. It is cold and wild, protected from the light even on the warmest days, and those are scarce. As she looks down, she feels a shadow, a strange fore-boding, but it passes like a cloud across the sun.

She secures the reins to a tree and scrambles down the rocks to him, conscious of his eyes on her, the feel of her body as she moves, the way something powerful in him sucks her close. It is an alien emotion for her to want to go to him; she is so used to pushing people away. The rocks are thick with springy green moss, watered by the endless spray where the falling river hits the plunge pool and bounces up again.

He catches her hand as she slides from the last rock, pulls her close, cradles her head as he kisses her.

'Found you,' he whispers. His hands slide beneath her jumper and she shudders with pleasure at the touch.

'I found *you*,' she points out, but the words distort beneath their lips and it doesn't matter. On impulse, Layla steps back and pulls her jumper and T-shirt over her head in one movement. Her eyes fixed on him, she slips out of her riding boots and jodhpurs, feels her toes sink into the soft ground. He waits. She loves that he waits, that he has that control. The boys she is used to rush to meet her, acting like she should be glad of their desperation. In truth, it only makes her despise them.

John steps forward and runs a finger slowly from her collarbone to her heart, tugging at her bra until she reaches back and unhooks it so it falls from his fingers. With one hand, he slips her underwear to her ankles and she steps free. Layla is naked, slick with spray, her chest rising and falling beneath his hands, his lips.

She loses all sense of time and all self-consciousness, safe in the cocoon of the rocks by the falls, cushioned by the mosses, the leaves that litter the ground. She grips him close to her, relishing the waves of pleasure and the sense of him being in her power. It overwhelms her, as if she has stepped into another world with him.

Afterwards they huddle together in his coat, both reluctant to leave, though he has to get back for a meeting and she is conscious of the horse tied to the tree, impatient and restless. Layla feels the opposite – an odd sort of peace washing over her. For once, her mind is quiet.

'I might know someone,' he says unexpectedly. 'He has a riding stables, show jumping. It's quite an operation. Maybe he needs some help. We could talk to him.'

'Really?'

'He owes me a favour. It would mean moving, though.' He traces a line on her cheek. 'Away from here.'

Layla dips her chin, takes a breath and a mental leap. He's finally asking her. Could she leave her parents, her life? After this afternoon it seems less of a decision. She'll do it, go with John, be with him, form a life.

'Yes. Call him.'

He seems surprised. Had he not expected her to agree?

'Where would we live?' she asks when he pauses to admire her, stroke her hair from her face.

His face knots in confusion, caution slides into his eyes. He doesn't pull away but his hands loosen their grip at the same second she realises she has it wrong.

'Layla...'

Warmth blooms on her cheeks. Her mind spins in embarrassment and pain.

'Oh, no, right, of course.'

He kisses her on the forehead, softens his tone, like he's talking to a child.

'I'd still like to see you, of course... if we can.'

She makes herself look him in the eye, smile, nod. How could she have been naive enough to think this was some sort of proposal? That it ever could be.

'There are lodgings at the stables... Layla, are you all right?'

'Yes!' Her laugh echoes from the rocks, sharp and insistent. 'It sounds perfect. You should go, you'll miss your meeting.' She steps back, sliding a little on the rocks, catching herself in time, retreating. 'I'll see you soon.'

She desperately needs him to leave so she can drop the mask. He gazes at her a moment.

'I'll call you later.'

It takes all she has, but she smiles.

'Bye, John.'

She doesn't want to watch him walk away. Focuses instead on Ruby, who is shaking her head up and down, her bit and bridle jangling. When she looks back, he is gone.

CHAPTER SIXTY-FOUR

CAL

Jean holds the crook of Cal's elbow as they proceed to the waterfall, less steady on her feet than the day she paced the moors with him and Mel, hoping to find her daughter. She seems to have used up all her reserves of energy. The sky is a clear-eyed blue, some consolation after days of rain. Tam so desperately wanted to come, but he had a bad night.

Behind him, Shona is walking with Chrissie and a small delegation of hotel workers, who have been corralled by Irene. He is surprised to see Archie James has bothered to join them, pristine red cords and clean wellies marking him out as a man who usually eschews the outdoors. Perhaps Cal has been unfair to judge him the way he has. But he notes that Archie keeps himself separate from the people who work for him. He has also come empty-handed, while all the others carry flowers to lay by the pool. There must be fifty people. He scans the faces, sees Bridget among them, but not Jim.

He looks down at Jean again and she grips his arm, tries to smile. Her face seems older but also smoother, the light catching the difference. The relief of knowing, he supposes. She has asked Chrissie to paint them a picture of the falls, so his daughter carries her art supplies with her, ready to capture the place as a memorial when everyone has gone.

Last night's episode has received a rapturous reception from fans and the national paper coverage today has been glowing. The success has been eclipsed, though, by the news that fellow inmates attacked John Knowles in the early hours, beating him so badly he is now handcuffed to a bed in Aberdeen Royal Infirmary with a punctured lung. Cal feels the raw sting of the consequences, a chain of events he unwittingly set in motion.

Even the attack hasn't induced Knowles to admit responsibility. Cal can only hope that, as the trial looms and the man realises that his life has crossed into another phase, he will choose to speak. But then again, some people are good at keeping secrets, and this is one that he has already kept for thirty-five years.

When they reach the waterfall, they form a semicircle on the ridge above, looking down on the water. It is louder than usual today, the flow full because of the recent rainfall; they strain to hear the words the minister speaks of the lost daughter. The service is brief yet beautiful, the congregation sheltered by the trees.

When the prayers are spoken, Cal feels a sudden yearning for Margot, the past crowding in around him. Unsettled, he looks for Shona, catches her eye across the group. She is sombre, but he senses the familiar charge between them and is bolstered by her presence. Chrissie's gaze is on the water, her artist's eye lost in the tumble of foam over rock.

'Layla's life on earth was too short,' the minister finishes. 'Today we remember her as she was and ask that justice is done in her name so that her parents may find peace.'

The minister crosses to Jean and shakes her hand, holding it in the two-handed grip that all churchmen seem to have perfected. Then she stands apart, reading the messages on the bouquets of flowers that have been laid. The rest of the crowd whisper in hushed tones, unsure if they should stay or go.

Over by the trees, Chrissie unfolds the easel she has carried, setting out her paints. Cal makes his way round to her. He sees Archie close by, shifting from foot to foot, his hands in his pockets, clearly desperate to leave.

'Lovely service,' Archie says to Cal.

'It was.' He smiles politely before turning to Chrissie.

'I'm going to walk Jean back to the car.' She is already sketching some lines on the canvas they bought together yesterday. 'I can come back for you after that. How long do you think you need?'

'Um, I'm not sure.'

Archie interjects before Cal has a chance to reply.

'Your daughter is welcome to take the easier path to the hotel and wait in the drawing room while they call a taxi, when she's finished.'

'That would work, Dad,' Chrissie says as she mixes colours. 'I just need to get the basics done here. I'll probably be done before you can get back anyway.'

Cal knows he is being irrational, not wanting to leave Chrissie in this place, with its history – as if trees can hold darkness.

'You sure?'

'Yes, fine,' she says, only half listening. He can see she is already lost, her mind on the paints.

As he leaves the clearing, he raises a hand to Archie, but the man has perched himself on a rock and is staring into the waters. Cal glances to where the other hotel workers are bidding goodbye to Jean, and realises the hotelier is deliberately waiting so that he can avoid walking back with the lower orders. He swallows his distaste.

–

It takes a long time to get back to where they have parked. Parking at the hotel would have made more sense, but Jean was adamant that she didn't want to go anywhere near the chef or his cottage. Off the hook for murder, Stephen is not forgiven for his violence.

Jean is slow, tired by the exertion and the emotion. They stop to rest several times. It is a relief to settle her into one of their neighbours' cars. The community has rallied to look after her and Tam. As Cal reaches to close the door, Jean grabs his hand. She squeezes it so tightly that the bones crack.

'Thank you.'

She fixes her eyes on his. It almost breaks him to see her gratitude. This is their goodbye for now.

'I'll be back up to see you soon,' he says. 'I promise.'

'You bring that girl of yours.'

'I will.'

He slams the door, watching as the car pulls away and Jean flops back, finished.

–

Getting everyone sorted has taken so long that he assumes Chrissie is probably done by now, on her way to the hotel. Perhaps he can intercept her. He scans the remaining cars, eager to speak to Shona, but then notices Irene waiting for him. She crosses the road, the tip of her nose pink, her eyes watery.

'You did it.'

She leans in and gives him a quick, tight hug.

'I couldn't have done it without you.'

Irene shakes her head.

'Too little, too late. But I'm glad we were able to piece it together.'

Cal feels emotional, knowing he is only the conduit for the truth. He nods towards the line of trees in the distance.

'It all came together, I suppose. In so many little ways. Even your boss was helpful. If he hadn't let me look at those old reservation books, we couldn't have worked it out.'

Irene's smile withers. The look in her eye makes something loosen, a swooping, falling sensation.

'What is it?'

'Nothing. It's just odd, that's all. That *he* would help.'

'I suppose? People generally want to help when they can.'

'No, I just mean, well, he hated Layla.'

Cal frowns, confused. 'He only took over the hotel five years ago.'

Irene shakes her head as if she is trying to dislodge something stuck.

'He knew her back then, though. He worked here for a brief spell when he was a teenager. He was the one I told you about – the debagging.' She swallows. 'I thought I told you it was him.'

Cal stares at Irene, his mind churning. What does it matter? It's all done now. But something inside him whispers a warning.

'No, you never said.'

'I'm sorry. I was just so ashamed of the way we behaved that day. I thought I did, but… him coming back. I've tried to put it out of my mind, to be honest. Like it didn't happen.'

'It's fine.' He tries to reassure her, unsettled but attempting to conceal it. Irene has done so much to help, after all. 'He still made a difference.'

As he waves at Irene, Cal thinks of the broken man in the hospital bed. The killer, in the place he should be. All the same, a terrible lurching dread sneaks into his body. He pivots on the spot, thoughts rushing, trying to slow them down and think clearly.

'That went well…' Shona's voice fades as she registers his expression. 'Cal?'

He forces himself to focus on her.

'I just found out something, from Irene. About Archie James, the hotelier.'

Her forehead creases. 'What?'

'He knew Layla. She did something to him and he hated her for it, but he's never even mentioned that he met her.' He scratches his head, trying to remember clearly. 'More than that. I'm sure he's gone out of his way not to tell me.'

'We've got Knowles,' Shona says. But he can feel her uncertainty.

'But Knowles isn't admitting it. What if…'

Their eyes meet. Shona's mouth forms a grim line. Neither of them wants to say it. The second profile.

Cal's voice rises in panic. 'I left him in the woods with Chrissie.'

'What?'

'She stayed to paint, and he was still there when I left.'

'I'm sure she's fine. We can go back for her.'

'Shit, Shona. Am I being ridiculous? I can't tell any more. I can't think. I don't know what to do.'

It's like he is nine years old again. Fear folds around him and he can't breathe.

'Can you call her?'

He shakes his head, hysteria bursting free.

'She doesn't have her phone. I have her phone.'

She's vulnerable. He knows this, and yet he's left her defenceless. What the fuck has he done?

Shona puts her hands on his arms, anchoring him. 'She's probably already at the hotel. Or he is. I'll drive there now. If she isn't there, I can walk down that path. You go the way we came and then we can't miss them.'

'Okay.'

Her words drift after him but he doesn't hear them. He's already running.

CHAPTER SIXTY-FIVE

LAYLA, 1986

'Okay, Ruby, steady girl.'

Layla unloops the reins from the branch and digs around in her pocket for a mint. The horse crunches it and nudges her for more, the distinctive clean smell spins around them. Out of the gorge and away from the fall, her head throbs with thoughts again, as if the fairy-spell of calm happiness has been broken.

But then she hears a branch snap further up the pathway. A loud crack as she is swinging her leg over the horse's back. John returning, unable to leave her, abandoning his meeting and his responsibilities, changing his mind? She feels a strange sort of rush, sudden faith in her ability to lure him to her.

But it isn't John who appears from the foliage. Disbelief races across her mind.

'What the fuck are you doing here?'

The horse skitters at the harshness in her tone and she draws the reins in tighter with one hand, patting and calming her with the other.

'It's interesting what you see in the woods.'

'Have you been watching me, like a Peeping Tom? That's probably as close as you'll ever get to a girl.'

She infuses her tone with disdain, but Layla feels rage travelling through her limbs at the thought he's been watching her, naked and moaning, bent over the rocks by the falls, abandoning herself in a way she never does with anyone. That he has been getting off on her. Her face flares with heat and horror.

'I've seen more than enough.' He throws his head back, miming her ecstasy. 'John, John...' His laugh is caustic, burning into her brain.

'Fuck off.'

But he doesn't. He advances towards her, a spasm of hatred on his face. The horse skips her steps, backing up and weaving, spooked by the sudden movement and the malevolence in the air.

'What are you doing?' Her voice is tight and high with panic.

He lunges for the reins and Ruby rears.

A moment of suspense. Rich colour all around her.

She never falls, has the strongest seat in the stables, but as Ruby thrusts away from him, Layla's shoulder hits a low-hanging branch, unsteadying her. Confused and ambushed, she feels herself plummeting, her foot tangled in the stirrup. She cries out as the horse bolts and the elastic of the safety stirrup fails to snap. Panic overwhelms her; she strikes a tree and finally feels the stirrup give way at the same time something in her leg cracks. She screams at the searing pain, nausea striking like lightning, black spots in her eyes.

She lies, dazed and overcome, on the damp ground, listening to the sound of Ruby thrashing in panic, colliding with branches and trees in her desperation to get away.

Layla's shoulder is raw and scraped, her leg pulses in agony. She hears the wheezing gasps for breath, lying flat on her back, and realises the sounds are coming from her. The roaring in her ears is indistinguishable from the sound of the water. All she can see is a thick canopy of leaves above her, the writhing branches twisted and black.

Then a face, over hers.

Layla draws in a proper breath and tries to sit but he pushes her back down with his foot.

'Get off.' The words come ghost-like from her mouth. Confusion courses through her, mingles with the hatred. She needs to get to Ruby – the mare will run for home and the stables, she guesses, miles away. She'll be terrified.

He straddles her and she gasps for air as his weight presses on her chest.

'Can't breathe.' The words take the last whisper of air.

He stares at her and the look in his eyes, the excitement she sees there, chills her.

'You're. A. Bitch.' He lifts her head and thuds it back down with each word, his teeth clenched. 'I. Hate. You.'

'Please.' She wheezes. 'I'm sorry…'

She can't get more words out, feels only the squeezing – his hands on her body: exploring, pinching and hurting, so different to John's caresses.

She shuts her mind down to a tiny patch of sky. A distant dream.

Then hands make their way to her neck and she jolts back to herself, fresh panic assaulting her. She scrabbles to reach, to push him away, but her arms are pinned down, her hands claw the dirt helplessly.

No.

Above, the leaves whisper their secrets and the last thoughts she has are of mossy rocks so bright and alluring that fairies dance on them at night.

CHAPTER SIXTY-SIX

CAL

Cal's legs don't move quickly enough. He's forgotten how the muscles work, can't make them go faster. The paths are uneven and he focuses on the ground in front of him, Chrissie in his mind, terror in his gut, knowing he cannot afford to fall. He smashes the green fronds of ferns that hang in the path out of his way, his breath heaving and sweat streaking down his back.

He has to scramble up a small incline, a stitch in his side and pain across his belly. He should be fitter. What if something happens to Chrissie because he couldn't get there fast enough? He can't live. If something happens to her, he won't live. It's like a threat or a bargain with a higher power. *Don't push me on this.*

Terrible thoughts run riot in his brain as his feet hit the path and his shins feel the impact of rock. Technicolour imaginings: the worst scenes, the worst outcomes. A combination of all the most horrible crimes he's covered. Rational thought deserts him.

He reaches the dip in the wall, hurdles the fallen rocks, every part of his body screaming in exhaustion. Tree branches whip his face as he tries to sprint through the undergrowth, failing, brambles tear his clothes, wrenching him back.

He's so convinced he will find the body of his daughter when he thunders into the clearing that he can't believe she's standing there, lifting her canvas from the easel, laying it carefully on a rock. It is a parallel world, a hallucination.

But Archie James is there too. Standing beside her, peering over her shoulder as she chatters. The sound of the waterfall has masked his approach, but when he lets out a warning cry, they both turn to stare at him. Cal doesn't care that he must look mad, hair standing on end, sweat pouring down his face.

'Dad? I thought we were meeting at the hotel? Mr James wanted to stay and see how the picture turned out.'

There's a hitch to her voice. It makes him cold.

He is conscious now that he needs to conceal his panic. He realises how close Archie is standing to Chrissie, how near they are to the edge of the falls.

'Oh. I forgot, of course we were,' Cal blusters. 'Ready to go, Chrissie? Come this way, will you?'

'Don't you need to sort these paints properly?' Archie says.

'No, it's fine.' She tumbles her precious colours into the bag. It is this more than anything that convinces him. She feels something is wrong.

'We'll sort them later.' He tries to keep his voice normal, but his desperation to get her away from Archie James is impossible to conceal. Reason and calm have left him, all he can think of is Margot, Layla.

'What's the rush?' Archie James' oiled tones make Cal's skin prickle.

He doesn't hide his distaste fast enough, sees suspicion dart into the hotelier's eyes, his bonhomie evaporating. Cal stretches out an arm to Chrissie, beckons. He has to get her away from the edge.

She lets her bag slide from her hand to the floor, her face chalk beneath the leaf canopy as she steps towards him. With a sigh, he reaches for his daughter, steers her behind him, his body between her and danger.

'Move to the path, Chris. I'm just coming. I'll get your things for you.'

She nods and he feels intense relief at every step she takes away from them. He has no desire to confront Archie James, to ask why he's lied by omission. All he wants is to get his daughter away.

But as he nears Archie, he sees the man's face contort with a cold knowledge and he cannot help himself. A wave of fury sweeps through him.

'You got away with it, then,' he hisses, as he picks up Chrissie's rucksack, angry for Layla, for every woman taken and tossed to the side by an arrogant killer. The memory of Dubois, his words, his teasing, echoes in his mind. What is it that compels them to gloat? Archie James has not had the grace to stay away, has stood at a memorial for Layla and watched her mother twisted in grief. Cal realises with a shock that earlier Archie was sitting on the rocks where she was found, where he hid her. He is an abomination.

Archie's smile is grim but satisfied. He keeps his voice low, but Cal is close enough to hear the hatred.

'I don't know what you're talking about.'

'Because you lost your trousers, she lost her life? Doesn't seem like a fair exchange.'

He isn't thinking, goading Archie, letting him know he knows. His gaze flicks to Chrissie. She's reached the edge of the trees. It's worth one last question.

'How did you even know Layla was here? She can't have been meeting you.'

The hotelier shrugs and slips his smug exterior back on like a coat. He is a skilful shapeshifter, though Cal can see the anger simmering beneath the façade now, wonders how he missed it before.

'So clever with your little podcast, and still you got it all wrong.'

John Knowles bruised and broken in a hospital bed. Dubois' lies. A bleak sense of guilt stirs Cal. He is right. All of this searching and the wrong man lies in jail. He is no closer to finding his sister. The terrible sense of failure. He meets the cruelty in Archie's eyes, finds rage and unfairness boiling up inside him.

He doesn't plan to do it, his daughter standing on the path behind them, but he can't help himself. When he lets his fist loose and punches Archie James, it is such a relief to let it all explode out of him.

'Dad!' At Chrissie's anguished cry, regret and reality flood back into his brain. But the world swivels and the sky rushes in as Archie retaliates, landing a punch that throws Cal off balance. His foot catches in a groove of slippery rock and he is pitched forward, too shocked to break his fall with his hands, blinding pain as his head hits a boulder. Stunned and groaning, he opens his eyes and sees only soft green moss, a splash of red on stone.

He's too groggy to register the sight of his own blood, not quick enough to respond to Chrissie's scream of warning. Archie stands above him, face pale and terrible, cheek swelling and wild calculation in his eyes. Cal groans and Archie's boot hits him in the ribs – the pain like lightning bolts inside him. Archie is incensed, knocked out of reason. This has been a terrible miscalculation.

He can't get off the ground, can't catch a breath to help himself as Archie kicks and roars in distress. His efforts to get away only roll him closer to the edge. The foaming brown-white of the water is thundering past so close to his head that his senses are overpowered, he can't call out a warning.

Run, he thinks, as he teeters on the cliff side and his daughter throws herself at Archie, screaming and beating her fists against his back. *Run, Chrissie, please run.*

It has all unravelled in an instant. The sight of her causes him such intense pain that as his legs slide into nothing he throws out both arms in a desperate, screaming attempt to reach her. He manages to grasp a large rock near the edge. His fingers strain to keep their purchase, to slow the momentum. His feet pedal frantically in space. He can see Archie fighting Chrissie off, pinning her to the floor so he is astride her, his hands on her neck and a contortion of fury and madness on his face.

'Shut up, Layla,' he screams.

Cal bellows like an animal in pain, unable to wrench himself higher. This is every nightmare that ever stalked him.

'Chrissie!'

As he swings his legs in one last attempt to regain solid ground, his toe catches the lip of the cliff and Cal forces all his weight onto it, yelling at the agony in his ribs, knowing he is passing out. He pulls through the pain and the blackness that takes his vision, using his last ounces of consciousness to drag himself over.

He can hear Chrissie thrashing, sees the blur of movement. Archie James is strangling his daughter and he can't help her. It's all his fault. Maybe, maybe if he reaches out, he can touch her and she will know he is here, that he loves her, that he's going with her.

He feels drops of rain on his palm. Then warmth, as other fingers find his, someone grasps his hand, words sound that can't filter into his head, only buzzing, noise. Shona? A drift from consciousness towards impenetrable black.

He's at the top of the stairs again, his face pressed tight, his father's hand meeting Margot's cheek, the cry and the ricochet from the wall. His father looking up and seeing him, face crumpling in regret, the front door swinging. 'Go to bed, Christopher.'

CHAPTER SIXTY-SEVEN

SIX MONTHS LATER

EPISODE EIGHT: AFTER THE FALL

Fans of the show will know that Cal Lovett is on compassionate leave following events earlier this year. I'm Sarah Travers, Cal's colleague and the producer of Finding Justice, *and I'm bringing this special one-off episode to you in his place.*

Six months ago, Archie James was charged with murder, thanks to Cal's efforts at uncovering the truth of what happened to Layla Mackie in 1986 when she rode her horse into the woods and never came out.

On the day that his daughter's killer is sentenced to life in prison, Tam Mackie isn't in Aberdeen High Court on Castle Street. He is miles away, working on the hills that surround his croft, the place he loves – in sight of the woods that swallowed his daughter. Recovering from a heart attack, Tam is still too weak to sit through the details.

Instead, his wife Jean has been in the public gallery for the duration of the ten-day trial. She has barely taken her eyes from the ex-hotelier, who sits before the judge with his head bowed. Supported by friends and family, she has listened to all of the details that have been gleaned about what happened to Layla that day beside the waterfall, as well as witness testimony about pranks at the hotel where Layla worked that the prosecution argued formed the motive for James' actions.

So far, Archie James has yet to break his silence about what happened that day in 1986. He has also yet to display any remorse for his actions. He will have a long time to think about it.

Also in the gallery for the verdict was John Knowles, previously arrested on suspicion of Layla's murder using evidence discovered by this podcast. We would like to reiterate our apology to John Knowles for the distress caused to him and his family. Knowles is not the only person to have suffered in this investigation, but we deeply regret our part in events. We understand he has recovered from his injuries and wish him well.

EPILOGUE

ONE MONTH LATER

The audience is laughably vast. Sarah has so far resisted the urge to crow about being right. She is ticking off tasks on a clipboard with her trademark efficiency, but her hands aren't totally steady. She stands to the edge of the stage, peering out from behind the curtains at the crowd, then turns back to the wings, catches him watching.

'What?'

Cal holds his hands in a surrender position.

'I'll go and check the slides,' she says, whisking away.

'It will be fine. I promise,' he tells the air she leaves behind.

He's even wearing a shirt and tie.

The final minutes are rushing past. Someone powders Cal's face and he lets them, suddenly afraid that his words and composure will desert him. His hands sweat like they sweated that day by the falls, when everything crashed down around him. He closes his eyes for a moment and pictures the girl with reddish curls and bright eyes, the one he will always miss. The thought of her is a wound that won't close. She is a hole inside him forever. But he must live around the void and he is determined to do that. Not to would be a betrayal.

He's spent his compassionate leave preparing for this moment, letting Sarah take on the final podcast while he took the time to try and recover his life. For a while he could walk away – he needed to – but it is a relief to be here now. Finding his skin. Three days ago, the inquest into the death of Marc Dubois recorded a verdict of suicide, drawing what Cal sees as a shaky line under the death. The man Cal was, the one who sat and jousted with the killer, is gone. He has to let go. It's time to move on.

As his name is announced, he steps into the brightness with memories at his back, pushing him into the light. He can feel the interest in the room, the intake of breath before the event.

He raises his eyes to the balcony. Though he will give this talk next week to a packed audience in Aberdeen and has told her she doesn't need to drive all the way down, he is glad Shona has ignored him. It calms him to know that she's there.

He has seen a lot of her recently, taking some of his leave of absence to walk in the Cairngorms, soothed by its granite tors and dancing rivers. He drove from there, legs still aching, to sit by Jean's side for the trial. The taste remains bitter, but at least Archie James is where he belongs.

Cal still cannot bring himself to dwell on the memory – Shona sprinting to the rocks, desperately hauling the hotelier off his beautiful girl.

He anchors himself at the podium but his mind is spinning, refusing to focus. He pours a glass of water with a shaking hand, glances up at the faces on the screen behind him: those red curls and that laughing smile. Next to her, a daredevil girl jumping a horse over a wide ditch, hatless and, finally, free. He can't let them down, he has to pull himself together.

And then he focuses on the audience.

There, in the front row, he finds her. Chrissie. So strong and resilient despite it all, a stunning reflection of the lost woman on the screen behind him. She is holding her grandmother's arm, Allie to the other side of her. The women in his life. It has been painful and difficult but they are wading into shallower waters.

Cal takes a deep breath and he fixes his gaze on her, his daughter, starting at sixth form college, no longer a child. She smiles a little, her eyes shining with apprehension and hope. He finds that is all he needs to be able to lift his head and speak.

'Unearthing the truth can feel impossible,' he says, 'but someone always knows. I'm Cal Lovett, and this is a live episode of *Finding Justice*.'

—

The last ripples of applause die away and the lights go down. Cal is hot, tired and exhilarated. When he staggers off stage, Sarah passes him a bottle of water and he tilts his head back, draining the cooling fluid. The producer is practically bouncing on her toes.

'Ratings are through the roof,' she says, and he laughs at how young she seems in comparison to her previous tough persona. He never would have imagined they'd enjoy working together.

'It's all down to you. Well done,' he says.

'Chrissie's gone across to the restaurant with the others,' Sarah tells him. 'They'll see you over there. But there's someone here to talk to you first.'

Cal looks up, expecting to see Shona, a smile already on his face at the thought of her. She said she'd have to dash off before the end to get back to Aberdeen, but maybe her plans have changed.

It isn't Shona. His forehead creases in confusion.

'Detective Foulds?'

'I admit it.' She laughs, holding her hands up. 'I'm a true crime podcast fan.'

Sarah ducks past them, excusing herself.

'So you did know who I was, that day we first spoke?' He laughs.

'Caught me.'

There's something tense around her eyes that makes him realise this isn't just a social call.

'You're here to tell me something.'

She nods. 'Something off the record, for now.'

Cal waits, feeling oddly detached from himself.

'Your scrapyard detail. It was bothering me. I've been looking into various things.' She has the sort of intensity Cal recognises, when something he's investigating becomes a fixation. His heart swells to realise he isn't the only person to care about finding Margot. Foulds ploughs on. 'Dubois once briefly shared a cell with a man called Jason Barr. Does that ring any bells?'

Cal remembers the ex-bouncer crowing about his connection to Dubois on television after he died. 'Sure. The nightclub bouncer who assaulted women on their way home after nights out. He was giving interviews a while back about knowing Dubois.'

'That's what made me wonder.' She nods. 'Unlike Dubois, Barr *was* in the area at the time your sister went missing. He *does* fit our profile. You were so sure that Dubois knew something. So, I thought what if, maybe…'

'There was a little pillow talk?'

'Exactly.' Foulds' eyes are shining.

'But Barr was done for GBH, not murder.'

'Yes, but I did some checking. Barr once boasted to another cellmate that he had gone too far and killed a woman. He said he left her in...'

'...a scrapyard?' Cal breathes out, reaches a hand to steady himself on the wall.

'Got it in one. This was years ago. The man informed, but there were no details, Barr clammed up and there was never anything concrete to go on. But if you add it all together, I think we have grounds to look into it.'

'Oh my God.'

Cal pictures the rows of cars weaved with grasses, the tiny hiding spaces, the acres of scrap. His eyes fill with tears at the thought that finally, they could get some answers. It doesn't surprise him in the least that Dubois took a kernel that interested him from Barr and treasured it, researched it, grew it into something else sick and depraved. The research he did into Cal and the podcast probably wasn't hard – the details online for anyone to find if they took the time – and they will have broken the sugar-filled monotony of his hours. For Cal, it explains the sadistic mischief in the man's eyes.

Without thinking, he steps forward and hugs the detective. After a second, he feels her arms return the hug, her hand patting his back.

'Sorry,' he says, embarrassed, pulling back. 'It's just...'

'I know.'

Cal rubs his eyes. Smiles a watery smile through the emotion.

'Look, I have to go,' Foulds says, clearing her throat. 'But I will be in touch with details. Okay?'

'Thank you. Thank you so much.'

The theatre is empty by the time he pulls himself together. Outside, a misty rain is hanging in the air, the streetlights illuminating inky puddles on the pavement. He crosses the road, then pauses as he sees his family displayed in the lit window of the art deco restaurant Chrissie has chosen. Sarah is there too, with some of the others, and they're all laughing at something she's said, faces bright. No one can see him, so he stops for a moment to drink them in – his colleagues, his mother, Allie, his daughter.

Maybe it's Chrissie's reddish curls, the turn of her face, her profile. Maybe it's the rush of emotion after speaking to Foulds. But as he stares at the window, it isn't his daughter he sees. It's his sister, for one moment parallel and alive. The way she should have been.

ACKNOWLEDGEMENTS

It's taken me a little while to get here, and I'm so grateful to all the people who have helped and supported me along the way. If you've picked up this book as a reader – thank you so much, you're making a dream come true.

Thank you to my agent Charlotte Seymour – whose skill, faith and tireless determination have carried me through. Charlotte, I'm so happy to be working with you and the fantastic team at Johnson & Alcock.

A huge thank you to Louise Cullen and the brilliant team at Canelo for taking Cal to your hearts and shepherding him to publication. It's so much fun working with you all. Thanks to Siân Heap, Alicia Pountney and Katy Loftus as well as Deborah Blake, Miranda Ward and Vicki Vrint for your editing magic. Thanks also to Fran and everyone working behind the scenes to get *Unsolved* out in the world. Thank you Andrew Davis for the beautiful cover.

Thank you to Bill Ryan for the transformational Writers & Artists course – kindness, insight and lots of yellow highlights! If it wasn't for W&A I would also never have met the dream writing support group of Chris May, Eugenia Hall, Gillian Anton and Tammye Huf. Thank you all for your wise words, insightful critiques and sweet potato fries.

For support, laughter and expertise on a daily basis, a massive jellyfish-laced thank you to the Criminal Minds crew: Adam Southward, Rachael Blok, Clare Empson, Dom Nolan, Elle Croft, Fliss Chester, James Delargy, Jo Furniss, Tim Kinsey, Susie Lynes, Niki Mackay, Simon Masters, Phoebe Morgan, Polly Phillips, Eleanor Ray, Kate Simants, Rob Scragg, Louisa Scarr, Victoria Selman and Harriet Tyce. It's a privilege to learn from you all and to be published together in the *Afraid of the Light* anthologies. Rachael – thank you also for reading *Unsolved* at a crucial moment and for picking me off the floor when I needed it!

Thank you to Sophie Hannah for the life-changing Dream Author programme. You're an inspiration on navigating the ups and downs of writing life. Thanks also to all the other DAs, especially Barbara Copperthwaite and Katrina Ritters, partners in crime at the Hewenden retreat.

Thank you to Caroline Green for reading a draft of *Unsolved* and giving invaluable feedback as part of the Books for Vaccines auction.

Unsolved was partly written at the Scottish Creative Writing Centre Moniack Mhor. Thank you to tutors Karen Campbell and Adam LeBor, the incredible team running the centre and all of my Moniack friends, especially Suzy Aspley, Sheena Cook and Rachelle Atalla. A truly special place and special people.

Closer to home, thank you to friends who've listened to me talk about writing (and probably wondered if I'll ever make it into print) for a very long time. Thank you for the long runs and moral support Laura Gazey and Michelle Fadil, for dog walks and weekly doses of sanity Lizzie Singer, and for looking after the whole family so many times Jennie Potts. Thanks also to the rest of the 'book' group for long evenings supposedly talking about books and definitely drinking Prosecco!

Geraldine DeRuiter and Rand Fishkin – thank you for being an amazing transatlantic cheerleading team. Your encouragement has lifted me.

Rebecca Rattue, Claire Linney and Laura Thomas – our escapes are such a source of joy. Thank you for all these years of friendship and here's to many more adventures together.

Genevieve Loveland – how lucky to have sat next to you on the bus that day. Thank you for knowing where all the bodies are buried and still being my friend.

Unsolved features a fictional country house hotel and is inspired by the landscape I lived in and explored as a teenager. To the people I waitressed with at Pittodrie House Hotel – thank you for all the lifts home and for being nothing like the characters in my imagined version! Thanks particularly to Maureen Forbes and Mark Fleming, who always looked out for me.

Finally, to my family. At the heart of every writer is a reader and that fire was fed by my parents who have encouraged me every step of the way. Thank you Mum, Dad and Daniel (especially for letting me max out your library card). Thank you to Lindsay, James, Stuart and the rest of the extended Murray-Greig-Smith clan. Thanks also to my Critchlow in-laws. Lesley you take the award for being the most prolific crime fiction reader I know!

Isobel Fettes, William Fettes, Edna Greig-Smith and Peter Greig-Smith. You aren't all still here but your impact is and your memories treasured. There's a lot of you in *Unsolved* and in me – from the love of the Scottish land-scape to the love of books. Thank you.

Duncan, Suzi, Edward and Jessica Morris – I always forget you aren't technically family but for these purposes you absolutely are. Thank you for everything.

Last, but definitely not least, Will, Rachel and Adam – your belief and love, plus endless patience with the hours spent writing and editing, are the reason this book is here. You are the best people in the world. Thank you.

Read on for an extract from the second book in the Cal Lovett Files series

PROLOGUE

BRYONY, 2007, WEST HIGHLANDS

Bryony tilts her face to the weak sunlight, trying to catch some warmth to stem the chill that is snaking through her veins. It's not the worst place to wait, but it is cold slumped on the doorstep. She lets her fingers fall to the slab of remorseless stone, worn smooth by centuries of farming feet. Her hands are sticky and warm, the blood congealing. Panic stirs inside her. Will someone come? Did they hear the shots? If so, they'll be here soon, with their false concern and judgement.

Her mind spirals, sending thoughts in loops and swirls. It would have been different if Robbie hadn't wet the bed, she realises. They wouldn't have been at home and this couldn't have happened. That it all comes down to one tiny detail is breathtaking. A sliding doors moment of fate. The moment her son slipped shamefaced into their bedroom this morning, gears slid into motion and darkness smiled.

Her fingers close tight, hands convulsing so that her nails pierce the skin in crescent moons. She was going to be better than this. She tried, but she failed. Since Robbie was born, she's had something else inside her. An ugliness that lay beneath the surface, undiscovered for so long, rearing up with motherhood. She shuts her eyes for a moment but the bloody image is imprinted on her brain, the smell in her nostrils. She's let everyone down. Her sons most of all.

Her breath sounds loud in the quiet.

Today was going to be a good day. They were going to go out. She was going to make an effort and take the boys to the green-watered lochan through the pine trees. She wasn't going to rush them or scold.

The bag she packed last night is just inside the doorway. Even with her eyes closed, she can see it: small swimming shorts and rash vests with dinosaurs on them; a box of Tunnocks tea cakes tucked in beside the good intentions. Sean loves the marshmallow. It was going to be an Enid Blyton-worthy adventure. Making the memories those Facebook bitches are always on about. She was going let them throw stones, get muddy, climb trees. She was going to be the kind of mother she had so much faith she would be – in those days before she truly knew herself.

The sun slips behind a cloud and she shivers at the sudden cold, unable to clutch the wisps of thought that pirouette in her brain.

She could tell by the look on Robbie's face that he'd wet the bed again. She didn't need him to confess, or to run her hand over the bottom sheet and find the damp patch, its penetrating odour roosting in the mattress, the room, his skin.

She should have been kind. Felt what normal mothers feel. The ones who can tuck a baby into the crook of one arm and wipe a kitchen surface with the other hand, all the while smiling like their life isn't the biggest heap of shite around. But she wasn't. She lost her temper. She ripped the sheets from the bed and she cancelled their plans. It wasn't that she didn't see the tears in his eyes, so much as she couldn't feel them.

Does she sleep? Her eyes jerk open and, against the greenery and the gravel and the hardness of the doorstep and the carnage in front of her, she sees *his* eyes. Haunting her. Blue and staring. Shock painted onto them. Robbie. Her oldest. Her complicated one. The child who deserved so much more.

'Robbie,' she whispers, her lips dry and cracking. 'I'm sorry, love.'

And she is. She really, really is.

She feels a sudden pain in her chest that blinds so bright it makes her fingers numb.

'Mummy's here,' she wants to say. 'Mummy's got you.'

But she doesn't, because nothing ever comes out right when it comes to Robbie. He's gone now. She can't go where he's going. She just hopes his brother will be waiting for him and they can hold tight to each other. Robbie and Sean. Her boys. The thought cracks her in two.

Is it later or is it now? She can hear a man shouting and the horrible crunching noise feet make on the gravel but she can't resolve the wailing into words. She thinks about putting her hands over her ears but she's just too damn tired.

She's always wishing for life to go faster, for the boys to grow, the drudgery to end. Time is interminably slow and awful. But just at the moment she changes her mind, it speeds up. Of course it fucking does. She just wants a few more minutes to sit here, to feel the wind on her face and hear the rush of the sea in the distance. To linger in regret.

But it's all louder now – the sirens, the feet, the slamming. She's finding it harder to stay calm. She can't breathe. They're all going to know. They're going to know how bad she truly is.

CHAPTER ONE

CAL, WEST MIDLANDS

Cal stands on the street corner, hesitating – or at least pretending to. He made a promise that he keeps on breaking. *Go home, Cal, go home.* Even muttering the words doesn't help. Where is home, anyway? Living back with his mother in a house he swore he would never return to, his marriage over. That's not home; it's necessity. Something stirs inside him, a compulsion that he can't shake. Even as he rehearses the arguments against it, he finds himself looping through the streets towards his prey, compelled to scratch the impossible itch.

The cafe is only open for another hour. There are few patrons left inside, just the dregs of the post-school pick up crowd. Fractious kids and tired mothers, a spaniel slumped on the floor, head on its paws in despair.

He orders a coffee – black, because it's quick and he isn't bothered about drinking it – then chooses a seat at a table with an abandoned highchair, dodging the scattered crumbs and half a banana squashed onto the floor.

His hands shake a little with adrenaline as he uses a napkin to wipe a clean spot for his laptop and pulls it from his bag, no intention of logging in, only of hiding behind it. He grips the hot mug between his hands and focuses his gaze on the garage over the road, where a recovery truck is unloading a dented car. A man in a luminous vest unclips cables, lowers a ramp. Then the man he's talking to rounds the vehicle and Cal's breath constricts. He can't prove it. She's been missing for thirty-six years so there isn't even a scrap of evidence, but this, he is sure, is the man who killed his sister.

As he watches ex-convict Jason Barr, something tightens inside Cal's chest, sucking the breath from him. He shouldn't be here. If the police knew what he was doing they'd be furious. He made a promise to Detective Foulds when she gave him privileged information in a moment of sympathy. He's abusing that trust. But he can't look away.

The man is thick set, walks a bit like he's sitting astride a horse – his thighs great trunks of muscle under jeans. The roll of fat on the back of Barr's neck beneath his shaved skull is one of the few changes that dates him from the pictures of him as a young man. The predator may have aged, but he's still ox-strong and muscular.

Cal's attention is absorbed by the tattooed arms that are now propped on the roof of the broken vehicle. Old patterns and declarations of love swirl and ripple there, an inked history of changing loyalties. Barr has altered them since doing time for assaulting women, hiding the man he was before.

As Cal stares at the hot metal beneath Barr's hands, he pictures the paleness of his sister's neck, the fragility of her collarbone, the red silk of her hair. He runs his fingers over the small tattoo of a swallow on the inside of his own wrist. A tiny memory of her.

'Excuse me.' Cal is wrenched back into the present by a woman bending forward to insert herself into his vision.

'Is this chair taken?' He can tell by the tone of her voice that this isn't the first time she's asked.

'Oh,' he says, his voice shaking. 'No. Sorry. It's not.'

By the time he shuffles so she can remove the chair from his table and carry it across to her own, Cal looks up to find that Barr and the battered car have gone. He feels a turn of wretchedness, a queasy sort of regret after giving into his compulsion. He comes here often, and for what? Watching, waiting, unable to do anything.

It bothers him, how close to his childhood home this garage lies. How close to where Margot was set down in the countryside after an argument with her boyfriend. Left to make her own way back. Never seen again. It's almost like Barr is taunting him with proximity, blatantly getting on with his life.

Detective Foulds promised the force were looking into things and yet it has been months. Impatience nags at Cal as he slugs back a few mouthfuls of the now-cold coffee and slides his untouched laptop into his bag. He should go to his mother's now; it's getting late. But, as he pauses on the pavement and inspects the dark clouds at the edge of the sky, Jason Barr steps from the dark cavern of the garage. His arms are stiff and swinging, a pack of cigarettes in his hand and his phone bulging in his back pocket. Barr saunters down the street and, even though Cal knows he shouldn't, that Barr may well recognise him from the papers, he can't help himself. The devil inside takes over and he trails him down the road, hurrying to match the length of the man's stride, heart pulling inside him, dread in his belly.

Dark fantasies descend: the going home traffic beside him is steady – a bus heaving with people ready for their tea. What if he pushed Barr in front of it? He can almost see the ensuing scene: the blood, the wailing, the *peace*. He feels his fingers twitch and his arm jerk slightly; a shadow movement of his deepest desires.

But then Barr halts, turning and peering back along the road as if looking for someone. Cal feels adrenaline tear through him, followed by shame and fear that make him every bit the nine-year-old boy whose older sister never came home. He bends and fiddles with the laces of his trainers. In a head to head between the two of them, it is easy to see who the loser would be.

When he glances up, Barr has moved on. The bus has stopped, disgorging passengers. People stream around him, tired and ready for home. He straightens and scans the distance, frantic to see over their heads. The ex-bouncer turns into a side street, vanishing from sight.

He should go home. Everything rational and sensible inside Cal's head is telling him to turn around, walk away. Instead, he finds himself jogging along the street, desperate to reach the corner before Barr slips away from him. He skids into the side street, sees the lumbering form in the distance and slows his pace, cursing his recklessness.

He falters when Barr turns to the side, but the man is just extracting and lighting a cigarette, barely pausing as he exhales. Cal follows the scent of the smoke in the air. Tailing him here is so risky. If Barr looks back he will see Cal, but he follows anyway, realising with a chill that he is mirroring his crimes, the way he stalked women in the early hours as they wound their way home after evenings out, late night working or arguments with their boyfriends. The thought makes Cal uneasy – makes him wonder if he is in some way becoming the predator he is shadowing.

But he shoves the misgivings aside because, as they thread their way through the streets in the direction of the river and the green swathes of willows dipping in the flow, he understands where Barr is going.

It seems too audacious, too insulting to be true. It's only when Barr pauses on the bank and stretches to peer over some bushes that Cal knows for sure he is right. The scrapyard is just across from where the bulky mechanic is rocking from foot to foot: rusting hulks of old machinery clothed in weed. A place that is usually still and silent with the remnants of the past rusting into the earth.

This is the place that serial killer Marc Dubois hinted Cal's sister is buried – information he and Foulds believe came from Jason Barr. At least, Foulds used to believe that. Who knows now? She's avoiding his calls.

Dubois and Barr only shared a cell for a short time, until Dubois was moved to a secure hospital setting, but it was enough time, Cal is sure, for a bored and manipulative serial killer to extract information for fun. The final piece of the puzzle as far as he is concerned, is the discovery that Barr once worked in this scrapyard. How many coincidences do you need before something becomes meaningful? Cal asks himself this question all the time.

The truth is, he knew the moment Dubois uttered Margot's name that there was a sick honesty behind the words. It is impossible to properly explain – he tried so many times with Allie before the divorce and she still saw room for doubt – but there was a gleeful kind of satisfaction in the way Dubois had dropped his crumbs. The pleasure of knowing something Cal didn't, and the plan to stretch it out and watch him suffer.

Cal drops back to the shadow of a bridge to watch, biting his lip as Barr circles the same patch of ground, grinding his cigarette butt into the grass with his heel, fists clenching and unclenching. When Barr moves off, Cal slips from his hiding place, tempted to follow, though he is increasingly uneasy at the man's erratic behaviour.

But then Barr spins to face him, turning back along the narrow river path, his face thick with twisted thunder. There is no time to move, or hide. Nothing to do but keep walking. A sense of terrible inevitability rises up inside Cal. His sister's laugh echoes in his mind as the man bears down on him.

Cal takes his hands from his pockets as Barr draws near. His heart shouts so loudly inside his chest that all he hears is the blood pumping in his ears, distant traffic fading away to nothing. Without choice, his gaze is pulled to the wide face, like metal to a magnet. As they meet on the path, Cal readies himself for a blow but, instead, the man he hates like death catches his eye and nods to him like he could be anyone.

Instinctively, Cal nods in response, everything in him immediately screaming out against this diabolical auto-pilot. As he steps to one side, too shocked to act, to block the path, to hurl abuse, he registers Barr's pale face and clammy expression: a million shades from the devil-may-care he's been watching for weeks.

'Cheers mate,' Barr says as he passes, but even the voice is out of kilter.

Something is wrong.

Rooted to the spot, Cal lets out an agonised breath, furious with himself for bottling this moment. He whirls round, fists clenched, suddenly suicidally determined to have it out, but Barr is fifty metres away, jogging in the other direction, as if fleeing for his life.

Bewildered, Cal folds at the waist, braces his hands on his knees and takes in shaky mouthfuls of air. His pulse steadying to a normal rate, his hearing returning. Sounds filtering through the haze. The crunch of metal, the whine of a motor, a shout.

He stands and edges towards the sound, the thing Barr saw that made him turn tail and run.

The police. They're digging in the scrapyard.